## "I should let the sea have you."

She stiffened, frightened he would carry through with his threat. However, she would not respond, would not give him the knowledge that she knew his language, a language her father often spoke when conversing with traders.

"Save me the trouble. Good coin spent on saving you from disgrace. Should have let the procurer have you. I would have been richer." He halted beside the ladder leading to the room and deposited her onto her feet. "Foolish, foolish woman, I'll bind you to the mast if need be."

Before she knew what she was about, she drew back her hand and slapped him.

Nicolaus furrowed his brow. "You do understand me."

Her eyes widened and he smiled. "It is as I thought, but how?"

A wave sloshed over the boat. Her pallor did not look well as his ship rocked back and forth.

"Come along, then." He lifted her into his arms and tucked her head beneath his chin. Her slight frame nestled perfectly against him when she wasn't pushing her palms against his chest. That part of him that had been cold for so many months began to beat, to breathe and to hope for a better future than the one he'd resigned himself to.

**Christina Rich** is a full-time housewife and mother. She lives in the Midwest with her husband and four children. She loves Jesus, history, researching her ancestry, fishing, reading and of course, writing romances woven with God's grace, mercy and truth. You can find more about her at authorchristinarich.com.

## Books by Christina Rich

### Love Inspired Historical

*The Guardian's Promise*
*The Warrior's Vow*
*Captive on the High Seas*

Visit the Author Profile page at Harlequin.com for more titles

# CHRISTINA RICH

## *Captive on the High Seas*

**HARLEQUIN**® LOVE INSPIRED® HISTORICAL

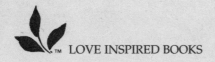 LOVE INSPIRED BOOKS

Recycling programs
for this product may
not exist in your area.

ISBN-13: 978-0-373-28321-7

Captive on the High Seas

www.Harlequin.com

**Printed in U.S.A.**

I will extol Thee, my God, O king; and I will bless Thy name for ever and ever. Every day will I bless Thee; and I will praise Thy name for ever and ever.
—*Psalms* 145:1–2

To Ami Jo, Jordan, Logan and Katie,
I love you much. Thank you for blessing my life.

# Chapter One

The shadow from the high mud tower loomed over Ada. Its shade broke the heat of the sun, causing her overheated skin to cool, stealing her anger. However, she knew the shivers racking her body had nothing to do with the coolness and everything to do with the fear coursing through her veins.

A young boy tugged on the lead bound around Ada's neck and hands, causing her to stumble. She bit the inside of her cheek to keep from crying out when her knees hit the wooden stairs. Before her bound hands hit the wood, a hand gripped ahold of her tunic and yanked her to her feet.

"You, there." The large brute released her and jabbed a finger into the boy's chest. "Take care with the merchandise."

The deep Philistine accent grated along Ada's nape. Waves from the great sea thrust against the port, filling her ears, roaring in her head. Breathing in through her mouth and out through her nose, she fought to calm the fear vibrating her limbs and risked a glare at the man through the mass of hair veiling her face.

"Come now, we don't have all day. These men would like to go home before the wind shifts again."

If she delayed the process, perhaps her brother would arrive and rescue her from her sisters' folly. Their jealousy had always been contained to biting words and foolish antics. Their last, a viper in her bed, had proven vicious, but selling her to an auctioneer in exchange for a gold band was beyond Ada's comprehension. How could her oldest sister, Dina, be so cruel? Because her sister, only half her blood, believed Ada nothing more than a daughter of a slave. All her sisters seemed to despise the way their father treated her as their equal, a daughter of a wealthy merchant. However, none treated her as poorly as Dina.

She shook the hair from her eyes and jerked her hands back. The rough rope cut into her wrists as the boy clung to the other end. The child stumbled and fell to his backside. His flushed cheeks, and beady black eyes quickly turned fearful when his master snatched him up by his tunic. The Philistine narrowed his eyes and Ada thought he'd clout the child, but he righted the boy and then patted him on the head like an obedient pet.

"See to the others." The Philistine's gaze settled on Ada. The corners of his mouth slid upward, revealing rotten teeth. He grabbed a handful of her hair and moved closer to sniff. The foul odor of his breath slammed against her cheek as he bent close to her ear. "If I did not need to feed the boy, I'd make you my bride just to teach you humility." He stepped back and swung his arm wide toward the gathering before them. Ada tried to jerk away, but the man kept a fisted grip on her hair. "Well now," he bellowed over the crowd. "Haven't we a lioness."

His thick arm snaked around her shoulders as he pulled her close. He made another show of smelling her with distaste. "And clean."

Ada was thankful for the platform she stood on as men of all likes surged forward. Their hands reached toward her feet, touching her toes. She scooted closer to her captor as she searched the crowd for her brother. *Almighty God, if You have mercy grant me rescue.*

"One piece of silver," a voice called from the crowd. The taunt was followed by a roar of laughter.

Ada glanced at the man who'd made the offer and sucked in a sharp breath. He was a short, burly man with a matted beard and a bevy of brightly dressed women clinging to his person. Their thick kohl and painted lips were tale enough of why the man would purchase her, but it was not their profession that left Ada shocked and even more angered. It was the five onlookers who stood behind the man. Her five sisters. Dina perched on the edge of a well; her hand propped on one hip, one corner of her mouth curved upward.

"Come now, certainly the girl is worth more," her captor roared.

"She is too thin." A man in the crowd spat as if disgusted with her appearance.

The Philistine gripped a handful of her tunic at her back and pulled it tight. "There now, not so skinny."

"Two, then."

Tears of anger fought their way to the back of Ada's eyes. As if losing her mother had not been enough…

Dina's jealousy had gone too far. The gold bangle around her sister's upper arm sparkling beneath the sun was worth more than two pieces of silver. Her captor no doubt knew this, which filled Ada with hope. Perhaps, the Philistine would fight for a higher bidder, especially since she'd cost him that gold band. Perhaps, the wicked man would pass.

"Throw in your best cow," her captor yelled.

Dina tilted her head, her gaze considering the lone bidder before glancing at Ada. Her sister ran a finger down the intricately woven shawl that had once covered Ada's shoulders and crown of glory, as her father had called her hair. A smile teased the corner of Dina's lips. Her nose curled as she squinted. Ada's other sisters paid her no heed. Their little elbow nudges and giggles told Ada they thought it all a game.

If only it were true. However, it seemed Dina was bent on revenge.

Why had she not listened to her mother's warnings? Because she wanted Dina to love her, wanted all her sisters to love her as she loved them. Loneliness filled the cavity within her chest. One tear welled. It filled her eye, but Ada refused to let it fall.

"What say you, man? My dinner grows cold." The Philistine pushed Ada forward. His fingers tangled in her hair. She pressed her lips together to keep her scream from pleasing Dina any further. The bidding man drew his hand over his beard. "Why spend so much on a weak and spoiled vessel? It is obvious she knows not of hard work. I keep my cow and give you one—" the man held up a small jar "—drink of wine."

Scanning the crowd, Ada looked for her brother

Asher, or anybody willing to save her. "Please, God," she whispered.

The Philistine leaned closer. His disgusting breath wafted over her. "No god will save you, sweet. Not even the goddess our city honors with such a magnificent shrine." Her captor motioned toward the mud-brick tower reaching into the darkening sky. "As you have no other bidders…"

The Philistine's words disappeared as Ada caught sight of a man pushing through the crowd. He was tall, even taller than many of the warriors patrolling the city gates, and imposing. A large gold pendant rested on one sinewy shoulder, holding together the pieces of his tunic. Besides the gold bands circling his upper arms, his other shoulder and both arms remained bare. A wide leather belt cinched at his waist revealed just how massive his chest was. His skin was gold, bronzed from the sun. Dark curls sheared at his nape framed a chiseled jaw. His body bore the marks of war, such as she'd seen on her father and Asher, but his clothing told her he was not a man of humble means.

Her gaze flitted to his, and she wished she could see their color. He tilted his head and spoke to his companion.

"Three pieces of silver, three omers of barley and four drinks of your finest wine," her captor called out.

Ada jerked her attention from the beautiful man and back to the burly bidder and the women giggling around him. She closed her eyes and dropped her chin to her chest as that wayward tear forced its way to her lashes. It was not a fair price, not nearly equal to that of the gold band now gracing her sister's arm, but she felt the Philistine's acceptance when he relaxed his hold on her.

How could she accept such a fate? It did not matter. If God chose not to save her she would pray and trust Him to mete out justice upon her sisters. And to comfort her father when she did not return home with them.

"Are we agreed?" The Philistine's voice bellowed with the power of a crashing wave, causing Ada to jump.

"Ay—" The bidder nodded.

"Two hundred pieces of silver."

Her head snapped up. She looked into the crowd for her brother, but her gaze somehow settled on the strange man towering above those around him. She drew in a slow breath. Dare she thank God for His mercy, yet?

"Two hundred pieces of silver," he repeated as he moved. The crowd quieted and parted like the wind blowing grains of sand. He halted in front of her. "Thirty omers of barley and four casks of Greece's finest olive oil."

Black. His eyes were the color of charred wood. Certainly they could offer warmth much like dying embers, but they were cold. Angry. His jaw clenched, hard as stone, and fear pricked her nape. Had God heard her prayer and granted her mercy, or had the Creator of the heavens and earth ignored her plea and delivered her into a worse fate?

Nicolaus willed calm into his tense muscles and forced the Sea Dragon to slumber. That man had died along with the skirmishes between Greece and neighboring islands. That man had died after he unknowingly sunk a ship filled with innocent people.

The ill treatment of the young woman reminded him of his own time as a slave, worse it reminded him of what he was certain his sister might be enduring. If she was still alive. He would not think on the fact that if he hadn't killed off the Sea Dragon his sister wouldn't have been taken from his vessel when his ship was boarded. Then again, it seemed he could lay the blame on the Sea Dragon, but why he was uncertain. Had it been revenge or something else altogether? It was a question David had never answered. All Nicolaus knew was a man he'd once called friend had betrayed him and had been a cruel master, not only to him but to all of his slaves, including the women. No matter how much he tried to ignore the fear, he could not, would not allow another woman to suffer. Not in his presence. Not again.

"What are you doing? You cannot think to use your father's merchandise to buy a woman, Nicolaus." His friend and best sailing mate, Xandros, laid a hand on his shoulder. "My friend, we do not have the time nor the resources to rescue maidens."

Ignoring Xandros and the dark clouds pushing against the sky, Nicolaus spoke to the Philistine who had yet to close his mouth. "Agreed?"

The Philistine's gaze dropped to the purse resting against Nicolaus's hip as if he could judge the amount hidden within the leather bag, and then buried his nose against the young woman's face. "She is clean." At least that is what Nicolaus thought he'd said. The man's dialect was thick and heavy as if he'd had too much wine. Of course, Nicolaus was not as familiar with the language of these people as he should be. "Three hundred pieces of silver, a hundred omers of barley and ten casks of your oil."

The game of bargaining was well known to Nicolaus. His father was among the finest merchants. Resisting the urge to weigh his purse in the palm of his hand, Nicolaus raised his eyebrows as he perused the young woman. He leaned toward Xandros, who spoke the language well. "Tell him there are many women in Greece who are clean and without such—" he made a motion with his hands as he glanced toward the woman "—curves."

Her lips parted with a soft gasp, and her dark eyes flamed with anger as Xandros repeated his words.

"A hundred pieces of silver. Twenty omers of barley and two casks of olive oil." Nicolaus crossed his arms over his chest and waited, a tactic he had often used when negotiating with adversaries. After a few moments of silence he turned on his heel to leave.

"A moment." The Philistine's words halted him. Nicolaus glanced over his shoulder. The young woman narrowed her gaze toward a spot in the crowd. Following the direction of her angered glare, he saw several young women pointing toward the platform. They seemed to be arguing with the oldest among them. Who were they? Rivals? Had this young woman stolen the affection of a man from them? Possible, but given how similar the one wearing the gold band looked to the woman being auctioned, he wondered if they were of some relation. Cousins, sisters perhaps?

"We have not all day," Nicolaus said as he turned his attention back to the Philistine. "You have no other bidders vying for this woman." He flicked a glance toward the first bidder. "None willing to pay what I am. Two hundred pieces of silver and one cask of oil. It is a fair price and more than the piece of jewelry you traded her for."

It did not take much to discern the trade, not when the one woman guarded the ornament with a raised brow and a smirk, and so he opted for his original bid of silver in an effort to halt all haggling. After dealing with the Philistine merchants in Ashkelon most of the day, he was done and ready to set his oars to the water. He was ready to return to his island home in Greece.

A low growl emitted from the Philistine. The hand grasping the woman's hair shook, pulling her hair if the signs of discomfort forming around her mouth and the lone tear were any indication. It took all of Nicolaus's will not to jump onto the platform and release the woman. The Sea Dragon would have and he was certain he would have, too, if the auctioneer had not conceded with a nod.

Nicolaus untied his purse, counted out the coins and handed them to Xandros. "See to it she is on the ship posthaste. We must leave before the storm comes in. Brison will fetch the oil."

He pushed his way through the crowd and toward the group of women he'd seen the slave glaring at. Standing before them, he took in their various features from exotic to plain. The oldest, bearing the intricate gold band with colorful stones around her arm, wore a veil over one shoulder. If it had not been sitting haphazard, Nicolaus would not have thought it out of place. However, the color and the weave seemed more suitable to the woman he hoped Xandros was securing. It also seemed to match the color of the slave's tunic.

"Your name?"

The woman lowered her eyes, her dark lashes brushing against her tanned cheeks. He wondered again if this woman was sister to the slave, the shape of their eyes, the slant of their mouths when they scowled were similar. However, the slave was much more beautiful. This woman's hair, cropped at her shoulders, was near the color of the sky the moment right before the night cloaked them in total darkness. The slave's hair, the color of wheat just as the sun begins to slip beyond the horizon, hung down her back in gilded waves. Her skin was much fairer, not as dark as the woman before him. This woman bore the lines of displeasure, sadness and spite, not those of a woman who'd known the love of family.

"Dina."

He pulled out a decent gold coin and flipped it between his fingers. Her greedy eyes followed the movement as she licked her lips as if starving for a meal. "I would purchase this from you." He touched the gold band. Although the stones glittered, the craftsmanship was not to be praised. It certainly was not worth the two pieces of silver the procurer used in his quest to acquire the slave, nor was it worth the gold coin Nicolaus offered her. He did not appreciate the way the band seemed to cause this woman to gloat, as if she'd been given a king's ransom. It did not seem fitting to leave her adorned with it.

Dina reached for the coin but Nicolaus pulled his hand back. "The band." The woman glanced at her companions before tugging the gold piece from her arm and dropping it into his palm. "What of the veil?" he added.

Dina touched her fingers to the piece of fabric and began to pull it from her shoulder. One of the other women laid a hand on her arm. "Dina, you cannot. What of Father?"

"Shhh, I will deal with him." Her eyes narrowed to slits as she thrust the fabric at him. Had these women sold their father's slave without his knowledge? His kin? For what cause?

Taking the veil, he handed it to the one who spoke. "Give this to your father if you must. Inform him she will be well cared for." He glanced at Dina and held the coin toward her. "As for you, my dear woman, riches are not everything."

She pinched it with her fingers, but he held on. Dina tilted her head as if to consider his words. Her gaze flitted to the bands on his arms and then to the clasp on his shoulder. The corner of her mouth curved upward. "It is obvious from your dress, good sir, that you have never been in want. Never wandered the desert smelling of sheep."

The woman could not be further from the truth. However, the wind pushing at his back reminded him time was short. "I hope your conscience can bear the guilt of your greed."

Did she understand the words he'd spoken in Greek? He could not tell, nor did he wait to determine her reaction. He turned toward the quay where his ship was tethered. The storm continued to cling to the horizon, but it would not do so much longer. It was time to leave Ashkelon and her heathenistic ways. He had a race to finish if he was to beat his Jasen, his twin brother, at their father's game. The prize—the ship and all merchandise aboard when they arrived home. His latest purchase only increased the stakes and sent a wave of urgency rushing through his blood.

He caught sight of Xandros's wide shoulders and the woman he tugged through the crowd. They were nearing the gates leading toward walkway that led to the ship when they stopped. The clenching of Xandros's jaw told Nicolaus all he needed to know. The woman refused to go any farther. Nicolaus pushed through the throngs of seafarers preparing to leave port until he reached his friend and the woman slave. Without a second thought he tossed her over his shoulder. Her bound fists thumped against his back causing him to smile.

He'd misjudged her size. She was much smaller than he had first believed, even if she did have curves, but curves would not help his mother with household chores, and her small stature would not be valuable to tending the vineyards. He would think on what position she would take in his mother's household as they traveled home. It was a shame he was not looking for a wife. He could imagine waking up to her beautiful, expressive eyes each morning. The warmth of her snuggled against him as he smoothed her hair behind the cup of her ear.

"Come, Xandros. Let us go home. I have a sudden urgency to win the race." For the first time in months, the burden of guilt began to lift from his shoulders and a smile formed. The air flowing to and from his lungs seemed freer. Perhaps, he could be redeemed. After all, if he could rescue one small maiden, perhaps there was hope to rescue more, including his own sister.

"It's good to see your competitiveness come back, Nicolaus. I had lost hope," Xandros called from behind him.

"As had I, Xandros, as had I." He stepped over the rail and jumped down onto the deck before turning toward his friend. "That bit of haggling with the Philistine." He puffed out his chest and smiled. A genuine smile, one that encompassed his entire being as freedom washed over him. Even the small fists—a swift reminder of purchasing a human, something he'd promised he'd never do—pounding against his back couldn't penetrate the first bit of happiness he'd felt in months. "And a prime purchase will do that to a man."

The fists beating his back halted. The woman stilled. Nicolaus slackened his hold until her toes touched the planks. The top of her head did not even reach his shoulders. She titled her head back. Her mouth scrunched into a scowl. Her eyes narrowed. Had she understood him? Did this Philistine woman understand his language?

"Do you speak Ionian?" he asked in his own language.

A shadow flickered through her eyes as her brows pulled together.

"Perhaps you paid too much for her," Xandros spoke in her language.

"Perhaps I did."

Before he realized what she was about, she swung her bound hands, clouting him against the jaw as she stomped her heel down on his foot. Nicolaus grabbed her hands before she could hit him again. Xandros doubled over in laughter. "I would have paid thrice the amount if I would have known she would clout you, my friend."

Ay, Nicolaus would have paid ten times. Mayhap even more. She had too much fire to be wasted on the likes of Ashkelon's wickedness. A fire that seemed to banish all his horrid memories and dare him to breathe again.

"The merchandise is all aboard and secured." Brison, his youngest brother and the man—if one could call seventeen summers a man—he'd placed in charge of their merchandise stood eager to please.

"All save one." Nicolaus nodded toward the slave as he loosened his fingers around her upper arm. Her anger vibrated through his fingertips, softening his own anger at her poor treatment. What was it about this woman that threatened to banish months of guilt and anguish from his thoughts?

Brison's mouth fell open, gaping as if confused. Xandros stepped closer as if to protect the young woman from Nicolaus's wrath, a wrath that was not geared toward her. But what shocked and filled Nicolaus with a sense of pride was the way his young brother straightened his shoulders as if to protect her, too. He glanced down at the little damsel. Her eyes glittered like the amber jewels he'd seen in Ashkelon's temple honoring one of Greece's goddesses, and he had the urge to see them spark even more. "Brison, do not place the woman below deck, place her in the captain's chamber. I would like to keep an eye on my most prized purchase."

Did she flinch? He was certain she had. Brison most certainly did, and if he didn't know better Xandros did, too. "Very well, Captain." Nicolaus caught the twist of his younger brother's mouth before he turned toward Xandros, who nodded his agreement. Brison took hold of the woman's arm and led her away. She tried to jerk from his brother, but Brison held firm. Even in her anger her stature was full of grace, and the sway of her hips was gentle, like the smooth motion of his vessel on a calm sea. The sight eased his irritation over his crew's obstinacy. What was wrong with his brother and friend? Was he such an incompetent commander that his brother must seek his second-in-command's permission before seeing his orders carried out?

"He thinks you've gone mad." Xandros tugged on a rope leading up to the mast. "I'm inclined to agree. Prized merchandise?"

A rumble of laughter bubbled from Nicolaus's stomach and burst forth. He clapped Xandros on the back, his mind sobered as he grasped hold of his own words, words that the Sea Dragon would have spoken. "Perhaps I have, my friend. Perhaps, I have."

"Mayhap the men should seek the mercies of the sea god before we leave port." The corner of Xandros's mouth lifted. It was only a jest, but it bothered Nicolaus nonetheless. He'd long ago given up the idea of gods. Much to Uncle's delight and his father's grief. Where had the gods been when he was beaten day after day? Where were the gods when his sister was taken from his protection? Those so-called gods his friends and family called upon were nothing more than falsehoods conjured in the minds of idle men.

"Tell them to be done with it." Nicolaus focused on the western horizon. The clouds grew darker and heavy. He did not have time for a storm. Not when he actually cared to beat his brother this time around.

All laughter left his friend's face as his jaw fell open. "You can't think to leave port with a storm coming toward us."

"I've not known you to shy away from a small

storm, my friend. Besides, we've not the time to waste if we're to beat my brother."

"You've drunk seawater to be mad as you are."

Nicolaus smacked his friend on the back. "Nay, I admit there's a risk, but I have the best sailors on board my ship who do not wish to be swallowed by the sea. If you look—" Nicolaus pointed "—the clouds are moving from the southwest. If we hold course and follow the coast north and then west, we'll get ahead of it and mayhap miss the squall altogether."

"It is a relief you don't intend to sail straight across the sea."

One corner of Nicolaus's mouth twitched. How would his friend feel when the skies cleared?

# Chapter Two

All reasoning had disappeared when the man had tossed her over his shoulder as if he were a barbarian and she nothing more than a sheep to slaughter. She had been fooled by his attire, richly dressed as he was, into believing he was kind, compassionate. She had hoped to convince him to return her to her father. Instead, he treated her no different than that Philistine when he had dragged her around by her hair.

And now she was being led around a boat. She'd heard of such vessels moving on the Great Sea, but she'd never seen one. Tales told by her father when she was naught but a girl had filled her with excitement. She had longed to experience such adventures until she recalled with clarity how his boat had splintered against rocks leaving him near death.

The crewman stopped beside a ladder and motioned for her to climb. She tilted her head back. It seemed as if the ladder led to a small room or a pyre. She'd heard the stories of these heathens, who even now lifted prayers to an unfamiliar god. She would not be their sacrifice, not to their god of the sea. As if one existed. Had they not heard of the one true God? The One who created the seas *and* all the beasts within.

The boat rocked. Although she understood the motion of the water, she was not prepared for the way it unsteadied her, causing her to stumble toward the wooden rail. White waves crashed against the boat. She sucked in a breath as the sailor lashed his arm around her waist and pulled her back from the edge. Fear clawed at her stomach, making it angry with each movement of the vessel. Her mouth began to water. Before she knew what was happening the man had her bent over the railing as she lost her morning's meal. She pressed her bound hands to her mouth and squeezed her eyes closed.

"Better?"

"My thanks." She nodded; grateful he'd spoken in her language and not that of her captor. She'd prefer the captain did not know she understood most of his language, especially if it helped her to escape.

The crewman pointed back toward the ladder. Ada wished to be as far from the sea as possible, yet… She glanced toward the port. If she could gain her freedom could she reach the shore before a sea monster attacked or the water swallowed her? There were people milling about. Would someone help her?

"Go on. It's the safest place for you." He pointed.

Ada's stomach once again rebelled. Hands once again pressed to her mouth, she shook her head.

A shout rose from below. Rows of oars poked through the side. Another shout and the boat lurched forward. Ada stumbled, but gripped the rail to keep from falling. She swallowed back the tears threatening to spill as the boat lurched again, and again. Each movement proceeded by a command. A command that took her farther away from home.

The man glanced around as if considering Ada's chance of escape. "Very well. However, you should sit over there." He tugged on her hands. Shaking his head, he led her to the back end of the boat. The one closest to the shore. "Here. Sit beneath the shade of the helmsman's perch. You won't get stepped on and the walls will keep you from falling into the sea. My brother will not be happy I disobeyed his orders and will have my head if anything should happen to you." He paused as he looked her over. "Considering your sickness, I am certain he will understand."

A wave splashed against the boat, spraying upon her face. She pressed her back against the side and slid until she sat on her heels.

"I have duties to attend. Nicolaus had hoped to leave before the storm." Nicolaus? This sailor's brother and captain? It was not one she imagined. More like Leviathan or Goliath. He needed a name that invoked fear in children, not one that made her want to champion him as if he were a hero. He most assuredly was not her hero. Heroes didn't steal maidens from their homes. It didn't matter that he didn't actually steal her, it didn't matter that he, in truth, saved her from that horrible man, she couldn't—wouldn't—think of him as a hero, especially not her hero.

The man looked toward the sky and Ada followed his gaze. Angry gray clouds hung low, gliding overhead.

"Seems we'll sail right into it." He planted his fists on his hips and shook his head. The boat jolted and then rocked. Could the tipping and tilting of the boat possibly worsen? Ada gasped at the thought, but before she could ponder the panic welling inside her, the boat rolled, jerking her to the side. Instinctively, she flung her bound hands out to keep her head from hitting the planks. The crewman seemed unaware of her predicament or the odd creaks and rolling of the boat. His feet remained planted as she struggled to right herself and keep her stomach from rebelling against the motion. Were the waves making her ill or was it the lingering fear from her father's tales?

"I will bring you a drink when I return. It should calm your nerves some." He turned to leave, and then halted. "Take care. The god of the sea will not likely return as comely a maid as you if you were to fall over." He left, scratching his head.

"Bah," she whispered beneath her breath. Her brother had oft teased her when she was little saying the fabled god would come steal her away to his kingdom if she did not behave. The memory burned the back of her throat. What would Asher say now? However, it was not she who had been about such mischief to cause her trouble.

The captain's brother halted near the middle of the boat and glanced at her over his shoulder before disappearing beneath the planks. Ada waited a few moments to see if he would return.

A shout from the platform above her caused the forward motion of the boat to quicken. Ada's pulse thundered harder with each jarring movement. She bit at the ropes binding her wrists in hopes of loosening them, but to no avail. Standing, she ducked beneath the helmsman's perch and leaned over the rail. Her gaze turned homeward. Merchants continued to busy themselves along the wharf. Some carried amphora vases toward the shore, others carried them onto boats. Waves rolled in from the sea, crashing against the stone piers, and her stomach roiled with the motion. She needed off this boat, needed to go home. Her brother had taught her to swim when she was little but never in such a vast body of water and never with her hands bound. All she need do was get into the water and swim on her back, kicking her legs.

The distance did not seem too far as she could still make out the arms and legs of the seafarers on shore. She gauged the incoming wave as her stomach threatened to unleash its fury. If she did it right, if she jumped before a wave passed, would it push her to shore as it did the pieces of drift being carried toward Ashkelon?

She pressed her face against her hands. Then what? Would she end up on the auction block again once she made it to the port city? This time to that horrible man with the matted beard and colorfully dressed women clinging to his arms. No doubt, especially since he had not seemed too happy to find himself outbid. At least she had a chance of returning to her father. And the sisters who had betrayed her.

Air hitched in her lungs. Had they acted on her father's wishes? He'd been angry over her mother's passing. Had he decided to rid himself of his youngest daughter, too? Was that why he had allowed her to journey into the city with Asher and her sisters when he had never done so before?

The thoughts ambushed her chest, tearing little pieces away from her heart. If she did not return home, she would never see her father again, never know if he had wished her gone from his presence.

She glanced down the side of the boat and watched the oars dig into the water, pushing the boat forward. If she jumped here, she would miss the oars and by God's mercy He would see her safely home.

A look around the deck told her only a few men remained above. The rest, she assumed, tended the oars. The sailor who had helped her earlier had yet to reappear. Armed warriors stood on either side of the captain on a platform at the head of the boat. Nicolaus's arms were crossed over his chest, his feet braced shoulder width apart. The strong wind tugged at his tunic, brushed back the curls of his hair.

Power and strength exuded from him and she could quite imagine him the son of one of his fabled gods. Her sisters had oft spoke of such men—half god, half man—with wistful smiles and wistful sighs. Mostly, they were larger than David's Goliath had been. And they always had some sort of gift. Ada had paid her sisters heed only to gain their acceptance, but she knew better. There were no gods other than the God of Heaven and earth. He was the only living, breathing God. A god not created by the hands of man.

As if he could feel her eyes on him, the captain turned. His gaze settled on her, warming her chilled limbs from the stiff, stormy breeze. If only they had met under different circumstances. If only he had not acted the barbarian and hauled her over his shoulder as though she was his property. Of course, she was. He paid a great price to own her. However, that did not mean she was not angered by his behavior. Was this how her mother felt when she was bought and taken from her home by Ada's father?

A shout drew his attention forward. The boat lifted, slamming Ada against the back of the craft and then to the side. A wave knocked her feet from beneath her and off the boat. She grabbed ahold of the rail and clenched her jaw, her feet dangling over the side. She glanced toward home, now a mere speck in the distance and she knew she'd not be able to swim the distance, not in the angry sea.

Her fingers ached with the effort to maintain her hold. She lifted her face to the sky. "Abba God, please, I just want to go home to my father."

The boat rocked one way, lifting her away, and then the other plunging her into the cold waters. A wave crashed into her forcing her fingers to let go. She was pushed and then pulled, the wave sucking at her and then rolling her. Her lungs caught fire as she kicked her legs, fighting against the sharp talons of the wave.

He had shifted only a bit when the delightful prick at his nape had changed to a gut instinct that something was abominably wrong. A flash of bare feet and legs caught his eye when the sun-bleached linen and waves of wheat-colored tresses thrust upward.

"Xandros! Brison!" He jumped from the command post and onto the deck. He did not wait to see if the two followed. Unhinging the clasp at his shoulder, he removed his outer cloak, leaving only his undertunic on, and ran toward the back of the ship. He grabbed hold of the end of the coiled rope, kept at either end of the boat in the instance a man fell overboard, and hopped over the rail. He dove into the water. He'd sailed since he was a young boy and never once imagined anyone would willingly throw themselves to the mercy of the sea. Had she preferred to take her chances with the waves, or had she slipped overboard?

He blew the salty water from his nose and kicked toward the surface. Relaxing his muscles, he allowed his body to bob with the waves while he tied the rope around his waist. Brison's bellow rose above the seas and the oarsmen reversed direction. Nicolaus would be thankful later that the coming storm had prevented them from unfurling the sail.

"Nicolaus!"

Xandros stood on the rail, pointing northward. The woman's bound hands rose above her head before disappearing in the choppy water. Nicolaus bit back a curse. Brison should have cut her loose, but then Nicolaus should have ordered him to cut her loose. Perhaps then she'd have a better chance against the sea.

Not that she would have much of a chance if she did not know how to swim. The sea often took humans captive. She bobbed above the water, gasping for air, and he realized she had been pulled farther away than he expected. He hoped the rope reached that far.

"Nicolaus!" He did not need to look at his friend to see the warning. The way the sea bubbled around his legs and rose against his chest, he knew a large wave was bearing down on them.

He dove beneath the water, beneath the fall of the wave until it passed. Kicking upward, he broke the surface and sucked in air before slicing his arms through the water toward the last place he'd seen her.

"Where?" There was no time for patience. However, his gut told him to wait a few beats of his pulse.

The water once again rose. *God, my uncle is certain You are real. I did not save the woman only to see her swallowed by the ocean.*

The wave tugged at him and crashed down upon his head before he could swim under it. He tumbled deeper away from the surface, slamming into a tangle of seaweed. No, it could not be seaweed, they were far enough away from the shore and he was not that close to the bottom.

Was he?

Something bumped against his leg. His eyes flew open. A mass of tresses expanded from either side of her heart-shaped face. The strands took on a life of their own as they obeyed the motion of the turbulent water. He wrapped his arms around her and kicked his legs until they broke the surface. Her body lay lifeless in his arms. Brushing her hair from her eyes, he willed them to open.

He spun her around so her back was pressed against his chest, and wrapped his arm tight around her stomach. He lay on his back and started to swim toward the boat when she began coughing. Her lids fluttered open and then widened in fear. She smacked her head against his shoulder as she arched against his chest. He tightened his hold on her as the sea began to bubble against his legs, but she managed to twist her body around to face him.

"Trust me." Staring into her eyes, he spoke her language and willed her to trust him. If only until they set foot on the boat. "Hold your breath. I am taking you under."

He glanced toward the large wave as it rolled toward them. Her muscles tensed.

"Now."

She sucked in air a moment before he propelled them beneath the wave. With his arms wrapped around her waist, he once again pushed them toward the surface. He shifted her against his side and sliced through the water toward the boat—her hair tangling with his arms and legs hindered him. After only three strokes, the woman tensed and began to struggle against his hold.

"Halt!"

She jabbed her elbow into his ribs, but he held tight.

"You will die."

She dug her heel against his shin. Twisting in his arms, she clouted his jaw, scratched at his eyes. He was a good swimmer, one thing he'd always beaten his brother at, but she was making it difficult. He seemed to be swallowing more water than usual.

"Halt," he growled near her ear, jerking her against him. If she did not stop they would both die, and then he'd, most assuredly, lose against his brother. A shame, given he'd just begun to feel alive again.

Her eyes filled with tears, or perhaps it was only the sea. Whatever it was, her fear and sadness reached into his soul and tugged with a greater force than any wave. He knew right then he'd do anything to protect her, even allow the sea to take him.

"I am scared." Her eyelids slid shut, pushing tears down her cheeks until the droplets fell into the bobbing water.

Did she wish to meet her maker? Was he so fearsome that she preferred death over his company?

"Home."

His gut constricted. He understood that one word,

had longed for home with great sickness during his own captivity. He glanced toward the shore, the large tower, a mere speck of sand on the horizon. However, with the sea once again rising he did not have time to span their language barrier and explain that he'd take her home after he'd beaten his brother in their quest.

As if guessing his intentions, she slammed her bound fists against his nose, forcing him to loosen his hold. Her arms flailed, and she kicked her legs against his as she struggled to keep her head above water.

Nicolaus grabbed hold of her tunic, her hair enslaving his forearm and chest. Tugging on the rope attached to his waist, he bound her arms to her sides and then to him. Even though it seemed the fight had drained from her limbs, he was not willing to risk losing. He hated losing, even when he gave up. But giving up was not possible. Not now.

With her back cradled against his chest, he twisted onto his back and kicked his legs. "Xandros, pull!"

After what seemed like long moments, Xandros and Brison pulled them onto the deck. Nicolaus untangled from her hair and loosened the rope from her body and then from himself. He lifted her into his arms, cradled her against his chest and carried her toward his chambers. He climbed the four rungs of the ladder, ducked beneath the beam and set her in the corner before returning to the portal.

"Brison, see the men work double time. We must get ahead of the storm. Xandros, report to the command post. Once the storm passes, we sail west across the Great Sea."

Nicolaus raked a shaking hand through his hair. Droplets of water splattered to the deck and pooled with the sea dripping from his tunic. He eased in a breath and blew it out slowly. Several times before facing her.

She huddled against the corner, cloaked in her glorious mane with her eyelids closed. He could almost believe she was a creature of the sea. A daughter of the fabled gods. However, her beauty was incomparable to the stories of the beautiful creatures luring sailors from their ships.

Drawing her knees into her chest, she shivered with a violence that shook even him and near caused him to lose his legs. As if sensing he watched her, she opened her eyes. Fire raged in the depths of her glittering jewels. The quivering of her jaw belied the fearless front etched on her face. If not for the rope around her neck and binding her hands she could have held court in the finest palaces. How could anyone sell their relative? Of course, he knew. He had seen the petty jealousy of the women watching this maid's fate. Who was she to them? A sister, a cousin? No doubt, a servant in their father's house. A cruel master to allow his daughters to send such a creature to the auction block and near into the hands of Ashkelon's darkness.

Had his sister suffered such a fate? The anger he'd fought to calm resurfaced. He clenched his fists, his nails biting into his palms. The maid lifted her chin as if to defy his anger.

Shaking his head in disbelief at the woman's misplaced courage and never-ending fight, he laughed. If the men accompanying him when they'd encountered the evil seafarers had had half her courage he never would have been captured, not even against the ten ships that had surrounded him, forcing him to surrender. And never would have been taken to Delos and suffered the shame of slavery. Nor would his father have suffered the loss of his daughter.

# Chapter Three

The captain's jaw hardened, his fists clenched at his sides. She tore her gaze from his angry glare only to lose her breath at the sight of his broad chest and thick arms. The contours glistened beneath the droplets of water sliding down the smooth skin of his arms. Ada swallowed the knot forming in her throat and blinked her eyes against the sting of tears. As much as she wanted to blame the sea, she knew better. The captain's cruel laughter had pierced the layers of brick and mud she had used to protect herself against her sisters' taunts. His laughter should not cause her this much pain, especially given he was nothing more than a stranger, but having gone from the daughter of a wealthy and much respected merchant to a slave and near drowning in a matter of hours was wreaking havoc on her emotions.

Certainly he had been kind enough to risk his life to save her. However, that reason alone was not enough for her to take offense at his mockery. Not when she'd learned as a small child to keep such things from hurting her.

Taking a step closer, he knelt and reached his hand out. She shrunk against the wall as he brushed her hair from her eyes. The warmth of his hand against her cooled skin sent another round of chattering to her teeth. And more despised tears.

"I will not hurt you." His slow, soothing tone and the rough pad of his thumb against her cheek as he wiped her tears made her want to believe him. The muscles in her shoulders even began to relax, but then he pulled a silver dagger with an intricately jeweled hilt from a sheath attached to his belt. "All right?"

Tensing once again, she darted her gaze around the small room in search of a weapon. A bench with brightly colored silk pillows and a small table, quite clearly attached to the floor, was all that decorated the room. Air refused to enter her chest as the knife neared her throat. The cold silver slid beneath the rope and against her skin. A different sort of fear gnawed at Ada's insides. Was this how she was to die? Why save her from drowning only to mess his tidy sanctuary by slitting her throat.

*Because he thinks to offer you as a sacrifice to one of his false gods.*

Uncontrollable tears welled in her eyes and slid down her cheeks. The edge of the knife pressed against her neck. She closed her eyes and swallowed.

"Hear my plea, *Adonai*, God of Heaven and earth."

The blade stilled. Ada opened her eyes. Nicolaus's dark eyes stared into hers. Where they had once been dark and cold, they now held curiosity and warmth. Like she thought they would. Droplets of water dripped from his curls and down into his thick-bearded jaw, before plopping onto a well-defined arm honed, no doubt, in battle if the scars marring it and the rest of his upper body were any indication.

His lips twitched as if he were about to say something, and then he refocused on her neck. His blade tugged against the corded rope. Slicing downward, the knife broke through the rope. He pulled it from her neck and then cut the binding from her wrists before sheathing his knife. Ada swallowed, and salt from the sea continued to invade the inside of her mouth.

Nicolaus grabbed hold of her wrists and turned them in his hands. His eyes darkened to match the night sky as his fingers trailed over the chafed flesh. He glanced at her neck. Lifting her hair off her shoulders, he murmured a few words she did not quite understand. He settled back on his heels and took her hands in his once again, his thumb smoothing over her wrists in a gentle motion. "These need tending."

Ada blinked several times, pretending she did not understand and pulled away from his touch before cradling her folded hands against her chest. She prayed he would leave her alone. His anger she could accept, but his gentle touch and the concern in his eyes reminded her of her mother's love. A love she would never again know. She wrapped her arms around her legs and buried her face against her knees.

If her mother had not gone to be with her ancestors, her father never would have left her to the care of her sisters and Ada would not be on a boat surrounded by increasingly violent waves.

The captain stood, raking his hand through his hair, sending bits of water splattering all around her. His jaw clenched. The creases at the corner of his right eye twitched together, and his nostrils flared. "You stay."

Ada feared to even breathe in his presence given he seemed to be angered easily at the sight of her, not to mention every time she inhaled she caught a whiff of sandalwood and wet leather. A heady combination to her sensitive emotions, especially considering she had wanted to throw her arms around him in gratitude when he released her bindings. However, his command, as if she were a dog, left a metallic tinge on her tongue as she bit back the rebuke.

His chest expanded as if he were about to speak, but he took a step back and then disappeared down the ladder.

Waiting a few breaths, Ada scrambled across the floor and peered down the opening. Nicolaus stood below her with his arms crossed over his bare chest. He was so close that if she reached out her fingers she could touch his hair. Rolling his shoulders, he turned his head, and she jerked back before he caught her.

"Large swell to the west."

Ada stood. Her legs threatened to buckle beneath her but she pushed forward toward the window and wrapped her hands around the edge for support. Strong winds tugged at her hair. Rain or bits of the sea stung her cheeks. The man Nicolaus had called Xandros stood on a platform at the front of the boat. Beyond him was nothing but gray sky and rising waves.

The gurgling in her stomach bubbled into her throat. She fought the sickness, but it continued upward. She knew there was nothing here to catch the contents of her stomach—if there was anything left— and she did not wish to dirty Nicolaus's pristine abode.

Gathering the hem of her sodden tunic, Ada climbed down the ladder and raced toward the back of the boat. She leaned over the rail and heaved. And heaved. With her arms against the top rail, she rested her head and fixed her thoughts on trying to breathe past the sickness overtaking her stomach.

The boat rolled to the left and she dug her nails into the wood railing. No sooner had it gone one way, it rolled the other. Seawater rushed over her bare feet as the boat tilted. Ada's feet slipped from beneath her and she found herself sliding, once again, between the rail and the decking.

A strong arm snaked around her midsection and jerked her away from the edge. Sandalwood, leather and sea salt engulfed her. She leaned her head against his chest and breathed a sigh of relief. "Thank You, God."

The sinewy arm banded around her waist flinched. "Your god has naught to do with your rescue, foolish woman."

Her relief quickly dispersed at his words. This Greek barbarian and his language grated her frayed nerves. Was her illness foolishness?

"I told you to stay." He tossed her over his shoulder. Her sensitive stomach rebelled and heaved. Fortunately for Nicolaus, her stomach was now empty. Although it would have served justice to soil his tunic. Her condition seemed to go unnoticed as he trudged across the deck.

"I should let the sea have you."

She stiffened, frightened he would carry through with his threat. However, she would not respond, would not give him a hint that she knew his language, a language her father often spoken when conversing with traders.

"Save me the trouble. Good coin spent on saving you from disgrace. Should have let the procurer have you. I would have been richer." He halted beside the ladder leading to the room and deposited her onto her feet. She noticed he had donned his outer tunic and was much drier than she was. "Foolish, foolish woman, I'll bind you to the mast if need be."

Before she knew what she was about, she drew back her hand and slapped him.

Nicolaus furrowed his brow. "You do understand me."

Her eyes widened, and he smiled. "It is as I thought, but how?"

A wave sloshed over the boat. Spray rained down upon them. Her pallor did not look well as his ship rocked back and forth. She clamped a hand over her mouth, her gaze darted around. "Ah, you do not like the sea."

She bent over, an arm clutched at her stomach.

"Come along, then." He lifted her into his arms and tucked her head beneath his chin. Her slight frame nestled perfectly against him, when she wasn't pushing her palms against his chest. That part of him that had been cold for so many months began to beat, to breathe and to hope for a better future than the one he'd resigned himself to.

"Hold still, lest I drop you."

Fire burned in her eyes as she glared at him. "I do not wish to be coddled. I am meant to be a slave and I should act as such, not as a maid in need of rescue as you so kindly put it."

Laughter tickled the back of his throat. It took much

effort to keep it from spilling forth. Strange how he'd felt happier since he'd brought her aboard his ship than he had in a long while. "If you are a slave, as you say, then I will coddle you if I so choose. As it stands, you are ill. I would not be a good merchant if I allowed my merchandise to waste away from sickness of the sea, now, would I?"

She lifted her chin a little higher, crossed her arms over her chest and released a huff. He gave in to the tugging at the corners of his lip. Fortunately, her eyes were closed else there would have been more from her viperous tongue. Admitting defeat was obviously not easy on this Philistine woman who called upon the Hebrew god, and he was certain their little sparring was not over, which pleased him more than it should. Especially given he looked forward to future matches with this mite of a woman.

"Brison, send a man for a cake of bread and fresh water. I need a bowl and a cloth and the lady needs dry clothing."

Tilting her head she glanced up at him. "I pray, do not waste your precious merchandise on a slave like me."

The constant reminder of how he'd acquired her burned in his belly. It wasn't as if he went about buying humans at will. He grabbed hold of the highest ladder rung and climbed into his captain's quarters. The woman shivered and then clamped a hand over her mouth. Nicolaus tossed the pillows onto the floor and then laid her down on the cushioned bedding of the bench. No sooner had he done so than she sat upright, clutching her stomach as it rebelled against the ship's motion.

He swept her hair from her face and tucked it behind her. Drawing her knees into her chest, she rested her cheek against them. Her amber eyes reached into him. He took comfort in the knowledge that she had not willingly jumped into the angry froth.

"I should not be here." The words were little more than a whisper, but they were like the snap of a sail as it unfurled into the wind. The vibration of her voice thundered against his palm, slammed against his conscience. He unfolded his length and crossed his arms over his chest before staring out at the choppy sea.

Had his sister said the very same words when she'd been taken from him? He dropped his arms, clenching his hands at his sides. The fear in his sister's eyes as she was taken would forever torment him. The fact that he had taken another young maid from her homeland did not ease the suffering. It did not matter that he thought to save her from an even more repugnant future than being bound to him.

"What is it you are called?" Nicolaus glanced down at her. Her tresses, darkened from the water, fell down her back and pooled onto the bench. He could not change what was. He was not the one who had placed her on the auction block. He only intervened in what fate had in store for her and for that he would not apologize. Somehow he'd make her see the truth. Preferably before they arrived at his father's house.

"Ada." Her body rocked with the waves. She leaned near the edge of the bench and would have fallen if he had not reached out a hand. Her eyes grew wide, and she jerked from his touch.

"Ada." He liked the sound of her name. "You should lie down and rest. It is fortunate this is a small storm and will blow over soon. No doubt your stomach will improve once the sea settles."

"How can one rest when being tossed about?"

Before he could respond, Brison entered. "I will see to her, Captain. Xandros has need of your assistance."

"Xandros is capable of guiding us through the worst of storms. What could be the problem?"

Brison shuffled his feet, his gaze never meeting Nicolaus's. "Do not keep your thoughts to yourself, Brison. Say what needs to be said."

His brother glanced at Ada before darting toward Nicolaus. "Er...there be ships approaching, Captain."

"What did you say?" His chest constricted in fear. The last time he sailed, ten ships had ambushed him, capturing him and his sister. He had not considered until this moment how his ship had been left to his crew and all of the gifts his father had sent along to his sister's future groom untouched. An action unheard of for a band of sea thieves. But then it was not just any band of thieves, but rather David of Delos, a man he once considered a friend. A man who had fought by his side. Why had his friend turned against him, stolen his sister and forced Nicolaus into bondage? Those were questions he could not ponder at the moment. Now, he would do all in his might to keep his ship, crew and especially Ada safe.

"A ship. Perhaps two. Xandros could not be certain. What, with the storm and all it's a mite hard to discern when they hide behind the waves."

Nicolaus breathed a sigh of relief, but still raked shaky fingers through his hair. He knew they'd encounter other ships, and he was thankful only one or two approached. However, he preferred not to encounter them with Ada and his youngest brother on board. He could not lose another sibling to thieves, and he wouldn't risk Ada.

## Chapter Four

Brison's words were mumbled beneath his breath, but she understood the tensing of Nicolaus's jaw. Whatever news Brison had brought with him wasn't good. The front of the ship lifted, and Ada gripped the edges of the bench to keep from tumbling to the floor. However, her gaze remained on Nicolaus as he braced his palms against either side of the entryway and swung his legs outward before jumping to the deck.

Once the boat dipped and then settled, Ada pushed from the bench and stumbled to the window. Rain stung her cheeks, like when her sisters had pelted her with pebbles whenever they had wanted her to leave them alone. She swiped the water from her face and shielded her eyes. Dark clouds mingled with the angry sea, making it difficult to distinguish one from the other. The dark wood of the boat was all that broke the dullness of the scenery. That, and the broad shoulders of Nicolaus, who stood on a platform at the front of the ship. His mass of dark curls, soaked from seawater and rain, clung to the contours of his corded neck.

His tunic molded to his broad shoulders and arms as wide as a large earthen jar.

The man standing next to Nicolaus lifted his arm and pointed. Ada caught site of a dark spot looming on the horizon. What it was she could not tell, but by Nicolaus's stance, she could only imagine. She'd heard the tales from merchants at her father's table. Some from her father who had personally encountered the ruthless warriors of the sea. Could it be a ship on the horizon? A ship filled with thieves?

She turned and slid down the wall. The violent rocking of the boat churned her stomach. Hugging her knees to her chest, she buried her face against her forearms. An unbidden tear dropped from the corner of her eye and merged with the salty water soaking her tunic. What did it matter if the ship held thieves? She'd been traded by her sisters for a gold armband to one master only to be sold to Nicolaus.

What did one more mean to her?

Nothing. Her future had never truly been hers to determine, and now it seemed even less so. She'd be thankful to have known a mother's love, which she'd hold in her heart as long as she breathed. She'd also known the spite of siblings who despised her for who her mother was, for who she was. A Hebrew.

Drawing in a shuddering breath, she lifted her face and looked at the rafters sheltering her from the storm. It seemed as if God had forgotten that she was supposed to be one of his. "Lord, have You no mercy? Who will protect me now?"

"*I* will protect you with my life." Ada glanced up at the man who spoke her language in broken pieces. Nicolaus firmed his jaw, and determination shone bright in his eyes. "As will every man under my command."

As much as she did not trust these men who'd taken her from her home, she believed this one. Believed that this man would do as he said and protect her with his life. However, the fact that he felt the need to reassure caused her pulse to rise.

"Are we in danger?"

A shout from below deck was stolen by the roaring of the wind and the crashing waves. Nicolaus crossed his arms over his chest, and his gaze shifted out the window. It seemed he preferred to be on deck with his men, and for some reason she wished for his presence right where it was, with her. As much as he angered her, he brought her comfort, made her feel secure.

"There is always danger at sea."

She pushed from the floor and gripped the window. The sea churned, swishing and swirling like the desert sand in the midst of a storm. The brush of fabric whispered over her nerves as Nicolaus moved closer. Although he had to be as soaked as she was, warmth radiated from him, inviting her to shift closer. She tried to focus on the activity on the deck, on the waves washing over the railing, but his scent drew her gaze. He leaned his forearms against the window and lifted his face to the rain as if accepting punishment from the sky. His eyes were hooded in such a way she could not tell if they were open or closed. Did it matter? She could blame her stare on curiosity. Sure she'd seen Greeks like him. Many had sought out her father's house for trade, but she'd never seen a man such as him. One that exuded a quiet strength and kindness. A rivulet of rain slid down his brow, down onto his cheek. An instinct to wipe it dry left a knot deep in her chest. What was she thinking wanting to touch this stranger, one who'd thus far proven kind, but a stranger who could command her death at any moment if he were so inclined.

She pulled her gaze from his profile and looked toward the object that now began to resemble a ship much like Nicolaus's. "And what of them?"

"It depends."

She tilted her chin and looked him in the eye. "On?"

"Whether they are friend or foe." His chest rose high and fell deep, much like that of the waves surrounding them. The warning in his voice and the concern in his gaze caused her knees to wobble. "I imagine they intend to port at Ashkelon and wait out the storm, but they are hours from land."

Ada drew her brows together. "We have not been at sea long. How can we be hours from land?"

Laughter rumbled from his chest, hitching her breath at the joyous sound. "We are farther than you think, Ada. The wind is now at our back pushing us while they fight against it. If they are friend they will most likely continue to fight toward your home. Although—" he squinted an eye as his lips pressed into a thin line "—it'd be easier for them to find refuge in another port such as Joppa."

"They are foe, then?"

"Possibly, and if so, they will head toward us as they seem to be doing. However, there is no certainty. We must wait to see what happens. Whatever be the case, Ada, you must hide and remain hidden. Do not make yourself known lest you wish to borrow more trouble. Even friends can lose their heads at the sight of a pretty maid."

Gasping, she pressed her lips together to keep from arguing. The idea that she had borrowed trouble was absurd, especially if he thought that sort of trouble had landed her on his vessel. She moved away from his commanding presence and flung her arms out to her sides. "Where is it you would have me hide, Captain? There is very little here to shield me."

The corner of his mouth twitched until he gave in and smiled. Strange how the turn of his lips broke the severity of the harsh contours of his jawline. Strange how such a thing caused a tickle of lamb's wool to fill her chest. It made her want to laugh, to dance like the village women when word of their bridegroom's approach met their ears. "I would see you belowdecks with the merchandise, but that is the first place anyone with nefarious intentions will look. You will remain here. Brison has brought you a dry tunic."

He moved toward the bench and slid a panel from the end of it. He pulled out two leather scabbards and attached them to the wide leather belt around his waist, and then he pulled out a torn piece of leather with pictures and strange letters scribe onto it. He tucked it beneath his tunic. "Once you are changed, hide in here. When they have left I will come for you."

He grabbed her shoulders and lifted her chin until she looked at him. "Ada, do you understand the importance of why you must remain hidden?"

She blinked. The crook of his finger against her chin was something she had never experienced. The warmth and gentleness made her want to follow him across a stormy sea. Even though she didn't quite understand what it was he meant, she nodded.

"It is unlikely any man sound of mind will try to board my ship in such weather, but we must be prepared. I'll not risk—"

A shout, followed by another halted his words, but she did not need to hear them to know he would not risk losing costly merchandise. After all, he'd risked his life to save her when the wave had swept her off the deck. Nicolaus glanced out the window. The color of his cheeks deepened in anger and his nostrils flared before turning his attention back to her. He held her firm as a wave smashed against the side. "Your vow, Ada."

It was not a question. She'd heard that same tone in her father's voice when he demanded obedience. She was fortunate Nicolaus did not sweep her off her feet and shove her inside the bench as her father would have done.

"Ay." It was the only word she could form before he'd left her to tend to his duties. His commands to his crew cut through the howling wind, causing her to hurry in the task he'd given her. It took her very little time to change into the dry clothing, and then she tossed the discarded pillows back onto the cushioned bench. The hollow darkness of the hidden space glared at her. Oft times she sought out small spaces, places she could hide from the animosity of her sisters, but the danger pressing upon them caused her fear to overwhelm her thoughts. What if aught should happen to Nicolaus? What would happen to her then?

The ship seemed close enough that Ada could make out blurred shapes of people on the other deck. Inhaling a deep breath of salty air, she gathered her wet clothing and scooted feetfirst into the empty space beneath the bench before sliding the panel closed until there was not even a sliver of light. She would do as he asked, and then pray God would rescue her from any seafarer warriors, and more important from falling in love with a man who would surely sell her as soon as he reached his destination. After all, she was no more than a possession, one that he'd paid a handsome price for.

Nicolaus climbed the ladder to the command post, stood next to Xandros and noticed the winds had shifted against them. He drew his hand down his beard. Could the situation worsen? "How does it look?"

"They are fighting against the wind as much as we are now."

"Aye, but something doesn't look right. Why would they head toward Ashkelon when Joppa is closer? Their sail is unfurled in a storm. A seasoned seaman would know that to be a deadly mistake."

"Unless they are bold in their attempt to overtake us."

Nicolaus narrowed his eyes. "It gives me the mind they are thieves, yet their vessel seems to be nothing more than a simple fishing boat, not one made for warfare as thieves are wont to sail." Nicolaus lifted his face toward the sky. "If only this storm would give way."

He felt more bound than he had when he'd been taken captive all those months ago, and he blamed it on Ada. Her innocent beauty had called to him, luring him to rescue her from the ways of men. If he hadn't rescued her, he would not care whether or not ten ships surrounded him, but something about her tempted him to live again, to breathe. He'd even smiled at her antics, a smile that warmed his innards, and that was something he hadn't done in a long while.

"We'd still need the wind behind us, not pushing at our side. Mayhap we should head due north."

Nicolaus shook his head. Although his ship was lighter than most vessels and could possibly outrun the one approaching once he unleashed his rowers he would not risk the consequences if he failed. Again. "I do not wish for them to think we are avoiding them. If they are about nefarious deeds they'll only give chase."

"Do you think they will attempt to board us in this storm?"

"I've seen men steal bread from a child while their bellies were full from a king's feast." Nicolaus twisted his lips. "Aye, if they are thieves a storm such as this will not halt them."

"If they attempt to board us?"

Vivid memories ambushed him. A day hadn't passed that he did not recall the events and wondered what he could have done to save his sister. He hoped this day would end differently, one where he didn't lose an innocent maid to a band of thieves and where he did not end up in shackles. "We will not raise arms unless their actions warrant such. We will not resist their efforts to steal our merchandise if they so choose." Nicolaus swallowed; the lump forming in his throat near choked his next words from him. He would not allow his emotions to sway him this day. "Xandros, if they require me for ransom you are to allow it. Take the maid to my father's house, ensure her freedom at all cost and care for her."

Xandros held his position without so much as a blink of his lashes, for which Nicolaus was grateful. His second-in-command would carry out his orders, not because Nicolaus was his captain, but because they were the best of friends and if anyone understood the battle weighing on his shoulders it was Xandros. It would not be easy for his friend to stand down and watch his captain once again be removed, just as it would not be easy for Nicolaus to allow another man to step foot on this boat after his last encounter with an approaching vessel.

The boat tossed upon the waves like a leaf in a creek after a heavy rain shower and as they moved closer Nicolaus could tell something was amiss. Whoever captained the ship had not been at it very long. "Do you notice something, Xandros?"

His second-in-command squinted. "Ay, I see women, lots of them now."

Tension knotted Nicolaus's shoulders as needles pricked his nape. He leaned his palms against the railing. He hadn't been able to make out man or woman, only shapes of bodies, bodies that seemed to be clinging to the rails. "What do you make of it?"

"A ruse?"

Thieves of the sea often consisted of ruthless women as well as children. Merchant ships, unless carrying slaves, did not.

Nicolaus drew his hand down his beard. "Could be. Tell the Haemon and Argos to stay on guard. It wouldn't do to be caught by trickery."

Patience was one thing his father had oft praised him for, but now was not one of those times as he waited for the confrontation to come. Were they friend or foe? Even though he was alert to the possible danger, instinct told him these people meant no harm. Given the way the women clung to the sides he was beginning to suspect they were a village in need of rescue. If so, what sort of danger had they encountered for them to be desperate enough to face the great unknown of the sea?

"Bring us to the right a little and toss the small anchor overboard to slow us down."

"You cannot think… Nicolaus, we'll head straight for them."

"Aye, be ready to reel it back in."

Xandros shouted his orders to one of the men. The helmsman shifted the steering oars and the ship turned just as Nicolaus had commanded. An order to anchor cried over the roaring of the storm and the vessel began to steady in place. As the single boat approached he could see the pale and sunken cheeks of her occupants. "They do not look well."

Although the words were more for himself than Xandros, his second-in-command grunted. "Still a ruse?"

"I do not believe so, my friend. We'll soon know the full of their adventure, and if not then we'll know their mischief." He rested his palms on the hilts of his daggers and hoped he would not have to use them. After the amount of torture he'd endured during his captivity, he didn't relish causing anyone harm, but if these people posed a threat to his brother or to Ada he would. His only comfort was that she was safely hidden. As for Brison, he'd grown up beneath two brothers and knew how to hold his own in battle.

He glanced over his shoulder and looked at the window of the captain's quarters just to ensure she'd done as he'd requested and breathed a sigh of relief when he found it empty. A small part of him was surprised, especially given her feisty nature when he'd brought her aboard.

"Toss another anchor to slow us even more."

In a matter of moments, the other ship neared enough for them to yell over the crashing of the waves. The condition of the approaching ship was not all right. It was obvious Xandros knew this, as well.

"What is it you wish to do, Captain?"

Nicolaus drew in a slow breath. Instinct told him these people held no danger for him or his crew. Yet, fear tried to grip hold of him, tempting him to order the anchors pulled and his rowers to reverse course, leaving the broken vessel to the mercies of the sea. Given its battered condition, it would not take long for it to completely splinter. Could he allow his fear to leave these people to certain death?

"Prepare the planks."

"You cannot think to bring them aboard."

"What choice do we have, Xandros? There are not that many of them. We cannot leave them to the mercies of fate. They'll die."

"They are not your responsibility."

"If not us, then whose? They are in need of rescue and we are able."

"The ruse?"

"Even I can see these people are in desperate need of help." Ada's lyrical accent curled around something in his chest and lifted his lips into a smile. Xandros growled and stalked away to do as bid.

Nicolaus kept his gaze focused on an old man waving in a frantic manner. "I thought I asked you to stay hidden."

She leaned against the rail, her hair blowing behind her like a sail in the wind. He could not recall seeing any woman as lovely as she, not even his sister and she had been a coveted prize among their neighbors as well as abroad. "I did hide, but…" She pressed her lips together, and he could only guess that she'd succumbed to another bout of sickness. "Besides, they look harmless."

Ay, they did. But could he be for certain? Once the ships were close enough his crew began throwing ropes to the other boat and began laying planks between them. What he saw on the faces of the occupants of the other boat left bile rising in his throat.

# Chapter Five

$A$da twisted her fingers together as Nicolaus's crew maneuvered the boats close. The space between them decreased, and just when she thought they'd bump into each other, several of Nicolaus's sailors attached laddering planks to the rails.

She bit the inside of her lip to keep from crying out when one sailor jumped onto a ladder and ran across to the other boat. She glanced at Nicolaus, who observed his men in silence. His body relaxed as they moved with swiftness and efficiency. Obviously he held great confidence in his men for he was not bellowing out commands as her father often did when overseeing his workers. "Is it not dangerous to tie the boats together in this storm?"

"There are always dangers, Ada. However, I must discern these peoples' intentions, and then ensure their safety. Do you wish their boat, if you can call it as such, to break apart and be washed away by the waves?"

"Of course not." She inspected the people, looking for signs of mischief. She'd never seen a thief up close, but she'd imagine that they would not look as if they'd been without food for weeks. "So, you have decided they are friends?"

He crossed his arms over his chest and scowled, never once looking at her. "Nay. My trust is not easily placed, especially in strangers who do not heed my warnings."

No doubt he spoke about her decision to defy his command and come out on deck. "Ay, I suppose the lack of trust can be true for strangers who steal others from their family."

He flinched, and she instantly stepped back. She knew her words were like a dagger. Knew if he hadn't intervened with the burly bidder she would have been in a much worse position. That didn't mean she liked her current situation.

"Remember this, Ada, I did not steal you and I did not sell you to be auctioned off like sheep. Correct me if I am wrong, but the women who looked much like you, perhaps your own sisters, did that to you. What I wonder is, why?" His last words were no more than a whisper above the wind and light rain, but she heard them as if he shouted them in the silence of a clear desert night. He tilted his chin and pierced her with his turbulent black eyes. "Why is it, Ada? Why did your sisters feel the need to sell you? Did you steal the affections of their marriage prospects?"

Ada's jaw dropped. How dare he, but why indeed? That was a question that had burned in her heart and roared in her thoughts since the moment Dina shoved her into the hands of the trader. One thing was for certain—no man had ever paid her heed. They'd always vied for her sisters' attentions whenever her father allowed interactions between them and prospective marriage partners. Her sisters disliked her and she never truly knew why, but Nicolaus's accusations were far from the truth. She could only assume their hate was born out of their dislike for who—what— Ada's mother was: a slave. Still, she was her father's daughter the same as her sisters. She was not at fault for her father's choice of concubines. "Ay, they hated me, due to no fault of my own."

She stomped across the deck as best she could, gripping the rail until her knuckles turned white so she would not slip and fall, or go for a swim as the captain believed. She was many things: stubborn ay, a fool nay. Her life may not be her own, and death one of the only choices left to her and her alone, but she did not choose it. The Lord of Heaven and earth reigned, and if her mother had been correct He would rescue her from a life of captivity. She believed it without doubt.

Reaching the ladder, she climbed the rungs, stepped into the small room and then threw herself onto the cushioned bench. For the first time since being brought to this boat, she was thankful for the crashing waves rocking the vessel and the noisy wind stealing her sobs. "God, You will rescue me, will You not? Or am I to endure the same fate as my mother? A slave with no will of my own?"

She wanted to go home, away from this man who both irritated and drew her like the soft lamb's wool of her bedding after a long day tending chores. It didn't matter that her sisters disliked her because her mother had been a Hebrew. At least she knew what to expect from them. Besides, they would all soon marry and have families of their own to tend, leaving her to her father's house. It was not what she longed for, but it was better than this—being swept away to a foreign land with a stranger who was kind one moment and condescending the next. Much as her mother had been treated by her father. A slave, no more, no less.

Ada dried her eyes, stretched out on the bench and folded her hands in front of her. The seams where the wood butted seemed to be flawless. They were coated with a yellow substance and not a single drop of rain leaked. The pine shone with a gloss, and she could not help but think the craftsmanship was much like the captain. He was a man of strength and purpose from all that she could tell, but he was also a man of rugged beauty. And if she were to look at the truth of it, his rudeness had gained her cooperation. Not once, but twice.

She twisted her lips. Perhaps *obedience* was not the word, not in the sense her father demanded with a rough hand. Her father never would have asked. He only demanded, and if anyone refused to comply they were punished. Sometimes left without food. Memories of her mother tied to a stake outside the village entrance burned in Ada's blood. After night had fallen, she'd taken her mother what little food and water could be procured without the watchful eye of her father's wife. Still, it had not been enough.

Nicolaus had not proven cruel since his purchase of her. His kindness, although soured by his insensitivity, elicited a longing within her chest. A longing that caused her to dream of things she'd never thought to before. A family of her own, a household to care for. Love did not matter. A caring husband, much like she imagined Nicolaus would be, did not matter.

A memory of him brushing back her hair with tenderness, of him holding her while her stomach heaved, the comforting circles he massaged on her back...she closed her eyes as a tear slid down her cheek. Her mother had offered her such tenderness when she could and suffered dire consequences when caught by her father's wife. How was it that her father mourned her mother's passing when his character toward her spoke of dislike? Of course, Ada would not have known the difference if not for Nicolaus. And for that, mayhap she should despise the captain.

She rose from the bench and drew close to the window. Sea spray bathed her face, and she was thankful the rain no longer poured from the skies to hinder her sight. Nicolaus grabbed the hand of a woman who teetered on a wide plank and helped her onto the deck. His lips moved as he spoke. The harsh lines etching his cheeks and furrowing his brow disappeared as the woman smiled and bowed her head. Brison gave her a cask and some bread before motioning to a small group of people huddled together near the command post.

Shame filled Ada's eyes, lodging in her throat. She was spoiled as her sisters oft claimed. Here she was bemoaning her fate, when these people were truly troubled, lost at sea. The heat of Nicolaus's gaze drew her attention, and the harsh lines reappeared. She straightened her posture. Lifting her chin, she moved from the window and descended the ladder. Careful not to bump any of the seafarers, she made her way toward Nicolaus's man and was pleased to discover if she kept her knees slightly bent she could maneuver the deck with ease.

She laid her hand on Brison's shoulder. He glanced at her, his eyes narrowed.

"I would help, if it pleases you?"

Brison shifted his gaze to his brother. It irritated her a little that he needed Nicolaus's permission, that *she* needed his permission, to help.

"Are you well?" The concern in Nicolaus's voice curled around her insides, leaving her feeling weak, but she would not allow it to discourage her. "I will not have you tumbling into the water."

Ada stiffened her spine and swallowed the bile rising in her throat. Of course he would think of nothing but the cost of losing her. What did she expect after knowing him a short amount of time? That his kindness toward her meant he cared for her as a person? His words proved otherwise, and oddly the sting in her chest hurt much worse than the pebbles her sisters were wont to toss at her. "Well enough."

The corners of his mouth slid upward. Something squeezed tight in her chest, trapping the air in her lungs. Had there been a more confusing man to ever cross her path?

Never. They were either outwardly cruel or showed false kindness in order to gain an appropriate trade with her father. This man seemed to approve of her actions. His words were both kind and biting. She'd oft longed for the approval of someone, anyone outside of her mother, and most important from her siblings as they had seemed to share the same lot as her. But for some reason, his smile meant more than she expected. It meant more than the need to go home.

A home where a strong arm ruled and kindness was absent. A home where it was near impossible to be accepted for the Hebrew woman she was. A home where there were few smiles unless she was being laughed at by her sisters.

* * *

An intense amount of joy built within his chest, much like it had the first time he had hit the mark with his arrow when he was no more than a boy. Ada's courage, especially in the midst of a turbulent sea and stomach, gave him hope, and yet made him pause. If his crew had had half the courage of this slip of a woman, the seafarers never would have boarded his ship and stolen his freedom and the greatest treasure he'd ever had care of, his sister. If his crew had had Ada's bravery, they never would have been taken captive by David's men.

He should not think so harshly of them. He could not fathom the burden his crew had carried with them. His own burden had been heavy during his captivity, but only because he did not know what sort of fate his dear sister had met. His brother Jasen had told him of his crew's determination and of their disappointment when their search gained them nothing. Of course, his crew had not suspected David of such a deception. No matter Nicolaus's assurances that there had been naught they could have done to save him and Desma, he could still see the wary looks on their faces. It was as if they no longer trusted him as their captain and perhaps they shouldn't.

Xandros danced across the beams connecting the boats as if he were a butterfly flitting from flower to flower with no cares in the world. His second-in-command leaped to the deck. "Their boat is worse than we first imagined, splintered in various places from a battering ram. They're carrying the weight of the sea. 'Tis why they're sitting so low."

Nicolaus pressed his lips together and pulled air in through his nose. "What is it you are not telling me?"

"You've allowed the woman out, I see." Xandros nodded toward Ada. Nicolaus's gaze followed. She knelt in front of two small children huddled in the corner by themselves and offered them water. "They have nothing but old women and crippled men. The one who acted as helm is a boy of no more than six or seven summers. A fine job he did, but he's weakened by their days at sea with no sustenance."

Nicolaus took in the haggard features of the child. The dark circles beneath his eyes and sunken cheeks reminded him of the young boys who'd been enslaved with him. Many of them had been worked until they fell to their deaths.

"What is it you suggest, Xandros?" Although they'd fewer rowers by half the norm, allowing them more room to store merchandise, there was little space left. The lower portions had been filled with goods from all over the Great Sea and bringing these people on board would only cause them problems if they did encounter thieves. It would also slow him down and cost him time. Time he did not possess. The sooner he arrived at his father's house the easier he would breathe knowing Ada would no longer be at risk, especially since they were not heavily guarded.

"If they continue as they have been they'll only meet their deaths."

"Are there no able-bodied men among them?"

The look in his friend's eyes worried him. What had happened to these people? He dared not ask, yet evidence poked out from all angles, telling him the answer. These people had met with the worst of seafarers. A shout of alarm from one of his men had Nicolaus drawing his dagger from its sheath until he noticed his man carrying a small bundle, and another of his men cradling a small, elderly woman in his arms. His men carried them toward the others and Ada with her golden tresses hanging over her shoulder rushed to attend them. "From what I can gather they left their island when the mountain caught fire."

Such an occurrence often happened. Many believed it was the gods' way of punishing the people for not honoring them correctly. Something Nicolaus had long ago given up on. The gods had paid little heed to him when he'd been captured, and he'd never strayed from the rituals to deserve their anger. Not until recently. He would no longer be a pawn in their games. If he denied their existence, they could not abuse their powers over him. "That does not explain where their men have gone."

"Ay, there were few to begin with. They rushed to the boats in order to save themselves. Many were left behind for there was no room left as I have seen with my own eyes. They had planned to return once the fire disappeared. Instead, thieves came upon them and took one of their ships and all strong enough to labor."

Nicolaus clenched his teeth together and forced his eyes to remain open. It was as he thought. "They fought well, it seems."

"Ay, as the nature of their vessel proves. It is unfortunate that those who fought are either dead or now captives," Xandros said.

Nicolaus's gut contorted. He'd been victim to such thieves. Their cruelty knew no end. He scanned the waters in search of a threat. However, the waves rose too high, and the rain from the storm kept all else shrouded in mist.

A heavy hand clasped his shoulder. "Do not fret so much, my friend. They've been drifting for days."

Another of his crew carried an old man whose eyes seemed not to see. Perhaps, it was fear that left him with a blank stare. "It is a mercy these were left alive."

"Ay, a mercy indeed. They've been left to fend for themselves with no one to care for them."

Nicolaus clenched his teeth together. "Will their vessel make it to Joppa for repairs?"

"There is little left to repair."

"Will it make it to Joppa?" There was little room for the rest of the people to board his vessel. He didn't relish throwing merchandise overboard but would if need be.

Xandros must have read his thoughts. He nodded his head, and said, "Are you thinking of purchasing another boat and bringing them to our village?"

Nicolaus glanced at his second. "I cannot very well leave them at Joppa if they do not wish to stay. They've nowhere to go. No men to support the needs of these people. Our island is large and prosperous. My father has never rejected those in need and would not do so now."

He had not rejected Nicolaus when he'd arrived after months of captivity a weak and broken vessel with the shame of losing his sister bearing down on his shoulders.

"In that you are correct."

"And I do not think any of the ports we'll stop at for provisions will accept them."

Xandros heaved in a breath. "What of the challenge? If you determine to take them with us, we will not move with the swiftness needed to win. We could be days behind Jasen's arrival. And what of their provisions? The cost will be no meager sum, my friend."

Nicolaus bowed his head and closed his eyes. He risked losing. It did not matter if he lost his ship and all the merchandise he'd acquired during the voyage, but if he lost the race he risked the means to move away from his family and the shame of having disappointed his father. He'd lose the ability to search for his sister without his father's constant watchful eye. And what of Ada? "This I know. What choice do I have? I cannot allow them to continue to a fate unknown."

"There is no other choice, my friend." Xandros clapped him on the back. "The sacrifice is much, one not many would give up. Your uncle would be proud."

Yes, Oceanus would be proud, but what of his father? Would he be proud as well, or would Nicolaus once again see disappointment crinkling the corners of his eyes?

"You have yet to answer my question, Xandros. Will the vessel make it to Joppa?"

White teeth showed through Xandros's thick beard. His eyes twinkled with mischief. "It is unlikely. However, with me at the command, it has a chance, as slight as it may be. In the event it does not make it, I have no doubt, you will champion us."

"Order the men to move enough water and cakes of bread for those left on board before we break planks."

"I fear that may deplete our resources."

Nicolaus tugged on his beard, and then nodded. "Take what you need. We've rationed before. Let us port at Joppa and renew our provisions."

An alarm from Brison drew his attention. Nicolaus left Xandros and climbed onto the command post. The sea rose on the horizon, rushing toward them. At their current angle the wave would roll them. "Break the planks, now!"

Xandros ran across to the other ship as the men removed the planks bridging the vessels. If they had moved all the women and children there would be no need to save the other boat, but they'd only transferred a few. "Euclid!" he called to his helmsman. "Turn the ship toward the south until we are facing the wave. Raise the anchors."

The cry of an infant reminded him that Ada, along with several of the women and children, remained on the deck. If the boat rolled… "Brison, move them all below, huddle them in the center around the mast. Go with haste."

He tied a rope around his waist as did his two armed warriors, Haemon and Argos, standing guard on either side of the command post's platform. Nicolaus glanced at the other boat. A few of his men remained with Xandros.

Nicolaus could only hope his friend's natural ability with the sea would keep them well. "Tell the rowers to push forward. We must get in front of the other boat in order to take the brunt of the wave." He clenched his teeth together knowing he risked the lives on his vessel to protect those on the weaker, but it was his duty. They were all under his protection. Nicolaus glanced at the other boat and breathed a sigh of relief at the sight of a few oars maneuvering it backward in order to fall in line behind him. Nicolaus wouldn't question the appearance of the oars or the providence that had left several of his men on the other boat. He was thankful that there was hope for the other ship's survival, if it held together against the wave.

Even with the cry of the babe and the soft cooing of Ada's voice as Brison ushered her toward the back of the ship, an eerie silence settled over them. He crossed his arms over his chest and stared at the blue wall as it rushed toward them, daring it to crash over the bow. His jaw twitched in irritation. Could their situation possibly get worse? Ay, he knew it could, but he hoped it wouldn't. "Almighty God of creation, my uncle believes in Your existence, I dare not test You lest You see us all washed into the sea, but if You are real, if You are living and breathing as Oceanus believes You to be, as Ada believes You to be, then I beseech You, save us."

The bow rose, lifting the bronze battering ram toward the murky sky. Nicolaus gripped the rail in front of him and dared the sea to take his ship, his crew and Ada from him. He would not see defeat this day. He would not. Could not. Assurance flooded his being, puffing out his chest. He held on to that thin thread of confidence as the wave lifted them high.

# Chapter Six

Ada handed the babe down to the waiting arms of a gruff-looking sailor standing on the stairs, her queasy stomach forgotten in the face of a greater need. She glanced toward the other boat. The arms and faces of the men in the small fishing vessel, including Nicolaus's friend Xandros, strained with each push and pull of the oars as it moved backward. Nicolaus shouted out a command, and Ada grasped hold of the rail to keep from falling as the force of their own vessel moved forward.

She brushed her hair from her eyes and stared at their captain. With his arms crossed, Nicolaus stood like a sentry near the city gates. Yet, he was much bigger for he hadn't the thick walls to offer him protection from the enemy. Nor had he an army to stand beside him. Only two warriors with shields at their backs and swords at their sides. Daggers hung from Nicolaus's leather belt. What kind of man stood against the sea as if to do battle?

An honorable one, no doubt. One who fought for those under his protection. Including the strangers in the hold. Including her, a mere slave. Had her father cared for his slaves in such a manner? Considering how he left her mother to die at the demands of his wife, she did not think so.

"Ada, you must get below." Brison's words must have carried on the wind for Nicolaus turned his head. The hard set of determination etching his jaw stole her breath. If the raging sea were a man it would, no doubt, beg for mercy. "He's a good sailor, Ada. You've no need to worry that we'll all drown."

She was fortunate to have Nicolaus as her protector— her master. After all she was no more than a slave. She bit down on the inside of her lip to keep it from quivering. A slave held no honor. Her own mother had been proof of that fact, working from before dawn until after dusk to keep her father's household as he'd expected, to do his wife's bidding until her fingers bled from the work she'd demanded of her. Ada recalled the anger of her sisters' mother at her father's distress when her mother had died. Was it possible that he loved her?

"Ada." Brison poked his finger against her shoulder. "We've no time to tarry."

Drawing in a breath of air, she descended the stairs and sat next to the other women. She squinted, peering into the shadows in search of the children. A whimper drew her gaze deeper into the shadows. The boy who had maneuvered these women to safety had his arm wrapped around the young girl. The babe, swaddled in soiled linen, lay at the children's feet. Looking from the group of women to the children and back again she had the feeling they didn't want anything to do with them.

Why?

They were children, innocent of any crimes. Ada rose from her spot near the mast and stumbled toward the children where they sat on the bare planks against the lattice. From all she could see it was one of the few spots that did not hold amphora jars. She scooped the babe into her arms and cradled it against her chest. Tufts of dark hair stood straight from the infant's head. Ada smoothed them back, before kissing the brow and then sat beside the girl child.

An elderly woman leaned forward, her finger pointing at the babe and then at the girl. Her toothless grunts caused Ada to scoot toward the girl as her arms gathered the babe closer. The rest of the women began to mumble among themselves. Their sneers left her chilled and heartbroken for the unwanted children. It was good Ada did not understand their words else she'd more than likely wish them back to their broken fishing vessel to face the angry sea on their own.

The old woman reached her arms out as she began to rise from her seat. Gray light streamed down upon the woman. The cruelty in her black eyes along with the angry tones spewing from her lips renewed the sickness in Ada's stomach and she pulled back.

"What is it you want?" Ada trembled as the woman wavered from side to side.

"They believe the child brings terror upon us."

Ada glanced at the young boy whose arm was wrapped around the little girl in protection. "What sort of nonsense is this?"

The old woman poked her finger in the air toward the young girl and released a mouthful of angry words.

The boy pulled the girl closer. "The mountain caught fire when she was born, as it did when the babe was. They believe them to be cursed. She says we should throw them to sea to appease the gods."

Ada flinched. Tears pricked the backs of her eyes. How could these women hold to such superstitions?

"What is it they call you?"

"Galen." He tilted his head toward the girl child. "Edith. She and the babe are my mother's children."

Ada was about to respond when the hold creaked as it lifted, rocking her forward with the force of the sea. Ada clutched the babe and settled her cheek against his chilled flesh. "Hold tight to the lattice. Do not let go."

Galen murmured something to the girl, and then swiveled around and stuck his feet and arms into the square holes. Edith squeezed herself between him and the lattice. Ada was about to do the same when the boat shifted, knocking her over. She righted herself and prayed. "Abba God, save us."

Ada slid away from the children and was flung against one of the women, crushing her against the mast as the boat continued to rise. Piercing screams filled the boat, echoing off the sealed planks and all the merchandise. Those closest to the mast clung to its thickness, the others grasped hold of the women anchored to the round piece of wood. The boat rocked left, and then right. Ada reached out with a hand to steady herself against the mast, but water rushed through the hole above them, sweeping her and the infant away from its solid strength and toward the back of the boat.

She grabbed hold of a piece of moored timber and clung to it with all her strength. The quivering cry from the baby tore at Ada's heart, but before she could adjust her perch and find a more comfortable seating a wave crashed against the side, tipping the vessel to its side with a loud crack. No sooner had they rolled one way than they were rolling the next.

Agonizing cries rose above the roaring of the sea, filling her ears with the terror. They were all being tossed around like leaves in a storm. It seemed as if her prayers had gone unheard. They were all going to die if the madness did not soon halt.

And what of Nicolaus? How was he enduring in the elements? Last she'd seen him he had been standing on the platform. Had the wave swept him into the sea?

As sudden as the violence had begun, it quit and the boat settled into a steady rocking. Ada closed her eyes. "Thank You, Lord."

She tore off a piece of her outer tunic and swaddled the babe inside before tying the ends around her neck. She peeked between the folds of the fabric. Innocent eyes peered up at her as the babe sucked on its fist. She couldn't help but smile at the warmth filling her heart, and she knew she would do anything to keep the infant safe. "Shall we see to our captain?"

Keeping her knees bent, she stood and on wobbly legs started to make her way toward the stairs. It was then she noticed the source of the cries and she nearly choked on her gasp of breath. The mast had severed. While the bottom half where the women had been remained intact, the top half laid at an angle pinning two of the women. Right where she and the babe had been. If the water hadn't rushed into the hold and shoved her toward the stern with its force, she had no doubt she would have died. She and the babe.

Ada rushed forward and tried to lift the wood, but it was no use. Even if it wasn't too heavy, the mast had fallen in such a way that it was wedged beneath a support beam.

"H-help me, please," one of the women croaked. Ada was surprised that the woman no longer spoke in little grunts but rather in Nicolaus's tongue.

Ada glanced into the pain-filled eyes of the old woman who had been determined to allow the babe to fend for itself. A gash split across the woman's brow and one of her legs was trapped beneath the mammoth wood. As much as she wanted to walk away and ignore her pleas for help, Ada's conscience just wouldn't allow it. Even if she couldn't move the mast, she could offer comfort.

Nicolaus pulled himself to his feet and peered over the railing. Although the skies remained gray and the waves washed over the deck, the turbulent sea no longer raged. A fortunate thing for his warriors since Haemon currently bobbed with each wave as Argos tugged on the rope tied around his waist. It was no surprise one of his men had fallen overboard. Nicolaus untied the rope from his own waist and glanced toward the helmsman's perch. However, the sight of his mast snapped in two stopped his search and left him speechless. The welfare of his helmsman and the men on smaller fishing vessel forgotten. His only concern was for the people below the deck. One woman in particular.

"Drop anchor!" Nicolaus rushed forward and pressed all his weight against the wood blocking the stairs into the hold. This was something he'd remedy when he designed his father's next ship. A woman's cry filtered through the broken debris. Nicolaus felt as if he'd been slammed in the chest with a battering ram. Had Ada been hurt? He should have kept her with him, held on to her...so that he'd know, know for sure if she was well. "Ada!" He shoved his palms against the mast and was met with an agonizing scream.

"Halt, you are hurting her." Even though he didn't like the thought of anyone in distress, the sweet sound of Ada's voice settled the panic in his blood.

Lying down on the deck, he looked through the opening and spied Ada's beautiful tear-streaked face staring up at him. "Are you well?"

"Ay. However, the mast has some of the women trapped."

"What of Brison?" If he could get his younger brother to lift the mast from below they might be able to free the women.

She turned her head as if to look around. Nicolaus hadn't seen his brother since he'd ordered him to take Ada below. "I haven't seen him."

"Did he not follow you down? What of the rowers? Are they free to move about?" Nicolaus prayed none had been swept from their positions. All of his rowers had been seated in the outriggers and susceptible to the elements. He hoped they'd not been washed away.

Ada nodded. "I will see to their condition. At least the ones I'm able to reach."

"Captain?"

Nicolaus lifted his head to find Euclid standing at his side and he relaxed a little more, thankful the helmsman hadn't been swept away in the waves as had Haemon. He rose to his full height and took in the damage to his ship. Besides the broken mast all seemed well enough. He hoped there was very little damage below deck, as well. "We need to lift the mast." He drew his fingers down his beard, wishing Xandros was on board, and yet hoping his friend was faring much better. "I am uncertain of the condition of the crew below and there are women trapped beneath the weight. Seems it is only the four of us once Haemon returns to the ship." He motioned toward Argos leaning over the rail. "And even then the mast is heavier than we can bear. Was Xandros able to shelter behind us?"

Euclid nodded. "They seem to have weathered much better. Seeing the damage, I have motioned to them our distress. I've no doubt Xandros will find a way to assist us."

The boat rocked a little, causing one of the women to cry out. His sea-hardened helmsman paled at the sound. "We may not have time. We've heard the cries of dying men before, Euclid, but coming from women it is much worse. We must free them posthaste and see to their injuries. We also need to reach Joppa with great speed, but I dare not order the rowers until we free the women and see if there is damage to the hold."

"Nicolaus."

He crouched down and peered down into the hole. Her wet hair clung to her shoulders and down her back, forming to her curves. A sling was tied around her neck with a lump cradled next to her chest. He had no doubt it was the babe wrapped against her. A darkening bruise began to form on her cheek beneath her eye and he wanted to reach down, pull her onto the deck and look her over for any other injuries, but more important the state of her attire told him there was water where there should be none, giving him a greater sense of urgency in his gut. "You are certain you are well?"

The corner of her mouth slid upward and she nodded. "I've found several rowers, and Brison."

A sigh of relief escaped his lungs. He did not wish to tell his father that he had lost another sibling to the sea.

"They did not realize the damage." Of course the rowers wouldn't have noticed the damage to the interior hold. In order to be a more efficient merchant, Nicolaus had walls built to form compartments throughout the center of the hold for merchandise. The rowers sat on the outriggers. "What of the children?"

Ada glanced over her shoulder and then lifted her beautiful face up to his. "They are well."

"Good. Take the infant and find a safe place until we can get the mast moved."

Nicolaus turned his attention out to sea, and then to Euclid. "I need you to take command—"

"Captain." Euclid shook his head. "The guards and I can manage."

"Euclid, it is a command." His helmsman's shoulders drooped. Someone needed to keep watch on the sea, and Nicolaus needed to be right here until the mast was removed from the stairs. He needed to be right here until he could fully see Ada. Until he could see for himself that she was truly well.

"Captain," Brison called up to him. "It does not look good. I don't mean to worry you, but the water is up to our ankles. I have a few of the men looking for holes."

"How are the women?" He knew what Ada had told him, but he didn't trust that she would tell him the truth, not because she meant to deceive him but because he didn't think she'd tell him if she was truly injured. Her concern being more for others than herself. He saw that admirable trait in her character when she pushed aside her seasickness and cared for the women and children they'd brought on board.

Nicolaus caught sight of Brison's lips twisting before he glanced away and then back again. "Two are trapped. One seems to be sleeping, her leg does not look good. The other…she's just staring like she's seen a sea monster."

*What of Ada?* he wanted to ask, but knew better. His concern should be for everyone under his protection, not just one woman, even if she did make him feel like living again. "Do you have enough men to lift it without causing them further discomfort?"

"Not sure, Captain. Let me get a better look."

"My thanks, brother." Nicolaus started to push himself up and then called back down. "Brison, let me know if the water rises any higher."

Nicolaus glanced around the deck for something that might offer them help, something to wedge beneath the mast and lift it from the trapped women. The problem was he couldn't see the portion of the mast below the deck. Using another piece of wood to lever against the mast may only cause more damage to his boat and further injury to those below.

"Captain, it's tight against a support beam. I don't see how we can move it from below. It would take most of the men down here to lift it, and there just isn't enough room."

Nicolaus shoved his fingers through his damp hair. It would have been easier if the mast would have been completely severed in two and not still attached to the lower half. He'd have to cut through the wood but the pressure might cause discomfort to the women pinned. He glanced over his shoulder at Argos as he held a thick rope in his hands. When Haemon made his way back on board would they have strength enough left in their arms after their struggle to lift the broken portion while he sawed through the break?

"Nicolaus." He looked down at his brother and saw the fear in his brother's eyes. "The water is rising."

# Chapter Seven

Ada dropped her gaze to the water lapping above her ankles. She knew she should have listened to Nicolaus and moved away. If she had, she wouldn't have overheard Brison tell his brother about the rising water, but she wanted to be close by in case she was needed. Besides, she couldn't move if she wanted. The need to see what was going on, the need to keep busy, even if it only meant holding the old lady's hand whenever she cried out or keeping a cloth pressed to her head, was too strong. She'd spent enough time hiding in the shadows when her sisters were in their awful moods, enough time hiding when scared. She wouldn't cower in a corner now.

However, if she'd listened to Nicolaus, she wouldn't know… She swallowed hard. They were all going to die, unless they removed the mast and stopped the water from filling the boat. If it had not been for the quiver in Brison's tone she would not have given in to the worry gnawing at her stomach and taken notice of just how dire their situation was. Grasping hold of the old woman's hand, Ada guided it to her brow. "Keep this pressed against your head."

Ada's knees shook as she stood, whether from the chilly water or fear she didn't know. The babe let out a little cry. She pulled the fabric and peered at the babe's innocent face. She'd never been more frightened in her life, not even when she stood on the auction block wondering if her sisters' cruelty would really see her spend the rest of her life in captivity or worse—prostitution. There was more than just her to fear for, there were the children, and these women who'd already suffered much in the past few days, if their sunken cheeks were any indication.

She stepped over a crate and laid her hand on Brison's shoulder. When he first turned toward her his eyes had been wide with fear, and then he blinked, replacing his concern with bravery. "You've nothing to worry over, Ada. My brother will see us safe."

A knot formed in her throat at the obvious pride in Brison's tone. She recalled their good-natured companionship. The affection between the two of them was strong. It was obvious Nicolaus loved his brother. What must it be like to have a sibling who not only liked you but cared? Of course, Asher had always done what he could to protect all of his sisters, but he was distant and somewhat cold, as if it were a burdensome task. There was no friendship between her and Asher, not like she'd witnessed between the captain and Brison. Poor Nicolaus, if they were lost at sea, he'd lose his brother, too. *Oh, Lord, please spare us from certain death. I beseech You to make a way.*

"Ada, is that you? I thought I told you to find a place of safety."

Ada tipped her head back. Nicolaus's eyebrows creased together and his lips pressed into a line. "Is he always glowering?"

Brison coughed, drawing Ada's attention. He smiled, and then covered his mouth with his fist before clearing his throat. "Only when he's disobeyed, which you seem to do a lot."

"Ay, that she does."

Ada glanced back at Nicolaus. The harsh lines of disapproval had relaxed. The man seemed to be smiling. How could he make merry when they were about to die? "I only wished to help."

The corners of Nicolaus's eyes crinkled as he narrowed them, his merriment gone. Growling, he yanked on his beard. He pushed away from the opening and disappeared. Boisterous words about her always wanting to help and disobeying his commands filtered through the hole in the deck, burning the tips of her ears. Brison's cheeks reddened at his brother's fury. Nicolaus crouched down, pressing his face near the hole, blocking what little light had shone through. "What help is it you, a mere maid, think you can be?"

She propped a fist on her hip. "I've eyes to see."

He shook his head as he raked his fingers through his curling hair. Droplets of water rained down upon them. "And what is it you see, Ada?"

Shocked, she blinked up at him. How many times had her father asked her opinion? None that she could recall. How many times had she disobeyed her father? None. She didn't dare. So why did she dare chance Nicolaus's wrath and disobey him? And why did he allow it?

"If you lift your end straight upward and Brison

and the others raise the broken piece lying across the women's legs, I can move them."

His eyebrows knitted closer together. If that was even possible. "That does not solve the problem of freeing you from the hold."

She heard his doubt and his hesitation as if her idea wouldn't work. Did all men think so little of women? "No, but if we are able to move their legs, there will be more room for your men down here to maneuver the broken pieces from the stairs."

Brison tilted his head to the side and then crouched down, roaming his hand around the splintered mast. He rose to his full height and looked up at his brother. "She may have the right of it, Nicolaus."

Light bathed her face as Nicolaus shifted, and she thought she heard more grumbling coming from him. His emotions seemed to shift as often as the wind. Did the captain scowl often or did he only do so now because his mind was perplexed by their situation? She guessed the former given it seemed as if his merry moods were unexpected by those around him, even himself.

"There is a problem with her plan." Although she could not see him she quite imagined him with his arms crossed as Nicolaus spoke in his native language to his brother. Blood rushed through her veins, thumping against the base of her neck and in her chest. Brison glanced at her before hanging his head. Ada offered him what little comfort she could by squeezing his hand, and then looked up at Nicolaus.

"What problem would that be?" she returned in his foreign tongue.

"Euclid cannot leave his position, and Argos is fishing Haemon out of the sea. I am only one man, Ada. I have not the strength of three or five to lift the mast."

She felt her eyes grow wide at the sound of defeat in his voice. "No, we cannot accept failure, Nicolaus. As captain you must save us." She stomped her foot in the cold water. "I do not wish to die in this watery grave, and I am certain your crew does not, either."

His face appeared through the opening. His cheeks bore the sting of rain and wind, his eyes cold with anger or perhaps determination. Whatever the cause, she prayed to God Almighty that Nicolaus would fight for their lives, much as he had when he'd rescued her from drowning. And soon. Given the water now lapped near her shins, they did not have much time. If only there was a way for some of the rowers to make their way on deck. "Who builds a ship with only one entrance?"

A rumble of laughter vibrated through the planks, filling the hold. The boat was sinking, and Nicolaus found humor in their situation. She glanced at Nicolaus's brother to see if he, too, thought his brother had gone mad. A smile lifted the corners of Brison's mouth, making him look even more a boy than she first thought. These Greeks, no doubt, had addled minds. That could be the only explanation for their good nature in the face of certain death.

"Brison, move the merchandise and make haste. I'll open the hatch." The pounding of Nicolaus's footsteps across the planks gave her hope that not all was lost.

"Move the stores from the back of the boat as well, to give us double access," Brison said to two rowers. The authority of his command made her wonder what sort of captain he would grow up to be, one much like his brother, capable and compassionate. From all that she'd seen, compassion wasn't common among men, especially toward their slaves.

Brison led two men toward the front of the boat and removed a panel. Ada watched as they began unloading crates and earthenware jars stacked higher than their heads. Breathing in a sigh of relief, she knelt beside the conscious woman trapped beneath the mast and patted her hand. She took in the scared faces of the women and children. Besides the time when they tried to keep Ada from picking up the infant, the group had been quiet without complaint. She understood their fear, the not knowing of what would happen to them.

"All will be well." She spoke in Nicolaus's language hoping to reassure them, but she was met with blank stares and animosity. What more could she do to gain their trust? Giving up the babe was out of the question, but she'd continue to show them the same kindness she did for the helpless infant.

How could he have forgotten about the entrances to the storerooms and the access into the center hold? He'd had compartments built at either end of the vessel in order to keep the merchandise secured. Of course, he had not figured on purchasing more than the compartments could contain, which left crates floating atop the water in the hold. It was fortunate the lattice kept the amphora jars in their places else they'd most assuredly break filling the water with all sorts of pleasant aromas. He didn't need sea creatures lured into the ship by their scents.

How long could his vessel keep afloat? He scrubbed his hand over his face. If Brison was correct, the water was rising too fast. If his men didn't find the hole and patch it, he wouldn't have to worry about winning his father's game. Right now all that mattered was saving as many people as possible. "Euclid, prepare the planks so Xandros can come aboard once they are close enough."

Nicolaus waited until his helmsman did as he commanded and then he bowed his head. If the water continued to rise, would they need the use of the dilapidated fishing boat? However, there was no possibility of moving his entire crew and Ada to the other boat. It wouldn't hold them. It barely held the villagers as it was. As much as it soured his stomach, his men would have to cast lots if repairs could not be made before it sunk. He could see no other way.

There was some solace knowing Ada would find safety in the decrepit boat. Even if the safety was not certain, some was better than none. He had confidence that Xandros would see that the broken vessel would make port at Joppa, but it was a double-edged sword knowing his brother must cast lots along with the crew. He would not dishonor Brison no matter how much he wanted to command him to the other boat.

There was no time to consider all the possible situations. His energies were better focused on survival, and that meant opening the hatch. He stalked toward the room beneath the helmsman's perch where he'd kept tools supplied in a built-in chest and then ran back toward the front of the boat. Since they had not planned on opening the hatches until they reached home at Andros, they had sealed them to keep water from entering that portion of the hold.

Nicolaus yanked on the handle, hoping the hatch

would simply release, but the seal had been done properly and held tight. He lined the chisel along the edge of the hatch and hammered to break the seal. The black tar dipped but did not break as he'd hoped. Digging his fingers into the seal he pulled at the sticky thickness. At this rate the vessel would rest at the sea bottom before he popped the hatch open.

He tried again with the chisel, gouging, digging, pulling, until all the little chunks broke away, but the hatch still would not open. Why did it seem whenever he sailed he faced difficult decisions? Perhaps he was not meant to be a sailing merchant as his father had been. Perhaps sailing should be left only to his brothers, Jasen and Brison. If they survived, he'd see his father's legacy passed to his brothers.

The temptation to bury his face into his hands and weep overwhelmed him, but he could not give up. He wanted to please his father, and he wanted to sail. The sea seemed to thrum in his blood. He'd never felt freer, more alive, than when standing on the commander's post with the ocean spray bathing his cheeks. At least he hadn't until he'd lost his sister to thieves.

Perhaps he should give up, walk away from his livelihood. Yet, his father depended on him, not for a simple game, but to bring Brison back alive. To bring him back a seasoned sailor. And Ada depended on him, whether she wanted to or not. Just as he depended on this great God his uncle spoke of, the one Ada trusted in and prayed to. Sucking in a sharp breath of air, Nicolaus looked toward the sky, the place his uncle believed this great God resided. If there was such a god, one who'd created the heavens and the earth, one who all other gods bowed to, then Nicolaus owed him his fidelity, but first they had to survive the sea. "Ay, if You are an all-knowing God, I seek Your forgiveness for my obstinate nature, but I pray You do not blame me for my lack of trust as of yet."

The gray clouds began to part. A single ray of light bathed the deck around him, warming his wind-cooled skin. If he were owned by superstitions as his parents and most of his sailors were, he'd think it was a sign. But he wasn't superstitious, and he'd just take it for the blessing that it was. The storm was breaking, and calmer seas were on the horizon. It still didn't fix the problems below his deck, but he sensed renewed hope within his mind. He could do this. He could save them all.

"Have you forgotten what you are about, Nicolaus?"

Nicolaus glanced over his shoulder. Relief cut through his bones much like the wave had broken the mast. It was good to see Xandros had been able to come to his aid. "The hatch won't open, even though I've loosened the seal."

White teeth gleamed in the midst of Xandros's dark beard. "Have you forgotten we latched the hatch from the inside?"

Nicolaus shook his head. "We've no time for jokes, Xandros. There are people trapped below. Brison, Ada..."

"It is not a joke. You ordered the ship to be built with the latches on the inside as a precaution against thieves finding your wares so easily."

He nodded. "Ay, I remember although I wish it was not so. What if Brison cannot remove the stores quickly enough?"

Xandros dropped a hand to his shoulder and squeezed.

"Have confidence in your brother, Nicolaus. This is not his first time sailing, and I'm quite certain that maid of yours will not allow him to rest. Now let us see what can be done about moving the mast now that we've able-bodied men to help."

Nicolaus stood and noticed the rowers who'd been caught on the fishing vessel were back on board. One man knelt near the entrance, his ear hovering over the opening. It was obvious he was listening to instructions and from the soft musical lilt, he had no doubt Ada was giving his men commands. Nicolaus smiled. "Since when did I lose command of my ship to a woman?"

Xandros nudged his shoulder against his. "Since you carried her aboard. Did your father not tell you to never challenge a woman else you're bound to lose all you hold dear—including your ship?"

No, his father had not given him such sage advice. If he had, Nicolaus wasn't sure he would have heeded it, especially where Ada was concerned. An image of her standing on the auction block forced its way into his thoughts, leaving a bitter taste in his mouth. He'd never interfered before—if he had he would have a fleet full of women and children rescued from slavery—but there was something about her. Perhaps it had been the proud tilt of her chin or the anger burning in her eyes. Perhaps it was because somehow he knew she didn't deserve the fate that seemed to befall her. Of course, no man, woman or child deserved to be treated as harshly as most slave masters were wont to do. So why save Ada? Why not the Egyptian woman from the previous port with the tresses the color of the night sky and eyes as dark as heated tar?

There was something about Ada that reminded him of his sister. What, he could not comprehend. Desma's hair was darker, her skin paler and her eyes lighter. She was much taller and more like willow than Ada. His sister was graceful as were most women of Ionian descent, not the curvaceous temptation Ada possessed. And his sister was obedient, compliant without fault. He chuckled to himself. Obviously Ada held nothing in common with his sister, and if that were true then he must be taken by her beauty. It was a good thing he did not believe in the Greek gods and goddesses else he'd believe they were playing tricks on his mind to make him besotted with Ada, a Philistine woman who called upon the Hebrew God.

If all he lost was his ship to her, he'd consider it a blessing. Although he'd never experienced that cursed emotion of love his mother continually harped about, he'd also never experienced half the emotions he'd encountered since crossing his path with Ada. The way his heart kicked against his chest—stealing his breath when she smiled, the way his gut contorted when he caught her gazing upon him as if he were more than a mere man, the way he had to continually halt himself from staring at her as if he'd never before seen a woman, and the worst, the disturbing sense of defeat at failing to protect her from the ails of this earth. Ay, he had a feeling he was close to losing something much greater than his ship to Ada, which was why it would be a good idea to put as much distance between them as possible, as soon as possible.

# *Chapter Eight*

Shadows appeared and disappeared as heavy footfalls pounded across the deck above. The desperate thumps should have alarmed Ada, but instead they brought relief to her frantic nerves.

"Brison," she called out to him over the noise of the men moving the stores and the pounding from above. He glanced at her, and she motioned for him to come closer. "Your brother has men above. Perhaps we can move the mast now."

He peered up at the hole and then back to where some of the sailors continued to clear the hold of crates. "We almost have it cleared."

She laid her hand on his shoulder to halt him from leaving. "No matter, Brison. The mast still needs to be moved." She knew she pleaded with him with her eyes, for his gaze shifted to the trapped women. "Your brother has a compassionate heart. He would not leave them to die. Nor will I."

With a nod, he leaped atop a few crates and jumped over a few more until he was speaking with the men emptying the compartment. She'd won a small victory. At least for now. Until Nicolaus discovered she'd caused his men to defy his orders by agreeing to her sound reason. He would, no doubt, command her to safety before the women were freed, but she meant what she'd said. She would not leave them.

"Are you giving orders to my men?"

Startled, Ada jumped. She tilted her head back. Although his tone had been deep and echoed throughout the hold, he was smiling. "I only thought to explain to your men how the mast should be moved. You're more than one man now, ay?"

"Ay, Ada, I'm more than one man now. Shall we get it out of the way, then, so you can tend to the wounded?"

The corners of her mouth slid upward, and a song took flight in her heart. She was far from understanding his ever-changing moods, but when he offered her his approval as he did now, his surly temper was long forgotten.

Brison and the sailors pressed into the small space waiting for word. Ada held up her hand. No doubt the releasing of the mast would cause the women great discomfort. "A moment, if you will. I'd like to pray."

"Ada," Nicolaus growled. "We've not the time for it."

She glared up at him. "It will only take a moment."

"You best let her, Nicolaus. You'll spend more time arguing with her than it will take for her to speak a few words," Brison said.

"No greater truth have you spoken, little brother."

Nicolaus did not say another word, only stared down at her, making her feel as if she were a spectacle back on the auction block. Closing her eyes, she lifted her face upward. "Almighty, Maker of the heavens and the earth, the sea and all that is within, happy is the one who has You as their help, O Lord. You love the righteous and preserve strangers. You relieveth the fatherless and the widow. Lord, help us now. Make these men swift in their rescue of these strangers among us. May their discomfort be as little as possible." She felt the warmth of Nicolaus's gaze upon her and the corners of her lips curved upward. She opened her eyes. "Almighty, please preserve this vessel until we reach land."

Nicolaus blinked, his mouth opened and closed as if he wished to say something, but no sound came out. Drawing in a relieved breath, Ada clapped her hands together. "Everyone will have to lift at the same time. It will take me a moment to move the women."

"Y'er no mor'an a mite. How're you to move them?" one of the sailors asked.

Ada felt her eyebrows knit together. Words rushed forward, but before they left her tongue she heard Nicolaus's voice. "She's stronger than she looks, and stubborn enough to carry this ship all the way to shore on her shoulders if need be."

"I will help." Galen unfurled himself from around his sister and pattered toward Ada.

"As will I." One of the old women rose from her seat and stood beside him.

"And I." A chorus of voices rose together as the rest of the women stood.

With them all offering their assistance, there would not be much room for Ada to help. And since they were kin or of the same community, Ada felt obligated to retreat to the shadows. Although joyful for the help, disappointment weighed down upon her shoulders.

She did not like being pushed to the shadows. The small bundle cradled against her chest whimpered. Ada smoothed her hand down its back. It was just as well she was not needed. She would not wish to bring harm to the babe while trying to help.

Ada squeezed past the sailors and the women preparing to move the mast and walked toward the front of the boat. She thought to sit beside the little girl, but the child's wide-eyed fear as she approached propelled Ada to find another place. She did not wish to cause the child more discomfort. She found a bench and curled her feet beneath her. The sodden hem of her tunic soaked through the rest of the cloth, but the chill did little to prompt her to move from her comforting position. If only she had purpose, a chore to keep her thoughts from straying to their dire situation and to what the future held in store for her. The infant wiggled against her chest. She pulled back the linen and peeked at the tiny rosy cheeks. Eyes the color of the bluest skies blinked up at her and she sucked in a sharp breath. Had they been this blue when he'd looked at her earlier? No wonder they didn't want anything to do with the child.

Where had he come from? Was he one of their own? "You are a boy child, are you not?" The baby cooed. Little bubbles formed on his lips. "I suppose we'll discover what you are when it's time to change your linens."

The innocent trust the babe offered warmed her heart. He did not know her, had never heard the sound of her voice, yet he did not cry or seem distressed with all the noise around them. "If God finds me favorable perhaps He'll allow me to keep you, tiny one."

"Ada." She jerked her head up and spied Nicolaus stalking toward her. His long strides cut through the rising water with ease.

"The women, are they free?"

"Ay." He bent down and scooped her and the babe into his arms.

"What are you doing?" She stopped herself from kicking her feet lest she cause him to drop her and the child.

"I am taking you to the deck."

"I can walk on my own feet, Nicolaus."

"Ay. I figured it would be quicker if I did not ask you to move and carried you."

"Why would it be quicker? I would have done as you asked."

A vibration rumbled against her side as he growled. "Have you once done as I asked?"

"Of course."

His arms tightened around her. His mouth hovered a small space above hers. If she wasn't holding tight to the babe, she was certain she'd run a finger over the seam of his lips to see if they were as warm as they looked. As if to remind her that her tunic was soaked with the sea, her body shivered. The obstinate man rolled her closer into his chest. "Without argument, Ada?"

She opened her mouth to argue, and then clamped it shut.

"Hence, the reason I am carrying you." He adjusted his hold on her, shifting her even closer. Her ear rested tight against the warmth of his chest and the smooth cadence of his heartbeat. "Hold on."

He grasped hold of the rail beside the stairs and climbed. Clear skies and the bright sun bathed her face when they emerged from the dark bowels of the ship. Nicolaus did not put her down as she'd expected, but rather carried her to the space beneath the helmsman's perch. Ada's cheeks heated when she realized the women from the fishing boat were already there watching with curiosity as Nicolaus set her down.

Nicolaus clenched his jaw, his nostrils flaring. "I've a feeling I've told you this before. Stay here. Do not move until I tell you to."

Swallowing past the knot in her throat, every bit of her wanted to argue, to demand an explanation, but after all they'd been through thus far, she'd heed him without question. Besides, his scent clung to her person as did the warmth of where his arms had been wrapped around her and she had not the wits to form a coherent thought. Words would not be forming on her tongue.

He opened a chest and pulled something from it. He knelt in front of her and wrapped a sheep blanket around her shoulders. "Ada, it is important for your safety and that of the children that you remain here until I come for you." He ran a finger over her brow, tucking a strand of hair behind her ear. Closing her eyes, she leaned into his touch, taking delight in the simplicity of his gesture. It was as if he cared for her. For Ada the Hebrew woman, not Ada the slave.

A cool breeze brushed over her and she flung her eyes open to find him stumbling backward as if she were a viper. He yanked on his beard and took several more steps away from her. Color rose high in his cheeks. Had she angered him somehow? "I must see what repairs can be made to halt the water from filling the hold before all the merchandise is ruined. I do not wish to worry over your safety, as well."

Ada bit the inside of her mouth to keep her lip from quivering. If only her wet clothing was to blame, but she knew different. How could she have thought he might care for her? She would do well to remember that he was a merchant, and she nothing more than his merchandise.

Nicolaus stalked away from the maddening woman and jumped down into the hold. Seemed whenever he set sights on her, he needed to touch her. He knew she could walk on her own, maneuver the ladder with ease, even with the babe snuggled tight against her breast. May the sea wash him overboard if he wasn't truly smitten with her. Once the barrier between them had been moved from the hatch, his blood pulsed with the need to carry her away, anywhere far from danger. Somehow he knew she wouldn't move from her isolated perch until all the others were back on deck, so he'd waited with arms crossed grunting out commands as he kept his eye on her.

Each emotion that had flitted across her face as she spoke to the babe had somehow seemed tied to him, especially her sadness. He did not like it. Not at all. Once he had her off this cursed vessel and placed some distance between them, he'd breathe easier. Relax, be more himself.

"Why the scowl, Nicolaus?"

Nicolaus snapped his head toward his smiling friend. He squeezed his hands into fists but kept them at his sides lest he clout the smirk from Xandros's face. "As much as I like to swim, I do not like standing in water. Not. On. My. Boat."

Perhaps if he bellowed loud enough his crew would

believe him. His scowl certainly had nothing to do with the slip of a maiden who wanted to keep the orphaned babe. The woman who made him want to smile, and even more, to make her smile. Before he knew it she'd want to keep the children, too. And how was he to give her that gift? They didn't belong to him.

Xandros laughed, filling the cavern and further irritating Nicolaus's mood. "Are you certain it has nothing to do with a stubborn woman?"

"Ay, and why should it? She means nothing to me other than more work to keep her out of trouble. The next time she disobeys a command, I'll throw her overboard myself." Nicolaus prided himself on not choking on the words, even if he did feel the blood drain from his face at the thought of losing her. Perhaps he could find a household in Joppa to take her in as a servant. It was far enough away from Andros.

He clenched his fists tighter and growled. Three days' travel in good weather was not far enough to halt the longing he felt where Ada was concerned.

"That is good news, my friend."

Nicolaus shook the disturbing thoughts from his head and focused on Xandros. "What is?"

"The hole was small and has been patched. The men are bailing out the water as we speak." Xandros twisted his lips. "Have you not been listening?"

"Ay, we're about to set sail again. We'll be in Andros in no time."

The corners of Xandros's mouth lifted as he shook his head. "Unfortunately, we need to port at Joppa. The mast needs to be repaired and we need to decide what to do with the fishing boat and her people."

"That could take days." Only moments before he

was ready to leave Ada at Joppa, to distance himself from her, but the thought of losing his father's game, losing the ship, his chance to stand out as a merchant on his own, Ada…it left a bitter taste of sour grapes in his mouth.

Xandros squeezed Nicolaus's shoulder. "We do not need a sail to make our way home. The rowers will do the job fine."

No, they did not need the sail. However, they still needed to port at Joppa. The storm, no doubt, had taxed his men. They needed a rest, and he needed time to think through his choices and hopefully make the right decisions. Distance from Ada was the only way to clear his head, or so he hoped. He had acquaintances in Joppa who would treat her well. "I've a boon to ask of you, my friend."

Scratching his beard, Xandros looked wary. "What is it you ask?"

"I have business to attend in Joppa. I would ask that you see to the repairs." Nicolaus lowered his chin and stared at the wet planks beneath his feet. Turning, he grasped the rail and climbed onto the deck before seeking out the commander's post.

"We have no more room for stores, Nicolaus." Xandros leaned his forearms against the railing. "What has such great importance that you'd abandon your duties?"

Nicolaus turned. His gaze sought the shadows where he'd left Ada. Even with the distance between them he could see the way the sun captured the strands of her hair, making them seem as if they were embracing. Was the sun captivated with her, too? "I am torn between the rights and the wrongs of what I have done.

After Desma was taken and I'd spent months in cruel bondage I vowed to never buy another human being, no matter the cause." He drew in a ragged breath. At least he spoke partial truths. When he found his sister, *if* he found her, he fully intended on purchasing her with all that he owned, even with his life if necessary. He had nothing to offer Ada, not even a position in his household since he didn't plan on remaining in Andros long. Of course, he had planned on setting her up in his mother's home. How was he to endure her presence so close, for however long it took him to find Desma? Of course, first he had to win his father's game if he was to claim this vessel and the merchandise within. He needed it to fund his mission. "Perhaps I shouldn't have taken the woman from her home."

Xandros swung around and looked toward Ada. "You saved her from a far worse fate. What wrong can be found in that?"

"I risked her life bringing her aboard this ship."

"No doubt death would be preferable to what that man had in store for her. I shudder to think of any woman being used in such a way, especially one as small as her."

Nicolaus gave in to the smile lifting the corner of his mouth. "Ay, even stubborn ones with tendencies to disobey." Recalling the quietness of his sister as she was taken away, he quickly sobered. Had his docile sister met with such a fate? He hoped not. Hoped she'd found a home with kindly masters who wouldn't crush her sweetness. "A maiden such as her should not be at sea."

"Ah," Xandros said as he twisted back around. "This has little to do with Ada and more to do with Desma."

Feeling the heat rise in his cheeks, Nicolaus scrubbed his hand over his face. "I should have listened to my instinct. I should not have agreed to travel to Rhodes so she could marry Knosis. The man is four times her age. I should have listened to Jasen and hidden her away. If I had, she wouldn't have been taken by David's men."

"You have captained many vessels and commanded hundreds of men, but there are some things you have no control over, my friend. Destiny, such as that dealt to Desma, is one. The nature of the sea is another. She flows to and from at her own will, not ours. She embraces us with calm waters, and tosses us about in her rages. She has no master to obey. If she chooses to take Ada from you, she will and there is nothing you can do about it."

Nicolaus followed Xandros's gaze. The waters had calmed. The once murky color now brightened to the unearthly hues he loved so much. There was a delicacy to the beauty, much as there was to Ada. And just as he could not command the sea to obedience when she was in a fit, neither could he command Ada. Even if it was for her own good.

"If the tales to be heard are true, your sister was to be Knosis's tenth wife. All the others, for reasons unknown, died."

Gentle waves splashed over the brass battering ram, bathing them in salty water. Nicolaus loved this about the sea, the peaceful tranquility of each roll and the drops of kisses upon his face. The sea was the only one to embrace his moods. His mother tried to coddle his moods, his father tried to command them, and Ada…she challenged them, firing his blood to anger and eliciting his softer side all at the same time.

He clenched his teeth. How was that even possible? He prided himself on having a sound mind. As the Sea Dragon he'd fought battles and conquered men. He turned a blind eye at the agonizing sounds of death because it threatened to weaken him. He ran from weakness, he despised it in his men as well as within himself. The emotion did not belong in the heart of a warrior, in the heart of a captain of the sea, especially in the heart of the infamous Sea Dragon.

Nicolaus cupped his hand at the base of his neck. The Sea Dragon had died. That part of him had died, but had it died enough to accept the weakness Ada made him feel?

Xandros nudged him with his shoulder. "Your father was not pleased about sending Desma to Knosis, but he'd had no other choice. Her destiny was changed when she was stolen."

As was Nicolaus's.

"For the better? We may never know. What we do know is that Knosis is still searching for his tenth wife. Perhaps, Ada's destiny was to become a slave, a prostitute in Ashkelon."

Nicolaus snapped his gaze to Xandros. How could his friend think as such?

"Then again, perhaps her destiny was to be rescued by a Greek merchant who means her no harm. One who is honorable and kindhearted."

Nicolaus may mean her no harm, but that seemed to be all he'd brought to her. She'd nearly been lost to the sea while under his command, not once but thrice. Then there was that small matter that he seemed to be losing himself each time his gaze touched hers. Surely he'd hoped to find a bit of his old self on this challenge of his father's, but it seemed as if he was discovering that the old him was truly dead and gone. Strange how she made him feel more alive than he'd felt in months, years even. And yet a part of him, the part that wanted to please his father by becoming a wealthy merchant, that part of him that needed to become more like the thieves of the Great Sea, to revive Sea Dragon in order to find his sister, seemed to be long gone, and all because of Ada. Was he willing to give up that part of himself completely in order to truly live? He just didn't know if he could since it would mean giving up on finding his sister.

# Chapter Nine

"You are husband and wife?"

Ada opened her eyes and jerked fully awake at the words spoken with ease in Nicolaus's language. She curled her legs beneath her and toyed with the soft sheep's skin cushioning her seat. "No, we are nothing of the sort. What makes you ask?"

Several toothless grins appeared at her response. "You've the look of a woman in love."

The constant thick knot in her throat dislodged and plummeted to her gut. Was she to suffer as her mother had, loving a man who could not, would not love her? It had taken all of her concentration to keep from giving in to the sickness plaguing her stomach, and now it came to life with a fierceness she could not tamp down. She had been fine when holding the babe, cooing whenever he began to cry, but her shoulders ached from the weight of the linen knotted at the base of her neck, and her eyes had grown tired. Each note sung out by the helmsman followed by the lurch of oars had lured her into laying the babe down on a blanket beside her and closing her eyes for a moment.

She would not be taken in by Nicolaus's kindness. She could not allow her curiosity about him to be misconstrued by these women. She did not love him. No matter how much she wanted to dance and sing with joy in his presence. She couldn't, wouldn't love him.

A whimper quivered from the baby's lips, cutting through her heart. He must be growing hungry, and she had not the means of feeding him, nor fresh linens to change his swaddling. She ignored the questioning looks, ignored the woman's words burning in Ada's chest. "What happened to the babe's mother?"

Ada tilted her chin and looked to each of the women when she was met with silence. The two who were injured from the splintered mast trapping their legs were beyond childbearing years. The others seemed just as old, or so the creased lines wrinkling their cheeks told her they were. Certainly one of these could not be the child's mother. "The mother?"

She might as well have spoken in her own language for all the response she received. A disappointed breath of air rushed out of her lungs. Edith peered around the side of Galen. Pale trails from her tears cut through the grimy cheeks. Knots of matted hair the color of the desert clumped at odd angles around the child's head. Galen tried to push her back, but she shoved the hand holding her away and stood. Dark lashes opened wide, revealing blue eyes. The same as the babe's.

Ada motioned for the child to move closer, but she shied back behind her little protector. "Would you like to hold him?"

"Leave the girl," one of the women croaked through parched lips. "Their mother is dead. Or she will be soon. The cursed seafarers. What care can we give the babe? They have taken all our young women among us. We have no one to care for or feed him. At least these young ones are old enough to care for us."

As if he understood the words spoken, the child began to cry. Ada crooked her finger and stuck it in the babe's mouth. "Shh, hush now, little one." She glanced at the woman brave enough to break her silence. "I am sorry for your trials. God has blessed you with the captain's help. He will see you well."

"Bah, the gods have abandoned us to our deaths. Most assuredly because we did not toss that wee one into the sea."

Heat filled Ada's cheeks. Her sisters worshiped many gods as did her father. She'd learned to keep her beliefs to herself, there was only one God. One who did not abandon his people in their time of need. "Ay, the babe lives, and Nicolaus found you. We have survived the storm and still breathe life into our bodies." Ada offered a smile. "We are blessed. Blessed by the one true God. Now, if you will hold the babe for a time I will find you water to drink and bread cakes to eat."

She'd also inquire about the infant's needs. With great reluctance, she deposited the babe into the older woman's arms. The child was one of them. He needed them, and no matter how much Ada wanted to keep him, she knew she couldn't. Ada straightened her tunic and then ducked beneath the canopy. She gasped at the beauty before her. What looked to be shimmering stars danced upon the surface of the crystalline water, but it was nothing more than the sun kissing the top of the waves.

She'd never seen anything like it. Certainly, she'd

seen the reflection of the sun upon the waters near her home, but the brilliant shades of blues were incomparable even to that of the morning sky.

A command came from the post, and she immediately sought out Nicolaus. Once again he stood with his feet braced shoulder width apart and his arms crossed over his chest. The breeze ruffled through his dark curls, and Ada knew a hint of jealousy for she wanted nothing more than to run her fingers through his hair, to see if the curls were as soft as they looked.

Long paddles cut through the water as the helmsman sang out orders in an odd cadence. The fishing boat, although smaller and with fewer rowers, glided beside them. Ada walked carefully to the ladder leading to Nicolaus's post. With one hand on the rung, she hesitated climbing. Not out of fear but rather she did not wish to anger Nicolaus. Nor did she wish to be in such a confined space with him, especially not after the observation of the other women. How was she to look at him without it seeming as if she were a woman in love? Before she could turn back she climbed the ladder. As soon as she stood on the platform, the brunt of the sea breeze brushed against her. "It is captivating."

Nicolaus snapped his gaze toward her. The corners of his eyes crinkled, and then he smiled. "I am surprised you stayed beneath the helmsman's perch as long as you did. My thanks for heeding my command even if it was for a short time."

"Nicolaus, I do not mean to tax your patience." She twisted her hands together.

He brushed his hand over her brow and down the

side of her cheek causing shivers to run along her arms. "Are you unwell again?"

"No." She looked to her feet. "The babe…they say his mother was taken by the thieves. He's—uh—hungry, and I know not what to do."

"And you think I would have knowledge of such things?"

She didn't know how to respond. Why had she assumed he would? "You have been capable and acted wisely in every trial we've met with thus far. I only assumed—"

"Come," he said grabbing hold of her hand. He pulled her close to the rail and pointed toward a spot on the horizon. His warmth encompassed her and she felt herself leaning closer. "Do you see those rocks and the city beyond?"

Squinting her eyes, she tried to see what he said was there but could not. She shook her head.

"It is Joppa. Not much longer and we'll be at port. I will send one of my men in search for a wet nurse. Perhaps, she'll be willing to travel with us and care for the child."

Ada's shoulders sunk in relief. Although she didn't relish giving up tending the babe, she also knew she was incapable.

"If she is not willing, then we'll continue to find wet nurses at each port until we reach Andros. Of course, we must seek the wishes of his people."

"They all but left him for dead, abandoning him in the hold to fend for himself," she snapped.

Nicolaus turned her to face him. With the crook of his finger he lifted her chin so she'd look him in the eye. "I am not your enemy, Ada. Nor do I wish harm to befall the child. These people have been through much, and it is only right to determine if they wish to keep the babe among them."

"My apologies, Nicolaus."

He rubbed his thumb over her chin and pulled her closer as he lured her in with the intensity of his dark eyes. Air caught in her throat, and her pulse sped. Anticipation, fear and joy swirled in her thoughts holding her captive.

"There is none needed, Ada. You've been through a trial yourself." He leaned down. The warmth of his mouth brushed against her brow, danced across her wind-cooled cheek and then hovered over her lips. An unexplained fire pressed against the wall of her chest and settled in the pit of her stomach. She shouldn't delight in the simple gesture, couldn't, but oh how she wanted him to touch his lips to hers, to know what it was that bound a man and woman together besides a marriage contract. What it was that had bound her mother's heart to her father.

A husband, children, a home to care for, those things were not the lot cast for her life. Even if her sisters hadn't sold her, even if she had remained in her father's house, marriage wouldn't have been possible, for no man wanted a Hebrew woman for a wife, even if her father was a Philistine. She'd heard that many times. None of that mattered, though, for she was a slave, a slave to this man who sparked a longing within her that she had no right to feel. Yet, here she was gazing into his eyes like a woman in love.

Pain, worse than any of her family's rejections, tore through her heart. The old woman was correct in her observation. Squeezing her eyes against the tears burning and threatening to spill, she shoved her palms against Nicolaus's chest and all but jumped from the platform. If God had any mercy on her at all he'd grant her a new master, one who didn't make her dream of things she shouldn't be dreaming of.

"Ada!" Nicolaus grabbed at her tunic to keep her from falling. Much to his surprise, especially given her earlier unsteadiness, the brash woman landed on her feet like a lioness pouncing on its prey. She didn't even hesitate before she was up and running away from him.

He jumped to the deck to give chase, but her golden tresses danced across her rigid back; the veil was more effective than any armor she could have donned. Blowing out a ragged breath, he lifted his hand and despised the way it shook. Frustrated by such weakness, he clenched his fist and dropped the offending limb to his side. A fool he'd been to try and kiss her. A fortunate fool at that. However, he wasn't certain if his fortune was because he'd almost tasted lips surely sweet as honey or because he hadn't. When her amber eyes had swirled with longing and she swayed closer, it was if he were a majestic eagle soaring over the seas ready to swoop in and catch his prey. If the confusion warring in his mind was any indication he was the one captured, tangled in a huntress's net with no escape.

No doubt he would have lost more than himself in that kiss, and he should be grateful the woman had kept her senses about her and halted him before he sealed their lips together. But curse his foolish hide if he didn't want that kiss more now than he had only moments before. He almost wanted it more than he wanted to win his father's game, more than he wanted his own ship. Almost. If it wasn't for his sister…there would be nothing stopping him from drawing Ada into his arms and kissing her. He wouldn't admit it, though, not even to himself, which was why he must find a willing family, one who wasn't overly cruel, to take her in, and the babe if the old women refused to care for him. It was the surest way to free himself from his growing obsession with the maddening woman.

"Nicolaus." Brison's call shook Nicolaus from his thoughts. Releasing his gaze from Ada, he focused on his brother. "We are nearly to port, and Euclid has been trying to gain your attention."

"My apologies, my thoughts were elsewhere."

"I can see that. If you no longer wish to be captain…" Brison winked as he punched Nicolaus in the arm. Although his brother joked, Nicolaus questioned whether or not his loyalty was to captaining this ship. If he continued to allow distractions to interfere with his duties he'd be good to no one.

"Your time will come soon enough, little brother. Trust me when I say, when it does there will be moments when you wish for insignificant tasks such as running errands around the boat." Nicolaus scrubbed his hand over his eyes, tired and burning from the constant salty sea spray. "What is it Euclid wishes?"

"With night about to fall, do you wish to continue on to port or anchor here? We've dropped the lead lines. The sea is a little more than ten fathoms deep."

"Have you checked the hole to see if it seeps?"

"Ay, the seal remains intact."

Nicolaus's gaze immediately sought out Ada. He drank her in like a man too long without sustenance. It was too dangerous for them to spend the night in the

port, especially with women on board, especially with
a beauty such as Ada. However, it would be torment
sitting under the same stars with nothing more than the
length of the ship between them. He'd want to share
the magnificent spectacle with her, to show her the
stars which would guide them home when they sailed
at night. Ay, certainly, she'd seen the twinkling gems
light up the night in her desert home, but they were
much more brilliant surrounded by the water. And if
the waters were gentle and they were close enough,
they could almost touch them. Of course, they'd only
touch the reflection of the brightest lights, but it was
the closest he'd come to placing the stars in the palm
of her hand.

"Drop the baskets. We'll anchor here until morning. The men will have to find their rest wherever they
can. We'll need enough blankets for the women and
children to shelter for the night."

"We have water and cakes of bread left."

"Ay, I'm sure they're all hungry. I purchased some
fruits when we were in Ashkelon. I'm sure the women
will enjoy those."

A soft cry whispered on the wind. Ada paced just
outside the shelter of the helmsman's perch, patting
the infant on the back. The babe wouldn't be appeased
with Ada's care much longer. He glanced up at the
evening sky. "How did I become the keeper of the
abandoned?"

Brison laughed. "I know not the answer to your
question, Nicolaus, but it has made life interesting."

Nicolaus joined in his brother's good humor and
received what he was sure was a glare from Ada for
his outburst. "That it has. Before you go about your

errands, would you motion for Xandros to draw the fishing vessel closer? I must have word with him."

All the muscles in Nicolaus's body relaxed when he spied a young woman returning with Xandros from Joppa. He knew Ada was tiring from her constant pacing in order to keep the infant calm. No doubt, her caring for the child had taxed her strength. Nicolaus was exhausted following her every move. The sitting, the standing, the pacing and bouncing. What was worse was the inability to relieve her of her burden. He didn't dare approach her. If he did, he didn't know if he could stop himself from drawing her into his arms and insisting she rest. Then he'd most certainly quench his fire by stealing that kiss, especially with her song mesmerizing his crew as she sang in a strange foreign tongue. It was as if they'd never heard a woman sing before. However, he could not blame them. He was captivated. Captivated by every note, every gesture of her hand as it smoothed over the infant's back, by her lips shaped like his bow as they nuzzled the babe's brow.

He raked a hand through his hair, his patience near an end as Xandros and the fishing boat rowed closer. Nicolaus had never understood men going to war over a woman, but he was beginning to. If another one of his crew gazed at her like a lovesick fool, he'd toss him overboard to contend with the great fish.

Propping his foot on the rail, Nicolaus rested his elbow against his thigh and glared at Xandros. The old women who'd gone ashore with him could row that fishing boat faster. If Xandros did not quicken the pace and bring the wet nurse aboard his ship, Nicolaus would soon be without a crew, and then where would he be? Stuck, outside Joppa with a maddening woman who tried his patience and tempted his resolve to restore his honor with his father, that was where he'd be. Perhaps he should command her to stop with her foreign song.

"Pfft, as if she would heed my wishes." She'd probably stand on the highest perch and sing for the masses, just to defy him. All of Joppa and every ship in port would no doubt fight to seize his ship just to get a glimpse of her to make sure she was not a mer creature.

Xandros maneuvered the fishing vessel beside them. White teeth gleamed in the midst of his beard. What did he have to be so joyous about? Nicolaus glanced around his boat and noticed not a single man moved about their duties.

"Prepare the planks!" He clenched his jaw at his own churlish behavior when his men jumped. He'd prided himself on being a kind commander, on never raising his voice unless necessity required it, even during his infamous Sea Dragon days. Then his men knew their duties, just as they did now. They were well trained, efficient. At least they had been before Ada stepped foot on the deck. Before he carried her aboard.

"It took you long enough. I could have swum home and back again in the time it took you to row here," he said as he met Xandros and the young woman at the edge of the plank. Nicolaus clasped his fingers around the woman's wrist, causing her to fall forward. Much to his displeasure he didn't quite wait until her feet were steady before he dragged her across the deck and presented her to Ada. He didn't like his behavior. He would have flayed one of his men for treating any woman with such harshness, but if he did not make haste and halt Ada's disruption of his crew, he'd go mad.

"Stop singing and give her the babe."

# Chapter Ten

Laughter bubbled within Ada's chest in relief even as tears of sadness threatened to spill forth. To make matters worse she had the sudden urge to clout Nicolaus with an earthenware jar. If he hadn't given her the command with such rudeness she would have fallen to her knees in gratitude. Even though the baby was tiny, he'd grown heavy over time and she was exhausted.

Rolling her shoulders back to ease her aches, she took in the young woman. Her tunic did not speak of wealth, nor did it speak of destitution. However, her red-rimmed eyes spoke of sadness. Why would she choose to leave her home? The question cleaved to her tongue, but it was not her place to ask. "Your name?"

"Chloe." The woman eyed the babe as she pulled her lip between her teeth.

"Are you the wet nurse?"

"Yes," Chloe responded. As if the babe understood the answer, he began to wail in earnest. Chloe's eyes watered. Ada patted the babe's back, but he wouldn't settle and she had no choice but to trust Chloe would offer him no harm.

"Nicolaus, she cannot feed the babe with your hand clamped around her arm."

He narrowed his eyes and released the wet nurse. Ada pressed a kiss the baby's brow and then looked Chloe in the eye, before handing the child to her. "My thanks, Chloe."

Since the older women had gone to Joppa, Chloe could have chosen one of the more comfortable spots on the cushions but instead chose a dark corner away from the two children. Perhaps to allow the tears clinging to her lashes to fall. Ada did not know, but her heart yearned to soothe the woman's sorrow.

"My apologies if my song caused offense. I only meant to calm the babe." His scowl deepened at her words. She clutched the shawl one of the older women had given her tighter around her shoulders and lifted her chin a little higher. Her fingers itched for an earthen jar. She pulled air in through her nose and willed her anger to calm. The longer their gazes locked, the harder her pulse pounded within her chest. She tried to step around him to place some distance between them, but he shifted. His commanding presence blocked her escape. She moved to step around his other side. He shifted once again. She dropped her hands to her sides, clenching them. If he did not allow her to pass soon she'd snatch up the jar full of honey Brison had given them earlier and drop it on his head.

"You need to eat." His tone was hard enough to chisel rock.

She turned on him, anger pumping in her blood. "I've eaten."

"I did not see you eat a morsel, Ada."

"And you were watching? I do not think you could

have kept an eye on me the entire time, not when you have waves to watch and a crew to command. I know how important your merchandise is to you. You need not worry that I'll expire."

His tanned cheeks deepened in color. He took a step toward her. "I would see you eat."

She stepped back and then took another for good measure.

"Arrrg!" She threw her hands down at her sides and turned toward the watchful gazes of the children and the wet nurse. A few sips of water was all the sustenance she could take before her stomach turned squeamish. If he wanted to see her eat, then he'd see her eat. She stalked toward the plate of bread cakes and the bowl of fruit beneath the helmsman's perch and grabbed two handfuls of sticky honey-covered dates and a cake. She turned back on him. Her heart pounded against her chest and the tips of her ears burned. "You want to see me eat a morsel?"

She shoved a handful of dates into her mouth and followed it with a whole cake. As if her stomach had not already suffered from her earlier sickness, the dates caused her mouth to water and her stomach to rebel, but she swallowed them down and prayed they'd stay until her master decided to find someone else to harass, but it was obvious she would not be granted such mercy. Taking what was left in her other hand she smacked them against his chest and ground them into his tunic. "There. You have seen me eat. Now go command your vessel and leave me be."

She rushed away from him and toward a basin of water. She sunk her hands into the depths and scrubbed the honey from her fingers. Crouching down beside the basin, she rested her arms over her knees and buried her face into the crook of her elbow. She'd sing to calm the monster clawing at her stomach as she had done so while walking the babe, but that would only draw the captain's attention. And further spur his anger.

"Ada." Any other time his attempt at a soothing voice would have lessened her irritation. It would have drawn her heart closer to wanting more of the kindness he sought to offer. Any other time she wouldn't have given in to her feelings of anger but would have left them lying dormant by focusing on a psalm her mother had taught her. It seemed as if several hours with an unsteady foundation beneath her feet was her breaking point.

The creak of his leather sandals and the soft whisper of his tunic met her ears above the lapping of waves against the vessel. She dried her eyes against her arm. Why wouldn't he just go away so she could suffer her disgrace alone? Was she to endure a lifetime of this man on her heels, watching her every move? Constantly drawing her gaze and pulling on her heartstrings? Was she to suffer his presence, he as her master, she the slave?

She was not her mother! She couldn't love a man who owned her, not when she'd watched her mother love her father with little in return. He'd honored his wife with gifts and servants. A home of her own to raise her children. Silks and jewels. Her mother was naught but a slave, her hands calloused, her fingers raw and bleeding from days of hard work. She'd died on a mat in the corner of a dark room after days bound to a piece of wood in the sun. No one had sought to ease her mother's torment. No one but Ada. And yet her father mourned her.

The touch of his fingers against her hand startled her. She lifted her face and gasped at the look in his eyes. They reflected concern and the turmoil burning in her soul. Certainly he wasn't concerned for her. Of course, that was a falsehood. He was a kind man when he wasn't being churlish. She'd seen the way he treated her, the way he treated the others. He even obtained a wet nurse for the babe when he could have easily taken the infant ashore and sold him into slavery or to a barren woman longing for a child of her own. Both were common practice.

"I did not mean to upset you, Ada." He gently squeezed her hand, drawing her to her feet, tugging on something in her heart. She pulled her hand from his and stood and wrapped her arms around her middle. The movement did little to sever the tie as she'd hoped. Strangely it seemed to cement the longing thrumming in her veins, the one that hungered for the comfort he sought to offer. "I had not considered that you may not be able to tolerate food. You need food to renew your strength."

He unfolded his length leaving her facing the dates and honey smashed into his tunic. He expanded his chest as he drew in a deep breath. A date slid down the front of his tunic. She followed it until it plopped to the wood between them.

"Ada, I—"

She burst into laughter. Nicolaus narrowed his gaze, and she clapped a hand over her mouth.

Her eyes grew wide when she covered those pink-tinted lips that beckoned him, tempted him beyond reason. He followed her finger as she pointed toward the deck, and then he looked at his chest to where honey and dates oozed. An unbecoming snort erupted from behind her fingers. Nicolaus glanced at her, merriment dancing in her rich amber eyes. He fought the twitch threatening the corner of his mouth as he swiped his palm across his chest and held out his hand for her inspection.

"You find this funny?" He took a step forward and pressed his lips together to keep from laughing when she realized there was no escape.

She held up her hand to halt him. "Nicolaus, my apologies. I was not thinking—"

He wiped his fingers over one of her cheeks and then the other. She drew in a sharp breath, her eyes growing wider. He gave in to the laughter building in his gut. "Now, that is funny."

Every fiber of his being longed to take her in his arms and kiss her, and if the lowering of her eyelashes were any indication, she'd welcome his affections. He lifted a shaky hand to cradle her honey-laden cheek. She grabbed hold of his wrist as her eyelids slid shut. The singe of her fingers branded him, leaving a trail of fire spurring up his arm and right to the center of his chest.

"Nicolaus." Her soft whisper did little to bank the flames burning in his blood. "I cannot willingly give you my affections. I beseech you, do not ask it of me."

He jerked his hand away from her and stumbled back. Her dousing cooled his longing more effectively than being tossed overboard. "I am not a thief, Ada. I do not steal, kill or destroy unless it is necessary for my survival. I do not need your affections, nor will I take them when they are not freely given."

He turned and stalked away, his hands clenched at his sides. He did not need her, did not need to hear her laughter and her song. He did not need to see her compassion and courage. And he most certainly did not need to touch her hand or feel the touch of her lips against his. She was not a necessity for his good nature, even though he'd had none prior to bringing her aboard. He could go back to the soulless existence he'd lived since losing his sister. He didn't need her to bring joy to his life, he did not need joy at all, and that was the truth.

"You've gone mad."

Nicolaus stopped midship and glared at his second-in-command. "What are you doing here? You have your own vessel to tend to."

"Brison said your temper was displaying itself and I see that he is correct. The villagers are taking their boat to Joppa. They no longer wish to be at the mercies of the sea but give their thanks for your aid. You will not be forgotten among them." Xandros scratched his chin. "You resemble your father, you know?"

"I do not take kindly to that statement."

"I didn't expect you would." His friend crossed his arms over his chest and exhaled. "What I'm about to tell you will sour you further."

"Be done with it and say what needs to be said. We've preparations to make before night descends on us."

"Knosis is in Joppa."

Air rushed from his lungs and weakened his knees. He didn't know what he had expected Xandros to say, but that wasn't it.

"Somehow word reached him at Rhodes that your

father's sons were sailing the seas. He's been searching for you and Jasen. He's demanding your father make good on his promise to provide him with a bride."

"I have no other sisters."

The corner of Xandros's eye twitched. "I am only the messenger."

"It is a blessing I have no women on board."

Xandros held his tongue, but Nicolaus could tell he had words he wished to speak. "What is it?"

"Ada."

"She is mine." Nicolaus flinched at the forcefulness of his own words. "I intend to set her free once we return to Andros." He'd hoped to find her a family here in Joppa, but with Knosis on the prowl...

"If Knosis discovers you purchased her..."

Nicolaus clenched his hands around the railing. He wouldn't allow Knosis to claim Ada as his own. "We cannot make port. We'll stay the evening here and then leave at first light."

"What of the repairs?"

"I have no other choice. Although the woman drives me mad and I was ready to throw her to the sea only moments ago, I cannot leave her to such a fate. I'd rather endure another year of slavery myself."

"Nicolaus, are you certain?"

"Ay." Nicolaus's shoulders slumped.

"I thought as much, 'tis why I purchased more supplies." Xandros grinned.

"My thanks, my friend."

"What will you do when we make port at Rhodes? If Knosis has his men looking for you—"

"I have a few days to consider my actions. Perhaps we shall port at Phaphos instead." The tension in his shoulders began to relax as did his anger with Ada. He'd prove to her he was an honorable and kind man and no longer a seafaring thief come to demand her affections, not that he ever had need of stealing affections from women, nor would he. Still, it remained, the Sea Dragon was long dead. "What of the wet nurse?"

"She's young with no home of her own and willing to leave Joppa."

Nicolaus clapped his friend on the shoulder. "You did well, my friend."

"Now—" Xandros laughed "—tell me how you've come to wear this latest adornment. Is that honey on your tunic? Are those dates?"

# Chapter Eleven

A bird's cry pierced through Ada's sleep, causing the pounding in her head to worsen. She pressed the tips of her fingers to her temples and drew in a breath. Her throat rebelled against the salty air, and she coughed. Her lungs burned with the spasm. She blinked her eyes open. The wooden canopy, so unlike the stone ceiling at her home, hovered above her. Much to her surprise she had had a good eve's sleep, even with the constant rocking, the song of the waves and the ever increasing aches in her body. How was she to hold the babe this day with her arms so weak?

Sitting up, she curled her legs beneath her and coughed. The pounding in her head turned to a roar. She was tempted to lie back down and close her eyes, but it was well past daybreak. She rubbed at her eyes and tried to focus. The babe was nestled beneath a sheep's blanket, the wet nurse curled beside him. Edith huddled in a corner next to the young boy who sought to protect her.

Their tunics were nothing more than filthy rags. If Nicolaus approached her, she'd find a way to ask after the children's needs, especially since their people had taken their boat and rowed into Joppa, leaving the three in Nicolaus's care. After what she'd said to Nicolaus last eve about stealing her affections, she had doubt Nicolaus would even speak to her again, which was fine with her. The more he kept his distance the better for her to keep her resolve. She would not become like her mother. No matter how much she wanted to seek out Nicolaus and his friendship.

A friendship was something she could accept. However, anything more was impossible. Her heart would never heal from the pain, not after she'd witnessed her mother's shame and the constant heartache forced upon her by Ada's father. Always loving, never loved. She rose from her bedding. Her knees wobbled, threatening to collapse. She braced her hand against the wall to keep from falling and drew in a few concentrated breaths until the dizziness abated. As soon as she thought she was no longer in danger of falling she slipped between the linen draped over the helmsman's perch. Another of Nicolaus's thoughtful acts of kindness to give her and the wet nurse privacy from his sailors' prying eyes.

Soft early morning light bathed the earth. Although more beautiful than she could have imagined, the brightness was like a blade to her skull. She stumbled toward the rail and squinted against the piercing light. The reflection of the sky rippled with each of the waves, distorting the perfect image. Yet, somehow it was just as beautiful if not more so.

Shivers raced down her neck and over her arms as a breezed brushed over her. She readjusted her shawl, pulling it tighter to ward off the chill in the air. It was a shame she could not stand near Nicolaus since he always seemed to bring warmth with him. She glanced toward the captain's post and lost her breath as she locked eyes with him. The distance between them did little to dispel the intensity of Nicolaus's gaze. It threatened to consume her. Her resolve of never being friends strengthened, but how could she even be enemies with him if he evoked such a reaction from her with just a look?

Tearing her gaze away, she rushed back to the alcove and slipped between the linen. She dropped onto her bedding, drew her knees in to her chest and then pulled the covers around her shoulders. What was she going to do? Beg him to send her home, back to the cruelty of her sisters and the neglect of her father? Could she go back to living under their constant rejection knowing such kindness existed with Nicolaus? Certainly it was better than being a slave, a slave falling for her master.

Would his kindness be enough?

"Lord, how am I to be content either way? If I go home I will always long for Nicolaus's kindness and laughter. If I stay, I will always long for something he will not give."

Perhaps she should have pleaded with the villagers to take her to Joppa. She shook her head. The pounding increased, making her stomach feel ill once again. She pulled her legs in tighter to her chest and buried her forehead against her knees. She would not have asked them to risk Nicolaus's wrath, and she did not think he would grant permission given he'd paid such a high price for her.

A shout boomed from the helmsman's perch above

her. The boat lurched into motion, knocking Ada onto her side. The vessel continued to lurch, turning and leaning, and lurching again with each tug of the oars. They were heading away from Joppa where she'd hoped to find solid ground and an end to her constant illness. Away from her last chance at freedom from Nicolaus.

She knew from Xandros, when he spoke to the older women last eve, that Nicolaus had chosen not to sail into the port in order to fix the mast. The repairs would have taken days, time Nicolaus did not have. She couldn't help the disappointment weighing on her shoulders. If Nicolaus would have taken them ashore while the repairs were made perhaps she could have found a messenger to send word to her father. And mayhap her father would have tried to rescue her from such madness. If he was inclined to do so.

According to Brison, who'd been speaking with another sailor, Nicolaus wished to make haste in hopes of beating his twin home in a challenge set by their father. It seemed as if Nicolaus's voyage was naught but a game, one he intended to win at any cost. She would have thought nothing of it except for the wagers made between Nicolaus's brother and the sailor.

If what she'd heard was true, Nicolaus had much to gain if he won and nothing to lose if he didn't. It stood to reason that was why he sailed into the storm. Did Nicolaus care so little about the cost of his wares that he'd lose them to the sea? She'd seen the multitude of crates, earthenware jars and the amphora jugs that hung in the lattice lining the walls of the ship. It was worth a king's ransom. A small one, but it made her father, one of the wealthiest men near Ashkelon, look destitute in comparison.

The one thing she was having problems believing was Nicolaus's lack of concern for his men. Was he so callous, so ruthless to put his men's lives at risk just to win a game? Her father would have been so focused on the prize that he wouldn't have given it a second thought, but all that she'd seen of Nicolaus proved otherwise.

The babe whimpered, pulling Ada from her thoughts. She scooted toward him and smiled. "Hello there. I suppose you're in need of fresh swaddling."

"I can do that," Chloe said as she yawned. Ada didn't mind changing the infant, she even wanted to, but the wet nurse seemed eager. Besides, the weakness invading Ada's limbs was worsening by the moment.

Ada sat back on her mat and leaned her head against the wall while Chloe cared for the babe. Chloe picked him up and readied him to feed. Ada looked to her lap and entwined her fingers into the folds of her tunic. The sting of longing for her own child made her sad.

"What is his name?" Chloe asked.

Ada snapped her gaze to the woman and the suckling child. The movement renewed the aches, and she pressed her hand to her head. "I—I don't know."

"Is he not yours?"

"No. He was on the boat with the women that were here last eve." She nodded toward the sleeping children in the corner. "The girl is his sister. Their mother was taken by sea thieves. The women wanted naught to do with him."

"As sad as it seems, I do not blame them," Chloe said as she brushed her hand over the babe's brow.

"They've not the means to care for him. Their only choices were to let him die or be sold into slavery. One offers more freedom over the other."

Ada pulled her lip in between her teeth. She understood that truth more than she wanted. Although she never said as much, Ada knew her mother longed for freedom from slavery. Was that why she gave up to death so easily?

"They granted him a mercy by leaving him with you."

Knitting her eyebrows together, Ada asked, "Why do you say that? I've not the means to care for the child." No matter how much she wanted to. "I am nothing more than a slave myself."

Chloe's eyes grew wide. "I do not understand. The captain does not treat you as a slave."

"Yet that is what I am." Ignoring the throb in her head, Ada stood and peeked between the pieces of linen. Nicolaus was where she'd last seen him commanding his ship. He seemed more at home on the open water than she'd ever felt under her father's household. "Two hundred pieces of silver and a cask of olive oil is what he paid for me."

Chloe gasped. "That price is unheard of."

Ada glanced at her over her shoulder, wondering how this woman knew as much.

"My father owned many slaves. I often traveled to market with him. He never paid more than a few pieces of silver." Chloe lifted the babe to her shoulder and began patting his back. "And never more than twenty for a woman."

Ada dropped her hand from the linen, allowing it to fall back into place, and turned to fully face the wet nurse. "You think I should see the high price as an honor?"

Chloe glanced back at the babe, her cheeks pink.

"Yester morn, I was the daughter of a wealthy merchant whose sisters suffered jealousy, for what reason I cannot discern other than my mother was my father's slave. Last eve, I found myself with a master. Although kind, he still owns me, owns my will and my freedom."

"He does not look at you as a master a slave, but as a man who loves a woman," Chloe said.

"He has not known me long enough to love me."

"Sometimes—" Chloe drew the tip of her finger over the babe's brow and then glanced at Ada "—all it takes is one look. It was that way with my husband. One look and he knew, as did I, that we loved each other. Although it did take him some time to convince me that my feelings were love."

Was it possible to know love with one glance? And what had happened to Chloe's husband to make her leave her home? Before she could ask, Ada began to cough and stumbled from the alcove so as to not disturb the children. It was just as well. She did not wish to hear falsehoods of love upon first sight. She knew nothing of love, knew nothing of how it looked or how it felt. All she knew was the confusion in her thoughts and her heart whenever he was near. She twisted her lips. Why did she insist on telling herself lies? Nicolaus agitated her even when he was not around.

She walked to the edge, leaned her head against the wooden rail and closed her eyes. If she didn't have to contend with the seasickness, as Nicolaus called it, she'd most certainly be able to think with a clear mind and be able to fight the pull the captain had on her heartstrings.

Nicolaus called out a command, and then the helmsman picked up the pace of his cadence. The rowers chanted. The vessel lurched with more force than she had experienced thus far, knocking her feet out from under her. Her head slammed against the deck. With her ears ringing, she stared at the morning sky until her eyes slid shut.

"Ada," Nicolaus hollered as he jumped down from his post and raced across the planks. He had hoped to avoid her until they had reached the next port, but his gaze kept falling to where he knew she slept. He'd somehow known when she woke, for anticipation filled him, waiting for her to appear. He'd been ready to seek her out to see how she'd fared the night when she'd stepped out onto the deck that first time.

Her unkempt hair poking at odd angles from her head put a hunger in his belly unlike any he'd known. He'd wanted to stalk over to her, pull her into his arms and smooth his hand over her hair and press his mouth to the top of her head. An entire vessel between them must not have been enough distance to guard his feelings from her since she'd run back to the alcove. If he hadn't been so captivated by her he would have noticed her pale, sunken cheeks and the way she shivered in the warmth of the morning.

Kneeling beside her, he shook her shoulder. "Ada. Ada, wake up."

He leaned closer to her mouth. Tiny breaths of air puffed against his ear.

"Is she all right?"

Nicolaus glanced up to see Xandros standing behind him. "Her skin burns. I need linens and water. See if we have any willow on board."

He scooped her limp body into his arms and rose. He pulled her tighter to his chest and rested his cheek against her forehead. "I should have forced her to eat and drink."

"This is not your doing, Nicolaus." Xandros tipped his chin toward her. "If I remember correctly, you tried and ended up wearing her meal."

"The willow, please." Nicolaus hastened toward his quarters, climbed the ladder and laid her on the cushioned bench. His pulse slammed against the wall of his chest as if he were about to go into battle. Ships he knew and could sail the Great Sea with linens over his eyes. Spears and swords he knew and could combat with the best Greek warriors, but this, whatever ailment she suffered was beyond his knowing.

Nicolaus bowed down. Grasping her hand, he lifted it to his cheek and rubbed it against his beard before holding her knuckles to his lips.

"What have I done?" he whispered, and then closed his eyes. "If there is an Almighty God, make Yourself known."

Ada made a soft groaning sound. Her eyelids fluttered open, revealing glazed emptiness. It was as if she was passing from this life. Nicolaus's heart stopped, fearful that she had done just that, but then she curled into a ball and began to shiver. Waves upon waves of shivers shook her, much like the sea had battered his vessel during the storm.

With great reluctance, her released her hand and took two strides to the door. "Brison! I need blankets, posthaste." He glanced at her small body in a constant tremble. He had never seen anyone suffer seasickness in such a way, which meant it was another ailment.

"Nicolaus," Xandros called from the deck, and the climbed the ladder when Nicolaus moved toward the bench. "I have the blankets, water and linens. Brison is searching for willow. Not an easy task after all was moved around from the storm."

"My thanks." Nicolaus snatched the blankets and covered Ada with several layers. He knelt beside the bench and ran his hands over her head.

"How is it she is cold? The temperature is warm."

"I do not know. I have heard of such sickness, but I do not know the whys of it." He raked a shaking hand down his face. "My mother always used willow in warm water to halt our fevers when we were children. I remember once when Desma was a mite, Mother would not allow us to see her. The servants prepared willow for her. My father's sadness was mournful. His joy overflowed when Desma recovered. 'Tis why my father was beside himself when she was taken."

"Nicolaus, you cannot take blame. Your father was sending her to Knosis and would have never seen her again."

"He was doing as he thought best. It is our way. You know this. Knosis is one of the wealthiest men. He would have provided well for her."

"With a nice tomb, no doubt."

"Xandros, please. I know you are correct. It is of little use to argue since Desma is no longer with us." He brushed his hand over Ada's damp brow. The heat of her skin was worrisome. He stood and glanced out the window. Although only half a day, there was still many leagues between them and the next port. However, if they turned around— He faced Xandros. "I would have a healer for her. We should return to Joppa."

"You risk running into Knosis."

"Captain!"

Nicolaus leaned out the door at his brother's urgent call and followed the line of his pointing finger. "How many?"

"Three, maybe more," Brison replied.

Nicolaus muttered a few curses beneath his breath and paced toward Ada, his arms crossed over his chest as Xandros poked his head out the door.

"It seems we're about to meet with him now," Nicolaus said.

"Ay, that it does, Captain."

# Chapter Twelve

He was in a raging squall if there ever was one. Brison had not lied when he said there were three ships. All of which were heavily armed and surrounding his own vessel. His fingers itched to draw his sword, but such an act would be certain death. Not only for him, but for his entire crew.

"What is it you think he wants?" Xandros asked.

"He most assuredly wishes to search my vessel in hopes of finding a bride." Nicolaus narrowed his eyes as Knosis prepared to board them. "Do not draw your weapons. No matter what Knosis demands."

Xandros looked at him out the corner of his eye with a slight smile turning his mouth upward. "Even if he threatens to take Ada."

Nicolaus pressed his lips together. Did his second-in-command miss the thrill of skirmishes? Nicolaus had to admit to a bit of excitement thrumming through his blood. If it had not been for Ada on board he would have welcomed a fight. "If he threatens such I will see to him myself, no matter the consequences. She is not his to take, nor is she my father's to give."

Xandros nodded toward the white-haired man maneuvering the plank boards between their ships. The man may be older than the sea itself but he was agile. "He may not see things that way, and it seems, given the vessels accompanying him, he has the law on his side."

Knosis stepped down onto the deck and eyed Nicolaus from head to toe. "So you're the one who lost my bride."

Nicolaus flinched but kept his tongue from spewing venom. No doubt the ruthless brute stole his sister himself and cried mishap for the loss.

"You've the look of your father. Strong chin and nose. A tall muscular build. How is it you allowed anyone to board your ship?"

The muscles Knosis spoke of twitched. The scars he bore from his time in captivity burned with rage at this man for his daring. "I allowed you on my ship."

Knosis rested his chin against his fist. "So you have."

"What is it you require, Knosis? I have little time for visits."

"I've heard about your father's challenge. He always did like his games. Did he tell you how I came to be your sister's betrothed?"

Nicolaus fought the urge to clench his fists. If Knosis thought to tempt him to anger with his insinuations, it was working. However, he could not allow it to show lest he end up in manacles.

"I see he hasn't." Knosis folded his hands behind his back and paced, his long white tunic dragging across the planks. "He wasn't much younger than you are now when we accepted the challenge of a merchant from Joppa. To Alexandria and back, much like I hear you and your brother are doing now. Whoever brought back the most merchandise won." Knosis folded his hands together. "The prize, your mother."

"My father is a fine sailor."

"I do not contest his abilities. However, your mother was a prize to be had. Enough for an Ionian to break tradition and marry a Dorian."

Nicolaus knew well the traditions of their people marrying only within their tribe. It had also been the source of many conflicts over the ages. Dorian women seemed to attract Ionian men.

"I suspected your father had somehow cheated, stealing your mother from me."

Nicolaus flinched at the accusation. No greater man of honor than his father could be found in all of Greece.

"It was not until after your birth that I discovered from one of your father's former crew exactly how he'd cheated. I gave your father the choice of prison—" Knosis halted in front of Nicolaus and looked him in the eye "—or his firstborn daughter as my bride."

"My father would do no such thing." Nicolaus gripped the hilt of the knife tucked in his belt. How dare this man disparage his father's honor.

"Yet, he sent you to deliver her to me."

All the air rushed out of his lungs. His hands fell to his sides. If Knosis told the truth—and for what other reason would his father have agreed to marry Desma to this relic—his anger was misplaced. How could his father have done such a thing? "He did."

"I kept my promise and did not have your father arrested. I can still do so. I have my doubts as to whether or not you were set upon by thieves. I cannot believe your sister, something precious to you, could have been stolen from the great Dragon."

"Doubts? You have doubts?" Nicolaus shook with anger. Whether at Knosis or his father, he did not know. One thing was for sure—because of their history he'd spent months chained to a wall and whipped daily to break his will, and his sister was nowhere to be found. Who knew what terror she was living at the moment. If the man wanted proof of his innocence he'd give it to him. Drawing in a deep breath, he gripped his tunic at the neck and rent it down the middle to bare his chest. He showed Knosis his back, and then turned back around. "Do you still have your doubts?"

Hesitation flickered through Knosis's eyes, and then they hardened. "Your scars do not prove anything, Nicolaus. The fact remains, your father owes me a bride and I mean to see that I receive one."

"You will not find her here."

"No?" Knosis smiled as he motioned for a few of his armed men to come forward. "We will see. I had wondered why you didn't make port at Joppa. I heard rumors of your mishap. I asked myself why a captain would avoid making port when he had need of repairs. Endangering your men is not a responsible action for a captain of your repute, Nicolaus."

Nicolaus narrowed his eyes. What did this man know of his reputation?

"I've no doubt your man here—" he pointed at Xandros "—told you I wished to speak with you. Then I hear tell this very morn that you've a slave woman on board. One that rightly belongs to me."

"That is not so."

"Is it not?" Knosis leaned in, piercing Nicolaus with his aged eyes. "You are either a coward or you are hiding something you wish me not to find. Which is it?"

"Perhaps it is neither."

"I intend to find out." He motioned his guards forward.

A sickening cough filtered from his quarters and echoed onto the deck. Knosis halted his soldiers with his hand, pulled back and glanced toward the upper room, his eyes wide with concern. "So there is a woman on board?"

"Ay, however I purchased her with my own coin and none of my father's. She belongs to me, not him."

"Are you not your father's son? His debts are yours, are they not?"

A sickening cough caused the hair on Nicolaus's nape to rise. She was worsening, but her illness may save them. "She has taken ill, Knosis. We did not make port for fear of infecting the whole of Joppa."

Of course, Nicolaus had no idea she'd been sick until after they'd left, but if it saved her from Knosis then he was fine with the lie he told.

"Leave me be," Ada hollered. Nicolaus's gut constricted and then released when heard Brison trying to soothe her.

"Ada, get back here."

Nicolaus glanced at the door to his quarters. Ada stood at the opening, her hands clenched to the posts, one foot dangling from the portal. Nicolaus's heart stopped, fearful that she'd fall until he saw his brother holding on to her. Her tunic clung to her curves. Her hair, soaked from fever, looked as if it hadn't been brushed in ages. However, what concerned him more than anything was the way her eyes darted from one place to another as if she were mad in the head. She kicked and screamed, clawing at Brison as he dragged her back inside.

Knosis cleared his throat, pulling Nicolaus's attention back to him. All the color had drained from the man's face. Knosis stepped away as if he, too, were afraid she was contagious. "I would speak to her, but I can see with my own eyes she is near death."

Something gripped hold of Nicolaus's innards at his fear being spoken aloud. He'd seen men rage with fevers while held captive. They lay where they fell until the fever passed, or they died. More often than he cared to recount it was the latter. He did not wish the same fate for Ada. She had too much spark, too much fire burning in her blood to be doused so soon.

"Ay," Nicolaus said, fearing what Knosis said was true. "It is my hope to get her home before it is too late." The last thing Nicolaus expected to see in his eyes before the old man traversed the planks back to his ship was sympathy, but it was there. Perhaps Nicolaus had misjudged him.

"I leave my vessel in your hands." Nicolaus began to run toward his quarters but was halted by Xandros. Bristling at the delay, Nicolaus crossed his arms over his chest. He needed to see her, to do all he could to calm her, to make sure she didn't bring harm to herself in her fevered fit. To make sure she didn't expire while on his ship. He would not lose another female under his protection. He couldn't.

"Would you have us sail back to Joppa or on to Paphos?"

Nicolaus clenched his teeth together as he glared at

Knosis. The man had nearly fallen into the water as he raced across the planks. He couldn't get off Nicolaus's vessel fast enough after seeing Ada's ill-well, yet for some reason he had yet to command his men to leave. He lifted a silent prayer that Knosis headed away from Joppa as it was the closer port to find a healer. However, Knosis was the greater of evils if he were to get his hands on Ada. "Wait until the ships have sailed, and then make haste in the opposite direction. Tell the men I'll pay thrice their wage for their hard work."

A tormented scream emitted from his quarters. Nicolaus felt the blood drain from his face and he started to leave again.

"Nicolaus, I've never seen the like, but she very well may have saved herself and you from Knosis. She will be fine. You must believe it. Do what you can to break the fever and give her sips of water. I will see us safe until she is well."

He prayed his friend was right because he didn't know what he'd do if he wasn't.

# *Chapter Thirteen*

Bright light filtered through Ada's heavy eyelids. A roar filled her ears, sounding as if the skies were in a constant rumble. It was much as if they were in the middle of another storm, except the boat wasn't being tossed from here to there with each crashing wave. Truth be told, she was not moving at all. She flung her eyes open. Pale gray stones created a canopy above her.

Was she no longer on the boat? She tossed the blankets to the side and sat up. The room whirled, blurring her sight. Closing her eyes, she drew in a few slow breaths to halt the dizziness in her head before opening them again. Wooden slats crossed over the windows and colorful pottery with scenes of life painted on them sat on a tiny table. There was little else to decorate the spacious room.

Footsteps shuffled outside the room and halted outside the door. Ada tossed herself back down to the thick cushion and closed her eyes just as the wooden door creaked opened. She kept her eyelids relaxed and her breathing steady trying to pretend she was asleep.

However, it did her no good when bony fingers peeled her lids open.

"Ay, I see you're finally awake." The gnarled hand smacked against Ada's brow, causing both her eyes to open. "Your fever's gone. Your eyes are clear. That's good. The captain was beside himself with worry, fearing you'd die."

"I've taken ill?"

The old woman ignored her and leaned in close, pressing her ear to Ada's chest. Was the woman mad? Ada sank deeper into the mattress.

"What are you doing?"

"Hold still. I'm checking your breaths."

"It is obvious I am alive."

"That you are." The old woman chuckled, straightened to her full height, which wasn't much more than a child, and shuffled toward the small table. She scooped some liquid from one of the pieces of pottery with a ladle and turned back to Ada. "They call me Dorca. I am a healer. Sit up."

"How long have I been here?" Ada propped onto her elbows and waited for the room to stop spinning again. Easing a little more, she realized slow movements lessened the whirlwind. Once she was sitting she grasped the wooden ladle and sipped. She grimaced. "That is foul. What is it?"

"Herbs to renew your strength. Your captain says you suffer from the sea."

Ada's stomach soured at the mention of the sea.

"No matter, it is quite common when one is not used to it. I've lived many years and have yet to leave this island. I'll die here, too."

Answers obviously weren't something Dorca liked to give, so Ada just smiled and took another sip.

"However, I do not think that is what caused your fever and cough."

She recalled the shivers and the heat, her unsteady feet, which she believed to be the lack of foundation. She recalled the spasms that had racked her body and then nothing more. The corner of her lip twitched as an image of Nicolaus hovered over her. The warmth of him as he carried her. The feeling of security as if he'd make all well. His soft murmured promises she dare not trust. Those were not memories she should recall, if they were even real. She was a slave, not a woman to be loved and cherished above all others. She drew the ladle to her lips. Better to taste the bitter herbs in the cup this woman offered than to long for what could never be.

"You've been here five days."

"Five days?" The wooden spoon shook as her hand trembled. Liquid spilled onto the cobblestones. Had Nicolaus left her here? Wherever here was. No doubt he had. Winning his father's challenge was important. It was why he sailed into the storm, risking all of their lives. She rose from the mattress and took a step toward the window, needing to know what was beyond the gray walls. What if he had left her? What was she to do then? Ada reached up to open the wooden slats.

"We had another storm, so I kept them closed to keep the breeze from further sickening you."

Ada bit the inside of her lip.

"He'll be back." The old woman pounded her hand against the mattress.

"When?" As if it mattered. It was better for her to never see him again. Especially since she seemed drawn to him in a way a slave shouldn't be drawn to her master. She crossed her arms over her stomach as if to keep herself from falling apart.

"Soon."

"Are we at Nicolaus's home, then?"

The old woman laughed. "No, child."

Ada nodded. Soon could be days. Weeks. Never. She had no idea what was worse, being close to him knowing he could never take her for a bride, or never seeing him again. Why couldn't Nicolaus have been one of the men visiting her father's house to trade, vying for her attentions? Things might have been different then. She drew in a shuddering breath. Of course they wouldn't have been. Her blood was impure. She was neither Hebrew nor Philistine, and she most assuredly was not Greek. What man wanted a woman without pure blood?

"Since he did not wish me to leave your side, I sent him to the market. You'll need sustenance soon."

Ada turned and glanced at the old woman. "You sent him where?"

Dorca reached her hand out and brushed it against Ada's brow. The corners of the old woman's eyes crinkled in concern. She nudged Ada toward the bed. "You must rest. Your fever—"

"I'm well." Ada waved her away and rushed to the door. Just as she was about the pull it open, it swung wide. Nicolaus ducked his head beneath the post and halted when he spied her, his broad shoulders angled in the entrance. One foot in, one out. The doorway wasn't made for so large a man.

"Ada, you are well?" With a smile curving his mouth, he thrust the basket at the healer and grabbed hold of Ada's arms. His dark hair, kissed by the sun, hung down into his eyes begging her fingers to brush it back into place. "You are truly well."

She pulled from him, hugging her arms around herself, and stared out the door to the lush greenery dividing Dorca's home from the sea. In the distance, fishing boats bobbed on the whitecaps as they rolled toward the island. Waves battered, pushing against the shore with a whispered roar. Over and over, again and again. Relentless in their soothing destruction, much like Nicolaus in her thoughts, and now in her presence. The vast sea and the man who sought to tame it fascinated her, captivating her thoughts, her soul and worst of all her heart.

Little by little, the breezes smoothing across her cheeks filled her with a sense of longing. *Of belonging.* As if this was truly her home. The call of the birds piercing through the air, the distinct sound of the waves…the man who loomed behind her, they were stealing everything that she ever was, making her forget her past—her mother's—they were giving her hope for a future. What happened to the days when her greatest worry was what trickery her sisters would play? How was she to fight the lure of him, the temptation to fall in love with him when her heart fluttered and took flight like a butterfly whenever he was around?

She hugged herself tighter and clenched her fingers in her tunic. "What are you doing here, Nicolaus?"

"I'll be outside only a moment," Dorca said as she slipped out of sight.

"What do you mean, Ada?" The soft cadence of his voice tugged her heartstrings, and then he laid his hand on her shoulder, his fingers gently squeezing. A longing deep within wanted to accept the comfort he offered, to spin herself around and fling herself into his arms, but she knew there could never be anything between them outside of master and slave. She wouldn't allow it. Even if it meant her death for her disobedience.

Tears stung the backs of her eyes. Life would have been much more endurable if he'd left and she'd never seen him again. She knew that now. Knew it the moment he smiled when he caught sight of her, knew it when she wanted to comb her fingers through his ruffled hair, but more than that, because of her illness he'd lose his father's challenge. She did not want to be the cause of their failures. Enough blame had been placed on her head where her sisters had been concerned and look where that had gotten her, on some island in the middle of the Great Sea, falling for a man who could never be hers. "Do you not have a race to win?"

His lips pressed together into a firm line. His jaw ticked. "I do not understand. Who told you—"

She shook her head. "I heard pieces of conversations among your crew. It was easy to gather the truth. Your ambition is admirable. My father would appreciate your tenacity. Not many would sail through a fierce storm, risking the lives of their men just to win a game."

His nostrils flared, and his muscles seemed to expand, making the spacious room grow small. The air around them crackled. She fought the urge to take a step back.

"And what of his daughter?" His frigid tone chilled her like the cool desert night. Had she angered him, pushed him too far? Just as well. Perhaps, his anger would distant him.

Lifting her chin, she looked him straight in the eye, sharing all of her built-up emotions over the past few days. Her confusion, her longing and most of all her anger at never having what her heart desired. A husband, children. Him. "His daughter is nothing more than a slave with no opinion of her own."

They stared at each other for several long seconds. His jaw twitched as he clenched his teeth. Her heartbeat thumped against her chest as she sought to steady her breaths. Somehow the space between them had closed. If she reached her hand up, she could touch his cheek and soothe the anger burning in his eyes. But if she did, like she very much wanted to, her world would no doubt turn into a raging fire. Never to be doused.

"That small detail has not stopped you thus far, Ada. However, I grant you the freedom to speak as you wish." His words vibrated through her, and she dropped her gaze to the intricately designed cobblestones at their feet. "Without consequence."

She walked to the window to place distance between them and opened the slats. The endless, blue field made her feel small, of little importance on this earth, and yet this man she'd grown to care for dared to tame its wildness. She drew in a deep breath of salty air in hopes of drowning the scent of him. Unfortunately for her, Nicolaus and the sea smelled much the same. "I do not pretend to know what it is like to be a man, to have to provide for his family. How-

ever—" not wanting him to think she was a coward, even though her insides quaked, she faced him
"—from all I've witnessed, the hunger for wealth
produces greed, greed eats the soul until the heart is
hardened. Hardened enough that there is no care for
anything beyond gaining more wealth, even at the cost
of other people's lives."

Had not her own mother been a victim to such
greed? Her father chased riches, leaving his slaves in
the care of his wife, leaving her mother to suffer her
cruelty.

Nicolaus's heart was far from stone, she knew
that. She'd seen his care for mere strangers, herself
included. He had even provided a wet nurse for the
babe. If Nicolaus hadn't been out in the storm those
people would have perished. So why did her mind insist on comparing him to her father and finding them
of similar thought?

"There are things you do not know, nor are they of
any concern to you. The merchandise aboard that vessel means nothing to me as it was purchased with my
father's coin. The ship is my chance at freedom, my
chance to do as I please without my father's games."
He moved closer, stalking her like a lion its prey.
"You've no idea what it is I risk by tarrying here waiting for you to get well. It is much more than a few
pieces of cloth and earthenware jars of honey and oil.
It is much more than a simple vessel owned by my father, which I designed and helped build with my own
two hands. Furthermore, *slave*, as you so often remind
me of your status, I had no real *care* to win my father's
game until I reached Ashkelon. Until I purchased *you*
with my own coin."

\* \* \*

That full bottom lip of hers fell open and then snapped shut. Her lashes fluttered, fanning against her cheeks. But he'd seen the amber of her eyes swirl to warm honey, the same color they'd turned right before he'd tried to kiss her only days before. She shifted forward, her hand hovering between them.

He gripped her wrist, the warmth of her skin, the beat of her pulse… Squeezing his eyes shut, he swallowed past the thick knot forming in his throat and then shoved her hand away. He yanked open the door and stalked from the cottage. The woman drove him to the brink of madness.

"Nicolaus." His grandmother stepped in front of him.

He rolled the tension from his shoulders.

"Not now, Yaya." He kept his gaze above his grandmother's head lest she see the turmoil in his soul. His vessel bobbed with each of the waves. His men had worked for days to repair the mast and from the looks of the unfurled sail, he'd say they succeeded. Now they could go home. "How soon before Ada can sail?"

"You intend to leave?"

He shifted his gaze to his grandmother's. Although the years weighed heavy on her face, disguising the beauty she'd once been, her eyes remained vibrant. "I must."

"Nicky," she said as she laid her hand on his forearm. His gaze flicked to hers. She hadn't called him that since he was but a boy. "You care for this woman?"

"It's not so easy as that." He cared more than he should, more than any sane man would given the way she made him want to kiss her and strangle her in one breath.

"No." She smiled. "Matters of the heart never are, but she has yet to regain her strength."

Nicolaus clenched his jaw. "My heart has nothing to do with how I care about this woman." He blew out a breath of air. "I am sorry, Yaya. She irritates me more than Jasen and Brison did when we were no more than boys."

His grandmother chuckled and patted his forearm as if to soothe him. "I can see that, Nicky."

"I give her the night to rest. We must leave on the morrow. It's fortunate for us home is half a day's sail." He leaned down and kissed her weathered cheek. "I am going for a walk, but will return before the sun disappears."

"Be careful, Nicky."

The corners of his mouth lifted. "Ay, Yaya. I'm always careful."

His grandmother always had a way about her that soothed. One gentle word from her when they were boys and their scuffles ended and he and his brothers became the best of friends. Although he'd been more than resentful when his father left them at Yaya's while he sailed the Great Sea, he now missed those days, wished they could go back to when things were simple. When his greatest challenge had been catching more fish than Jasen or swimming the fastest.

Nicolaus cut through the greenery and sprinted over the rocky terrain. He climbed onto the tallest rock and stared out at the expanse of nothingness before him. How many times had he stood in this very spot watching the sail of his father's ship until it disappeared?

Waiting for him to return? Such was the life of a sea merchant.

He tipped his head back and bathed his face in the sun. Would his children watch him leave and wait anxiously for his return? Would Ada? He jerked his chin back to the sea. Where had that thought come from? He shoved a shaking hand through his hair and jumped from the rock.

Nicolaus raced to the edge of where the foam crawled. He removed his sandals and stripped down to his loincloth, leaving his tunic, daggers and the scrap of leather his father had given him upon his first sea voyage as a child on the rocky shore. The map held wistful adventures and tales of treasure. David had stolen the map from him upon Nicolaus's captivity. Nicolaus had retrieved it shortly after Jasen had paid a ransom for his release. It had been a moonless night when Nicolaus entered David's home and threatened to break David's will until he confessed Desma's destination. Even under the worse torture Nicolaus could think of, David had remained silent, which led him to believe David did not know where Desma was. He never once confessed who he'd given Desma to, which left Nicolaus wondering and longing to search the seas for her.

His bare feet hit the water as he ran into the surf. Waves swirled around his legs, pushing and pulling, but he kept moving forward until the water swirled around his chest, and then he dove beneath the water.

He thrust his hands out in front of him, cutting through the water as he kicked his feet. Wave after wave crashed over his head but he kept swimming until he neared one of the rocks rising up out of the sea. Treading water, he inspected the rock that had seemed so massive when he was a boy. New crevices had formed over the years; others had deepened, creating windows for the sunlight.

Standing against the sea as he sailed from one port to the next had changed him. In some ways it'd made his heart hard, as Ada had so rightly determined. Yet, in other ways, it had created a longing, a desire to furl the sails and keep his vessel moored. Looking at this rock, he knew he didn't want to be battered and broken until there was nothing left of him. However, that was not a choice for him to make. Not until he found Desma. Even then, he was beginning to think the only woman he longed to be moored to was Ada. No other made him long for the freedom of her arms over the freedom of sailing.

He swiped the droplets from his eyes and sighed. His father would never allow such a union, which left him as he was, adrift with no real port to call home. He stretched out his arms and legs and floated on his back. The sky, as blue as the water, consumed him. He was nothing more than a small speck in the earth and the sea. Was there an Almighty Maker of the heavens and the earth, the sea and all that was within as Ada believed? Lying here on his back, cradled by the sea, he could almost believe it. Did this God truly love the righteous and preserve strangers such as he? A Greek even?

He laughed. What else had Ada prayed? *Happy is the one who has You as their help, O Lord.*

"Lord, if You truly exist will You help me find happiness?"

Turning over onto his stomach, he dove down into

the water. Thrusting his hands outward, he swam down as far as he could until his lungs felt as if they'd burst, and then he somersaulted and kicked his feet. With his arms tight at his sides, he shot upward like an arrow from its bow. He broke the surface, took a deep cleansing breath and swam back to shore.

He didn't have the answers he sought. He hadn't expected any. It seemed his best course was to keep distance from Ada, especially if he was to keep this madness from plaguing him.

He had picked up his sandals and donned his tunic, leaving the shoulders to drape around his hips, when he spied the bright pink blooms his sister had always worn in her hair. Picking his way across the stones, he plucked the largest bloom and cradled it in his palm. He crept back to the rock he'd claimed when he was a boy and sat The high sun soaked the droplets from his skin. The waters were calmer than they'd been earlier in the morn. Unfortunately, he was not. The duty to his sister weighed heavy on his shoulders. There was no guarantee he'd find her but he had to try, and he'd search the known world if he had to, which meant he had to go home.

Home. Now that was a source of confusion. If only he could remain here with Yaya. With Ada. To learn more about the woman beneath the fire. The one he knew held compassion for those less fortunate. He smiled. And those undeserving. Tenting his elbows on his knees, he twirled the stem between his fingers. Desma was delicate, much like the pink petals. She'd perish under the cruelty of slavery. Ada, although small in stature, was strong and courageous. And if truth were to be told, she was capturing his heart as efficiently as any seasoned fisherman.

"Ay, I best find a way to rid myself of the woman before I forget my duty to Desma."

# Chapter Fourteen

Ada followed the path leading to where Nicolaus sat. Her feet came to an abrupt halt and she gasped when she spied the red, welted lines slashing across Nicolaus's back. He jumped to his feet.

"You should not be here, Ada." His muscles expanded as he pulled his tunic into place but not before she'd seen the mark branded on his chest. "There are snakes crawling about."

Her gaze flew to the ground as she shuffled her feet.

"You would not wish to get bitten." He climbed from the rock and stood in front of her. "How did you find me?"

She ignored his question. She'd sought him out for a reason and it was not to argue as his tone suggested he was prepared to do. "I wished to apologize."

Nicolaus bent to tie his sandal, but glanced up at her. "There is none needed, Ada." He unfolded his length, his height imposing. "You were correct. It takes a certain kind of man to be a merchant. One that is ruthless with no care for others. As am I."

"Nicolaus." She searched his eyes, looking for something to belie his words. However, she knew differently, knew Nicolaus was nothing like the man he described. She knew him to be kind and compassionate even if he was grumpy at times.

He stepped around her and headed up the path she'd come down. She gathered the hem of her tunic and raced after him. "Nicolaus, stop."

He turned toward her. Vulnerability glittered in the dark depths of his eyes. She dared not examine why he resembled a child fearful of rejection. It was obvious the wounds marring his flesh were nothing compared to the ones buried within his soul.

Her hand reached up. The tips of her fingers brushed over his brow. The curls blanketing his skin were as soft as she'd imagined, even dripping wet. She caressed her thumb over a small white scar above his eyebrow. A ripple of warmth cloaked over her hand, spiraling up her arm and straight to her heartstrings. She jerked her hand away, dropping it to her side. "What happened to your back? I've seen many such scars. I have treated them among my father's slaves."

His eyes narrowed, his nostrils flared. "Then you've no need for my answer." He turned away and took giant strides up the hillside.

"They are recent."

Nicolaus continued his trek until he disappeared between the greenery. Rocks slid from beneath her feet as she tried to catch up to him. She slid, and she cried out when her hands scraped against the stones. She inhaled a breath and released it as she pushed herself up from the ground and sat. Facing the water, she pulled her legs into her chest. She rested her chin on her knees and stared out at the endless blue waters.

"What are you doing?" Even though she jumped, his deep timbre soothed an ache in her chest, one that longed to be cared for, watched over. He sat beside her, nudging her with his shoulder. "You know, you have a habit of sitting like that whenever you are upset?"

She drew in a shuddering breath. The sun shone so brightly against the waters that it was near blinding, much like the blooming emotions she felt toward Nicolaus. If she were not careful she'd love him like her mother had her father. "It makes me small. Sometimes small enough not to be seen."

"And why would you wish to hide, Ada?"

"How did you become a slave?"

He laughed but did not answer her. For which she was glad else she'd have to share her secrets, as well.

"It is beautiful here. The most beautiful thing I've ever seen."

"Then you are sorely deprived, Ada."

She turned her head, laying it on her knees, and looked at him. His eyes reminded her of obsidian. His hair, still wet from his swim, curled around his jaw and dripped onto his tunic. "The old woman seems fond of you?"

White teeth gleamed when he smiled. "Ay, she should. I'm her only grandchild who continues to visit."

"Your grandmother?"

"We call her Yaya. She's my mother's mother. Brison refuses to leave the ship since he has duties, but I believe he fears Yaya will beg him to stay. He and Xandros will arrive to break the evening meal."

"I am sorry, Nicolaus. I should not have spoken as

I did. Your grandmother says you have much on your mind. I haven't considered others."

"That is far from the truth, Ada." He tucked a lock of hair behind her ear, sending shivers racing down her back. "You've done nothing but consider others, even in your illness. And—" he turned his gaze toward the sea "—I understand what it is like to be scared. Several months ago I was sailing to this very island. My sister was to marry a wealthy merchant in a neighboring village. Although we were heavily armed we were overcome by thieves. They took everything, including her. I later discovered a man I had considered a friend had hired them to take her."

Waves rolled ashore. A lone, white bird screeched overhead. Her heart thundered in her ears. A tear slid down her cheek at his loss and at the words he'd left unspoken. She had no doubt he'd been taken captive, too. She sensed the scars marring his skin from his time in bondage were nothing compared to the ones residing in his chest. She took his hand in hers. What must it have been like for the strong, brave man to have his sister stolen from him? "I am sorry, Nicolaus."

He stilled, his gaze on their hands. He drew in air, and then twined his fingers with hers. His tanned calloused skin next to her paleness spoke of the differences between them, spoke of how she should not be giving him her heart. Yet, somehow this was more right than anything she'd ever known. It was as if she'd found her place in this magnificent world, here on this island, next to him. He lifted her hand and pressed his lips to her knuckles. The warmth of his breath whispered across her skin like finely woven silk. The pleasure stole her breath, threatened to steal her resolve to keep her distance.

"Nico—"

"Ada," he said as he clasped his hands together, cradling hers between them. "You must know, I do not purchase slaves, not since my time in captivity and even before only for my father and they were treated fairly."

Her heart sank at the thought of this proud man chained and beaten as his scars spoke.

"It is a way of life, Nicolaus. My father has many." She thought of her mother and how all of his concubines were treated differently. The beatings they'd received for small offenses. Nicolaus wouldn't be so cruel to his concubines. However, she did not think she'd like to share his attentions with a wife. Her fingers itched to pull away, but he squeezed, holding firm.

"It does not matter, Ada. I'd made a vow to never buy a slave, but then I saw you. The man bidding on you would not have been kind. Life would not have been kind."

She gazed at the waves, rolling in and then out. "I thank you for that."

He released one of her hands and crooked a finger beneath her chin, drawing her gaze toward his, and then tucked another strand behind her ear. "When my father issued the challenge between me and my brother, I did not want to sail again, but Xandros convinced me that I could search for my sister in each port. Jasen had already scoured every port known on the Great Sea, with no sign of her, but I had to try." His gaze shifted beyond her shoulder. "I do not care about possessions or my father's merchandise. I failed Desma in the worst way. There is little hope of finding her, but when I laid eyes on you and that distasteful procurer bidding on you I knew I had to try. I can't leave my sister to such a fate. If I win this challenge, if I beat Jasen, then I'll have my own vessel to search for her, to do as I wish."

He stared into her eyes. The glassy blackness swirled deep with emotion. He cupped her cheek with his hand and leaned his forehead to hers.

"I can do as I wish," he whispered against her mouth. His lips touched hers, light as silk. The air around them sizzled. He shifted back a little and gazed into her eyes. He caressed her cheek with his thumb. "If I win, I can do as I wish, Ada. I can continue to seek out my sister and save her, too."

The longing in his eyes tugged her heartstrings. Wanting—needing—more of his touch, she leaned closer. He sealed his lips to hers. Her heart soared like the griffin flying over the desert in search of its evening meal. Was this what it was like to be loved? To be wanted? She wrapped her arms around his neck and wove her fingers into his hair.

"Nicolaus," Xandros called from the path. Ada scrambled away and jumped to her feet. A rock caught her sandal. She wobbled, but Nicolaus caught her arm to steady her. The emotion in the look he gave her caught her off guard. She'd seen that look before, the one that consumed her father when he watched her mother, but there was something more, something she did not quite understand. It unnerved her and it left her more scared than when she was just his slave. It was as if he were a starved lion ready to pounce on his prey.

She jerked from his touch and ran. One thing she knew for certain—that kiss, still burning on her lips, proved she was no better than her mother, and that was something she could not allow. Ever again.

Nicolaus watched her disappear between the greenery and then Xandros emerged.

"Yaya said I'd find you here." Xandros glanced over his shoulder. "What did you do to her?"

The corner of his eye twitched at his friend's tone. "Have you become her defender?"

Xandros crossed his arms over his chest and glared. "If I need be, I will. It seems you are always upsetting her."

Twisting his lips, Nicolaus shook his head. "I do not know what has upset her."

Xandros smacked him on the shoulder. "You don't look happy, either. No matter, soon we'll spread the sails and be home. I look forward to your mother's table."

Nicolaus laughed. "Yaya has prepared you a meal fit for a king."

His friend didn't try to hide his pained grimace. "I mean no offense, but even the dogs turn their noses up at Yaya's cooking."

Nicolaus laughed as he traipsed up the hill, Xandros at his side. "Her skills have waned with her age. However, she has a new guest, one I'm certain she'll seek to impress. Besides, I went to the market myself. There will be cakes and honey and fruit."

"That is all I need."

"Is the mast repaired?" He'd seen the sail expand and knew it must be. However, he wanted to ensure there were no problems.

"Ay, and the men are rested. We worked in shifts.

After all their hard work and getting us here in good time, I decided to give them leave to explore Karimos."

"It is beautiful here, is it not?"

"A treasure unlike any other. There is smoke rising from your head. What is it you are thinking, my friend?"

Nicolaus stopped and faced the sea. "You know my grandfather has left all of this to me, but I had no thoughts beyond pleasing my father and becoming a merchant. Yaya's home was nothing more than a prison I longed to escape from while my father sailed off to grand adventures. I'm beginning to see it differently now. I could be happy here."

"What is it you're saying?"

"Karimos is a strong port. My grandfather's land is fertile. He had dreams of cultivating it." He swung back around, his hand swinging up toward the higher ground. "I could plant grapes. There is a valley on the other side of the main house where I could plant wheat, not much, but enough for the locals."

Xandros laughed. "I've never thought you to be a farmer, Nicolaus. You blood flows with the waters of this world. You are happiest when sailing. It is who the gods meant you to be."

Cringing at Xandros's use of *gods*, Nicolaus pierced his friend with a hard glare. "Is it? What if there is only one God, Xandros? A god who created the heavens, the earth and the seas? What if that God wishes me to grow roots here?" With Ada.

"You sound like your uncle."

"He may have the right of it, my friend. The gods our people have worshiped for hundreds of years are no more than statues made by our own hands." Joy filled him to overflowing. The excitement vibrated around him. "This God Oceanus speaks of, the one Ada calls upon, he is not made by our hands, he just is. How else do you explain that?" He motioned toward the vast sea. "And the sun, the ground we stand on. The thousands upon thousands of stars lighting the night sky. What if this Almighty God is calling me, a perfect stranger, to something more than what my father wished? If I do not win the challenge, Xandros, I'm making this place my home."

And if Ada was willing, if his father allowed such a union, he'd make one with her.

"I am not sure about this God you speak of, but I think it is wise. Yaya is aging and should not be alone. However, I do not think that is your reasoning."

He wanted to build a life here. To raise his children where he'd spent much time as a boy. To watch the sun set over the waters with Ada by his side, but he could not tell his friend the truth of it, not yet.

"What will you do if you win?"

A stone settled in his stomach. "Then I will own a vessel I built with my own hands. One my father has little control over, and I will have no choice but to search for Desma. I owe it to her enough to try."

"What of Ada?"

Nicolaus plucked a bloom from a branch. "I would free her and see her to her family, but the abuse she suffered at the hands of her sisters… How long before they sold her again? Then where would she be, a prostitute?" Nicolaus shook his head. "There are few options for a woman without the protection of her father. As my slave she will be protected."

"Until you marry. I cannot see a wife, no matter

how considerate, approving of Ada in your household. And I cannot see you setting her up as a concubine."

The thought of disgracing Ada in such a way soured his stomach.

"You've too much honor to dishonor your vows. Your brother would have no such qualms. It only stands to reason that you should free her, and then marry her."

Nicolaus halted his steps. Even as the Sea Dragon he'd held a code of honor as did his brother. "She is not Greek. I do not think my father would allow it and I will not dishonor my father in such a way. Even if she were Greek and I were to win I could not leave a wife at home while I spend weeks, months even, at sea. My mother suffered greatly during my father's absences. It is why he brought us here to Yaya's. It is why he quit sailing once Jasen and I could do so on our own."

"Then I guess you should pray to that Almighty God you speak of that you lose."

Would he be able to marry her if he lost? His father would not approve. He'd want Nicolaus to marry a girl from Andros, would he not? A girl who was nothing like Ada. But his father had broken with tradition and married his mother. Yes, she was Greek, but she was not Ionian.

None of it seemed possible. Perhaps it would be better if he won, then his choice would be made for him.

# Chapter Fifteen

Ada caught her breath at the sight of the rising mountain in the water. "What is it?"

"They are islands."

She sipped the water doused with ground ginger and honey that Nicolaus's grandmother had sent along for the journey wondering about these islands. "Do people live there?"

Nicolaus nodded. "Some, and some have been abandoned. Oft times, bands of thieves raid the villages, leaving them desolate. Those who escape have little choice but to leave if they can."

She took a small bite of honey cake, and then glanced at him, her eyes wide. She'd worried over thieves their entire journey and now it seemed as if they were entering their lair. "Do you live on an island?"

"I do. See?" He pointed to a piece of land in the distance.

"Is it as small as these?"

He shook his head. "We've several mountains forming our home. You've nothing to worry over, Ada. The island is heavily guarded with some of Greece's finest warriors. Me included." The twinkle in his eye momentarily disappeared as he winked at her.

A piece of cake lodged in her throat, and her pulse skidded to a halt.

"Any man would be a fool to attack us." She took another sip of water and watched as they sailed by island after island. They were nothing more than large gray rocks. Void of vegetation. They seemed lifeless. Not a place she would like to call home. At least the desert had some trees. She hoped Nicolaus's home wasn't as colorless.

"I am glad Yaya's herbs have calmed your sickness."

She smiled. "I, as well. Although, at first I did not think they would. Once the waters lost their waves, I much improved." She dropped her gaze to where the water separated as the ramming post cut through it. "I must thank you for seeing to the children while I was ill. It is a burden you did not ask to bear."

He grabbed hold of her hand. "It was no burden. Chloe has more than earned her pay."

"It is fortunate then that Xandros found her. What will you do with them?"

Nicolaus twisted his lips. "I haven't thought on it much. Most abandons become slaves, and that is something I cannot do. However, I do not know how my father will feel about my decision."

"You could raise them as your own, Nicolaus."

His laughter filled the air around them. "I've nothing more than a room to call my own. One I share with my brother, Ada."

"If you beat your brother, you'll have this boat."

The laughter drained from his face and his eyes

took on a serious glint. "Ay, I'll have this boat, but then I will have duties to attend."

He walked away, his shoulders slightly hunched. She drew her eyebrows together as she tilted her head. What had she said to upset him? Winning the challenge was what he wanted, wasn't it? How else was he to find his sister and find peace for his troubled soul?

Besides the embarrassment after their kiss yester noon overlooking the water, there had been little strife between them. Their meal with Yaya, Brison and Xandros had been entertaining and surprising when Nicolaus had invited her and Yaya to eat with them. She'd learned much about Nicolaus and his family. The constant competition between him and his brother Jasen was often fueled by their father.

Nicolaus's grandmother had grown distant when they spoke of her daughter, Nicolaus's mother. Although she didn't say anything, her grandson must have known of her sadness. If Ada hadn't been in love with Nicolaus before, the way he comforted his grandmother by patting her hand as the conversation flowed around them sealed her love tighter than any tomb in Ashkelon.

She leaned her elbows against the rail. The wind tugged her hair from her shoulders. As long as he did not offer her any more kisses she could pretend her pulse didn't beat a little faster in his presence. That her eyes didn't constantly draw to him or her knees grow week at the sound of his voice.

They approached another island, this one lush with vibrant greens rising way above the sea. Could the Almighty's creation be any more breathtaking?

Nicolaus called out a command. The oars halted, no longer splashing into the water. Men moved around the deck, wrapping the sail around the mast. She closed her eyes and listened to the waves lapping against the boat, carrying them forward. A sense of peace washed over her and she knew she'd never be content living in the desert away from the sea. She'd grown accustomed to these new sights and sounds over the past few days. The waves seemed to dance in her blood, the way thoughts of Nicolaus danced in her heart.

She leaned over the side to see around the front of the ship and once again caught her breath. They glided over the bluest of waters toward a cove filled with other ships of various sizes. Many looked ready for battle. Nicolaus hadn't lied when he said they were well protected.

Even Ashkelon with its thick walls almost as high as the lower mountains was not as well fortified.

"It is exciting."

She looked down beside her. Two pairs of eyes beamed up at her. The boy and the girl who'd stayed together when their people chose to abandon them.

"Come." She gathered their hands in hers and maneuvered toward the other side of the boat. She lifted the girl onto her hip and pointed to the water. "Look, you can see the fish."

"There are many boats. Is this where the raiders come from?" Galen asked.

Ada snapped her gaze to the boy and blinked and then back to the armed vessels. She hadn't thought of such a thing, but couldn't imagine Nicolaus stealing from the likes of these children and their village. "You will have to ask the captain."

"Look at the houses," Edith said. "They are much

bigger than the ones we had. Do you think we can sleep in one?"

Ada bit the inside of her lip and allowed the girl to slide down. "I do not know, Edith."

The girl slipped her hand into hers. "I will ask the captain if we can stay together." Edith rewarded her with a smile.

"Not me. I want to sleep on the boat. Nicolaus let me when you were sick."

She ruffled Galen's hair. "Is that so? No doubt you will sleep where the captain tells you to."

The boy lowered his chin, but not before she'd seen the pink tint of embarrassment. "Yes, Ada."

"Look!" Edith jumped up and down, pointing toward the front of the ship. "Mermaids."

Ada's mouth fell open at the multiple gray creatures bursting from the water and diving back down again.

"There's no such thing," Galen said as he leaned his head over for a look. "What are they?"

"I—I don't know." The creatures disappeared only to reappear in front of them. Their long glassy noses bobbing back and forth as they chattered. Edith giggled. Galen climbed onto the lower railing. Ada pulled him back down.

"I see you've met our friends."

Ada's knees turned to honey, but somehow she managed to keep standing. She glanced over her shoulder. "What are they?"

"Dolphins." Nicolaus smiled, his teeth gleaming in the sun. "Creatures of the sea."

"I cannot believe it."

"Believe it, Ada. They are a creation of your God,

the Maker of Heaven and earth, the sea and all that is within."

She could not tear her gaze from his. The same look he had given her right before he had kissed her swirled in the depths. Hearing the psalm taught to her by her mother, spoken in his foreign language, sent shivers over her arms. It was beautiful and magnificent, but more important, did he believe in the Almighty, that there was only one God?

"Where did they go?" Edith asked.

Ada tore her gaze from Nicolaus's and looked out at the sea. The dolphins were nowhere to be found.

"Oh, look!" Ada followed Galen's pointing finger a good distance from the boat and watched as the dolphins jumped out of the water and then dove back down.

"They are often here, greeting me when I return. It makes the coming home nice."

How much greater his return home would be to have Ada waiting. With her eyes shining the way they were just now, full of wonder and perhaps even love. His spine went rigid. Could he accept her love and not give in return?

Leaning over the rail, she giggled with the children. Her face beamed with excitement like the beacon sitting on yond hill beckoning the sailors to come home for the night. Her waist-length hair, the color of the wheat fields in the valley when the sun hit them just as it was slipping behind the mountains, tangled around his arm, ensnaring him.

He picked the strands from his wrist and took a step back. "Ada."

She glanced over her shoulder. The joy radiating from her felt like a battering ram to the chest. He raked his fingers through his hair. "We are about to make port. You and the children should seek shelter beneath the helmsman's perch. I would not want them to get caught underfoot and become hurt."

She blinked, all the excitement disappeared and her eyes lost the glitter of the night's stars. "Yes, of course."

She slipped past him, her hand clasped in the girl child's, her arm around the boy's shoulder. A pang of jealousy rocked him back on his heels. She seemed to control his emotions, the very air he breathed.

Ay, he'd long to sit with her at Yaya's and watch the sun slip beyond the horizon. The thought of marriage, although impossible without severing ties with his father, had made him happy. He wanted to set his eyes upon her beauty every minute of the day, to hear the soft cadence of her breaths throughout the night as he'd done tending her during her illness. But to allow her such control over him—that one look from her set his knees to quaking like the earth oft times did—could not be done.

He wouldn't allow it. A man controlled his household. It was the Greek way. His only hope of rescue from Ada would be if he won his father's challenge and left her at his mother's while he sailed away until he could decide what to do with her. With long strides, he walked across the deck and climbed on the command post. Many boats filled the port, but he didn't see his brother's. Did that mean he'd won?

His gut clenched at the thought of never seeing Ada again, but it was just as well. Perhaps he'd take her back to Yaya, or to her own family even. What concern was it of his if her sisters decided to sell her to another slave trader? None, yet he was concerned. He pressed his palms against the rail and clenched his fingers around the wood. Perhaps, Jasen had already returned, and then left again. His brother was never one to stay on land very long, even to gloat.

"Lord, Almighty Creator of all, I've no thought beyond Ada. A part of me wants to wrap her in my arms and never let her go, the other wants to run as far as possible from her. I do not wish to keep her if I cannot love her." To marry her, to hold her hand, to kiss her, to watch her cradle their child in her arms much as she'd done the babe. "Help me to know in my being the course I should take."

If he lost to Jasen, he'd proceed with his plans to move to Yaya's with Ada and the children. If he won... could he let her go? Either way he'd lose something of great importance.

# Chapter Sixteen

Needing to keep his mind on something other than Ada, Nicolaus climbed down into the hold. Unloading crates, working his muscles to exhaustion would force him to focus on something other than his need to be near her.

"You do not trust me to see the merchandise ashore?" Brison blocked the entryway to their stores.

"Get out of my way, little brother." He didn't want to hurt Brison's pride, but he didn't feel the need to explain his reasons for taking over, either. "I've no patience for argument at the moment."

Brison dropped his hands to his sides, his shoulders hunched. "Have I failed in my duties thus far?"

All the irritation knotting in his muscles disappeared at his younger brother's look of defeat. Nicolaus clapped a hand on Brison's shoulder, giving him a gentle squeeze. "You've done all I've asked and more. I've found the need to keep busy."

Brison held the keys, but Nicolaus couldn't find it in him to take them. He smiled. "It is your duty, Brison."

"Are you certain?" Brison's eyebrows rose, disappearing beneath his hair.

"Ay, I'm certain. I am yours to command." Nicolaus winked at his brother, who near jumped with excitement. "At least for now."

Brison stuck the key into the lock and it opened with a click, but Nicolaus tilted his head, listening for footsteps above, waiting to hear the lighter ones of Ada's.

"Nicolaus."

He shook his head and looked to Brison. "What?"

"You wanted to work. Why are you standing there staring at the ceiling?"

Nicolaus growled and took the crate from Brison's hands. He climbed the stairs. Edith giggled, followed by Ada's lyrical tones. It took a moment for his eyes to adjust to the sunlight and when they did he near dropped his crate. Ada's tunic was gathered in her hands, hiked above her ankles as she danced around in circles with Edith. Their joy had infected his crew over the past few days as Ada and the children grew closer. Even the sternest of his crew broke into laughter at times. At least before most of his men had been below deck and away from the image of Ada's and Edith's brilliant smiles, now they all stood around staring with mouths gaping.

Anger surged through his blood. His fingers constricted around the edge of the crate.

"What is going on?"

Nicolaus narrowed his eyes when not a single member of his crew acknowledged his presence. "You've duties to attend which are required if you wish to see your pay."

It took his men a few seconds too long to pull their eyes away and get back to their chores. They could have at least looked ashamed for their impertinent gazes.

Ada released the fabric balled up in her hands and halted their dance. She sucked her bottom lip between her teeth as she was wont to do when nervous. Edith, the poor child, looked scared to death, and he felt like a cur for causing the little one such fear after all she'd endured.

"You there." Nicolaus tipped his chin toward a young man, no more than fifteen summers, tossing a rope over the side for them to be moored. "Take this crate down to the wharf and then report to Brison for further instructions. Tell him you are there in my stead."

"Yes, Captain." The boy wobbled beneath the weight of the crate as he took it but managed well enough. Nicolaus fought the smile curving his lips. The crate was full of gold figurines he'd purchased for his mother.

"My mother will not be pleased if you drop it."

"Yes, Captain." The boy readjusted his hold.

"Ada, gather the children and Chloe. Make haste."

Her bottom lip quivered as her eyes filled with tears and he instantly regretted his harsh command, but he wouldn't soften toward her yet. Not until she understood she couldn't distract his men from their work, that she couldn't distract him. Singing and dancing, what would the woman do next?

He gritted his teeth together to keep from apologizing and then glanced at the ships moored around his. He knew the moment she'd turned away, for the air seemed to chill. He was tempted to call her back, tempted to ease any concerns she may have about his anger. His jealousy.

He swallowed past the knot in his throat. How would he react when Jasen caught sight of Ada? Although Jasen was his equal in many ways, including his looks, he had an easy speech with the ladies. He knew how to talk with them without being commanding or insulting them. Not that Nicolaus meant to offend, but that seemed to be all he did where Ada was concerned.

"Captain, do I have to go?" Bare feet pattered across the deck as Galen ran toward him. The boy slipped, but Nicolaus caught his elbow and held him upright.

"There is to be no running on my ship, Galen. Is that understood?"

"Yes, Nicolau—" Galen dropped his gaze to his feet. "Captain."

"What is the problem?"

Galen popped his head up. He jumped up and down. "Can't I stay here and sleep on the ship?"

Ada came up behind the boy, Edith's hand held in hers. The babe cradled against her chest. She'd make a wonderful mother to these children. "Chloe is packing the items your grandmother sent along."

"That is fine. I will have Xandros bring her when he comes." Nicolaus ruffled Galen's hair. "As for you, there are people I wish you to meet."

Ada was becoming quite confused with Nicolaus's change of behavior. One moment he was glaring and barking demands, the next he was smiling and teasing the children. Or he was smiling and teasing her and then stalking away with his fists clenched at his sides. It was a good thing she'd decided she couldn't be like her mother and fall in love with her master else she would be driven mad with the swift changes of his moods.

Nicolaus led them to the trestle. Ada gasped and took a few steps back. Although wide enough for two men to walk abreast, the steep wooden walkway looked dangerous. It was not something she wanted the children to traverse by themselves. Nor was it something she wanted to descend herself. One wobble and she would tumble into the water. She hadn't recalled the one upon leaving Ashkelon being so steep, nor did she recall it not having rails to keep her from falling. Perhaps that was because she'd been carried over Nicolaus's shoulder and had the blessing of her hair veiling her sight. "I think Galen has a good idea. I would not mind staying on the ship."

Laughter burst from Nicolaus. "Is that so? You who can barely sip water without becoming seasick?" He winked at her as the corners of his mouth turned upward. Her knees seemed to turn to honey. "Besides, there will be no one here to guard you, Ada. No one to keep thieves from stealing you away in the night."

She squeezed Edith's hand tighter and darted her gaze around the other vessels bobbing in the water. "I am willing to take that risk."

Nicolaus leaned in close and whispered, "However, I am not, Ada."

Her name rolled off his tongue, and his breath caressed the curls near her ear, causing her to shiver.

His face hardened to stone as he clamped a hand on Galen's shoulder and she near feared he was going to push the boy down the trestle, but he surprised her by kneeling in front of the boy and looking him in the eye. "Galen, you will not run. You must walk in the center as carefully as possible. Do you understand?"

Galen nodded.

"Good. I would not wish you to fall into the water. If you do as told and are careful, I'll take you to the beacon when morning comes." Nicolaus pointed to the mountaintop in the distance with a stone structure rising into the sky. Although it reminded her of the high towers at home, it was unlike anything she'd ever seen.

Galen's eyes grew wide with excitement, and he started to vibrate. Nicolaus squeezed his shoulder. "Remember, do not run. Walk with care, but wait until I tell you to go."

"Ay, Ni— Captain."

"Now," Nicolaus said as he loosened his hold on Galen and wrapped his hands around Edith's waist. "How would you like to go for a ride?"

The smile on Edith's face consumed her chubby cheeks. She started to dance. "Really?"

"Ay, come here." Nicolaus lifted her into the air and swung her around so that she sat on his shoulders. "You must hold on."

Edit began to bounce. Nicolaus grabbed hold of her feet and held them tight to his chest.

"Nicolaus." Ada took a step closer and then thought better of it once she caught sight of the trestle's steepness. She rooted her feet to the planks as he looked at her. "It is dangerous."

"No more so than going to the market." His words were a swift reminder of the last time she'd been to the market, the only time she'd been to the market. "I will return for you and the babe in a moment."

"B-be careful, please."

"Of course I will. I would not want to risk the lady's wrath."

She held her breath until the moment Galen stepped onto the quay, and then she found a new cause to worry. Men carrying large crates, earthenware jars and amphoras hustled to and fro, and from where she stood, the rocky ledge did not look as wide as the trestle. What if one of the men accidentally knocked the children into the water? It would be much better if Nicolaus stayed with Edith and Galen to make sure they did not get under the foot of a sailor.

She kissed the babe's crown and pulled in a shaky breath of air. She stepped closer to the trestle and squeezed her eyes closed against the queasiness forming in her stomach. Now was not the time to fall ill. She opened her eyes and looked down the trestle. Nicolaus had almost reached the bottom. If she waited another moment he'd set Edith down and return.

"Would you like some help, Ada?" She turned to find Xandros at her shoulder. Her body shook with relief as she nodded. "Here, I'll take the babe if you wish and you can crook your arm through mine. One step at a time," Xandros said when she threaded her arm around his.

She bit the inside of her lip and forced her eyes to remain open by keeping them on Nicolaus's back. He set Edith down and turned around. The mirth in his eyes dulled and color rose high in his cheeks. He walked back up the trestle until he stood in front of them. His gaze bored into hers, the intensity of it burning through her.

"My thanks," he ground out through clenched teeth. "I will escort Ada."

Xandros chuckled. "I should thank you, my friend, else I'd have no flesh left on my arm."

Ada gasped at the nail marks she'd dug into Xandros. "My apologies."

Before she could finish her words she was swept off her feet and into Nicolaus's arms. His pulse pounded against hers. The fear plaguing her disappeared and her heart sang at being so close to him. "I asked you to wait for my return."

"I know, Nicolaus, but I worried over the children. I did not wish them to get in the way of the sailors moving about and thought to go down the trestle on my own. I am thankful Xandros offered his assistance."

Nicolaus grumbled a few words, something about friends being helpful. "Do you underestimate my ability to give commands and have them obeyed?" He shook his head. "Of course you do else you would have obeyed me."

His beard bristled against her cheek and she found herself snuggling closer. "The next time you give me a command I will listen. I vow it."

"Pfft, do not make vows you do not intend to keep, Ada." They reached the bottom and he set her on her feet, and then he took the babe from Xandros, who seemed to be happy to be home. "See to it the wet nurse finds her way to the house."

Nicolaus glanced at Galen. "Hold your sister's hand and take care to follow my steps." He grabbed hold of Ada's hand. The warmth of his palm against hers caused her stomach to flop. She glanced over her shoulder to Xandros as he climbed back up the trestle. She did not have this same reaction when she touched his arm. Was it too late for her, had she already given her heart to this man who so easily carried a babe as if it was his very own?

The toe of her sandal caught against one of the stones and she tripped. Nicolaus caught her against his side to steady her. The closeness stole her breath. Heat rose into her cheeks.

"Take care with your steps, Ada. I would not wish to jump into the water and save you again."

She halted her feet. Pulling her hand from his, she propped her fists onto her hips and glared at him. "I did not ask you to rescue me, *Captain*, and I am very capable of walking on my own, thank you."

She slipped past him and hastened her steps to where the quay met the island. Sailors stopped their works. Some stared with laughter in their eyes as she walked by, others had the good manners to avert their gazes. It wasn't until she neared the end that she noticed one who wasn't laughing or averting his gaze. Her feet rooted to the stones. She tossed a glance over her shoulder to be sure Nicolaus remained behind her and then back to the man before her. They both had the same curling hair and thick beard. They also had the same stony jaw. They were the same in many ways, all ways, excepting this man did not cause her heart to soar like the great griffin. The man before her could only be Nicolaus's twin brother.

Nicolaus caught up to her and placed his palm against the small of her back to nudge her forward. His protection wrapped around her and the children and she wondered if they had anything to fear from this obvious relation of Nicolaus's. Her eyes widened and she dragged her feet as the truth hit her. The man before them could only be Nicolaus's brother Jasen, which meant Nicolaus had lost his father's challenge.

# Chapter Seventeen

Nicolaus gritted his teeth. He was happy to see his brother, but he would rather have waited to see him after his father had declared Nicolaus the winner of the challenge. Jasen's presence could only mean he'd lost, which meant he lost his chance to search for Desma. He would not ask his father for use of one of his ships, granting him false hope. Witnessing his heartache once had been enough.

"Have you treated your crew so awful that you've reverted to using women and children?" Jasen asked with a teasing glint in his eye. It was good to see his brother.

"No. We came across a fishing boat near Joppa in need of repairs."

"And you thought it necessary to bring them home?"

"Only these," Nicolaus said as he handed the babe to Ada, and then gripped his brother in a hug. "Since Mother has been hounding us to marry so she can experience grandchildren I figured having these little ones will pacify her for a time."

Jasen patted him on the back. "It is good to see you home. When you did not return..."

"I am well, brother. I am well."

Nicolaus pulled back from Jasen and motioned for the children to move forward. "This is Edith and Galen, and that—" he pointed to the babe "—is their brother. It seems they fled their island when a volcano erupted and were met by thieves. Their mother was taken."

Jasen's nostrils flared as color rose into his cheeks. "These children were left to fend for themselves?"

"They were left along with many old women and a few old men. They had not the resources to care for them. I could not leave them to the mercies of another."

Jasen nodded, and then tipped his chin toward Ada. "What of her? She has not the look of a Greek, and I cannot see any thief leaving her behind."

"This is Ada. She is from Ashkelon." Nicolaus chose not to say any more. His brother did not need to know he had purchased her, not yet.

"I was preparing the vessel to leave on the morrow to go in search of you."

"We sailed into a storm, and Ada became sick with fever. We ported near Yaya's until the repairs to the mast could be made and Ada recovered."

"I had wondered. I may beat you at father's challenges when it comes to sailing but not by days. You caused me great concern."

"My apologies, Jasen. I did not mean to worry you."

"Come, I would ease our parents' worry."

Although he didn't wish for Ada to be out of his sight, he wasn't yet ready to face his father and the constant sadness, especially in light of what he'd learned from Knosis. "I have duties to tend to before I can release the men. I only wished to remove the children from the dangers on deck as we unload the merchandise." Nicolaus smiled. "You'll be pleased with all you've won."

"I already am." Jasen's lips turned up at the corners as he puffed out his chest.

"All that is on board belongs to you except Ada and the crate from Egypt."

"Egypt? You could not have sailed so far."

It was Nicolaus's turn to puff out his chest and grin. "Could I have not? The proof is in the goods."

"There may still be hope for you to win yet, Nicolaus, as Father goes over our records. Go finish your tasks before Father wears a hole in the tiles waiting for your arrival and Mother burns another meal."

Nicolaus stilled. His pulse even halted. Could it be his parents actually worried over his absence? With the grief marring his mother's face and his father's eyes the last he saw them, he thought it would be little consequence for him to leave. Of course, their youngest son was beneath his care. That could be the only cause for their worry. "I will bring Brison before long, as well."

He quickly turned away and stalked toward his ship so his jealousy wouldn't get the best of him as his brother escorted Ada toward his parents' home. He met Chloe and Xandros halfway and pointed them toward Jasen. When he spied Ada with her shoulders hunched around the babe as if she were scared, he had second thoughts about leaving her to his brother's care. Truth was, he couldn't leave his vessel until it was emptied of all cargo and the decks scrubbed down.

No matter how much he wanted to walk away from his duties and stand by Ada's side.

"Do you speak?" Nicolaus's brother, an exact image of him, asked in a language spoken often by her father, eyeing her as if she were a leper.

"Yes," She returned in his language.

His eyes grew wide. He began to smile and then he laughed. "I see, and even in our own dialect. Who taught you such?"

"My father."

"Are you lame, then?"

Ada shook her head, not understanding why he would think she suffered some ailment.

"My brother did not say he purchased you, but since no thief would leave a prize such as yourself on board a ship, I can only assume he did. Are you his slave?" He sounded perplexed.

"Ay."

"Hmm."

Her cheeks heated over his assessment.

"Well, come along." He crouched near Edith, and she hid behind Ada's legs. "Would you like me to carry you? It is a long walk for such a little girl."

Ada caught her breath as she followed his pointing finger. It was so high and big. Imposing. "Is that yo-your home?"

Jasen laughed. "My parents' home. Nicolaus and I live in a room above the storehouses when we are in port so no one will be tempted to steal from us."

She couldn't take her eyes off the home. Nicolaus's parents must be important to have a house overlooking the village and the port. It was as if they owned it all.

"It is all right, Edith. This is the captain's brother."

The little girl peeked around her leg and shook her head.

"She's never seen two of anyone a'fore," Galen said. "Can we go to the tower?"

"The captain said he'd take you tomorrow as long as you listened."

Galen bounced up and down. "I am listening."

Jasen swung Edith up onto his shoulders. "Are you ready?"

Ada glanced at the house once more and nodded her head. They climbed up a cobbled path that twisted and turned, but was not any more burdensome than walking from her home to Ashkelon had been. Besides, the scenery, much different from her own home, kept her occupied. The lush green trees, patches of colorful flowers and the most breathtaking were the glimpses of mountains standing sentry in the sea. She'd always been taken with the things of God's creation. The animals, the grains of sand, the blooms on the olive tree plants, the sweetness of honey, but this—this was beyond anything she could have imagined. How could God grant these people such a blessing and yet they not call on his name?

They halted on a paved entryway, which gave her an open view of the mountains in the sea, the many boats bobbing in the port below. The sky and sea seemed to go on and on, coming together as one at the end.

"Ada," Jasen said as he swung Edith to the ground, "I will return in a moment. I must prepare my parents for their unexpected guests."

Her cheeks flamed, and she wished Nicolaus was here to ease her fears, but with his ever changing mood would her fears only heighten? Although she'd had many chores at home, they were nothing compared to what would be expected as a slave. She pushed back her reservations and determined to face her future with as much grace as her mother had carried during her own captivity.

"Hello." Ada turned to find the most stunning woman approaching her. Although her hair had long lost its color, it was intricately braided with a gold band wrapping around its length. She wore a white gown, much like Nicolaus's, but it was sealed over both shoulders with broaches and draped past her ankles.

Ada fought the urge to look at her feet and ankles, knowing her tunic didn't look as lovely as this woman's gown.

"I am Rena, Nicolaus's mother."

Ada felt her mouth open as she stared. Rena motioned for a servant to come forward. "The children will go with Agnes, and you'll come with me."

Ada held back the tears as Agnes took the children from her. The woman seemed kind but she would have liked a chance to give the children her blessings before never seeing them again.

"All will be well, you will see," Rena said. Although her voice spoke calm and truth, Ada was little reassured. "Come along now. There's a bath waiting."

Ada pulled her bottom lip between her teeth. After days of sea salt clinging to her skin, she looked forward to bathing but had little hopes of it given her status. She silently thanked God for the blessing and followed Nicolaus's mother through a courtyard and into a bathing chamber. A delicious aroma, one she could not discern, filled the air. She closed her eyes and sniffed.

"'Tis juniper leaves and lavender. It will help you to relax and cleanse any illness remaining in your body."

Ada drew her eyebrows together. How did she know of her illness? As if she read her mind, she answered. "Jasen told me you were ill and treated at my mother's home."

"Yes, that is true."

Tiles of various colors formed pictures of men and animals on the walls and the floor, but that was not what caught her eye. Two gold medallions hung on the wall, spewing water into two separate pottery basins large enough for her to sit. There was a fire beneath one, causing steam to rise into the chamber. A servant dipped a bucket into the steaming water and dumped it into a cistern.

"Is that dangerous?" She'd heard of such a thing before while she served a meal to her father and his guests, but her imaginings never conjured something so grand. Her short dips in the stream were pleasant enough when she chanced to get one, but most times she had to make do with a basin of water and a cloth.

"No, dear, it is quite pleasant." Smiling, Rena grabbed hold of Ada's hand, led her to the cistern. She knelt beside the pool and swirled her fingers into the water. Glancing at Ada, she motioned for her to kneel, as well. "See, it is warm. This time of the year can leave a chill in the air."

Ada knelt beside Nicolaus's mother. Her hand hovered above the water. It seemed too much to ask for a slave such as she to enjoy something so beautiful. Before she gave in to the urge to flee, she dipped her fingers into the water. Her eyes widened. "It is much warmer than the sea."

Rena laughed. "Is that where you bathe at home?"

Ada rose. Her eyes went back to the water trickling out of the walls. "No. I became ill, and a—a wave swept me off the boat and into the water."

"Oh, dear." Rena grabbed hold of Ada's hands and stepping back, looked her over from head to toe. "What was my son thinking?"

"He—"

"No matter. I am quite certain what was on my son's mind. However, I wonder if he had a clue himself." Rena squeezed her fingers and smiled. "Laurel will see to your needs." Nicolaus's mother walked away, her head high and shoulders straight. Ada had never seen a queen, but she imagined they would look like Rena. Ada's insides shook. The tears pressing against the backs of her eyes stung. Rena stopped and glanced over her shoulder. "Ada, you are a guest in my home."

A guest? Not a slave? Ada worried her lip. She gazed out the window overlooking the valley and sea below. What sort of place was this where slaves were treated as guests?

# Chapter Eighteen

Nicolaus slipped off his sandals and hooked his fingers through the straps. The pathway made of small stones cooled his feet, bringing relief to them after standing on the deck for so long. The small creek bubbled nearby, and he longed to show Ada the delicate beauty hidden beneath the canopy of trees.

It had taken longer than Nicolaus would have liked to get the ship unloaded and the goods locked in the storehouse, but he had allowed Brison to take command of the merchandise. Although he was slower than Nicolaus and Jasen, he had categorized the crates and made notes by each entry with great ability. Their father would be pleased, but Nicolaus couldn't help but wonder if Brison would be better suited to another profession. One that required him to keep his feet on land, one where he'd be less likely to encounter dangerous storms and villains.

He glanced up the hill to see how much farther they had to go. They should have been home already except Brison ascended the pathway ahead of him. His brother's muscles strained against the weight in his arms, which he insisted he carry. It was near too heavy for Nicolaus, but his brother seemed to manage. "Would you like me to carry that, little brother?"

"I've got it," he grunted through gasps of air.

"You would not wish to drop Mother's gifts."

An indistinguishable mutter made Nicolaus laugh. "You know, Father will be pleased to see whiskers on your chin. After seventeen years of gracing us with your presence it is about time, too."

Perhaps his jests would frustrate Brison and cause his feet to move faster. Now that he'd had time away from Ada, he was certain he was ready to see her and not lose his mind like a lunatic. However, if Brison did not hurry, Nicolaus would never know, especially considering each passing moment made him more anxious to lay eyes on her, to see how she was faring in his father's household.

His brother came to an abrupt stop and peeked around the crate. "Would you like to go around? You must be anxious to see Mother." An impertinent smile curved Brison's mouth. "No. Perhaps it is Father you're in such a haste to see. Hmm, I think not. I'm guessing it's Ada who has you dreaming with your eyes open and muttering in your sleep."

"I've done no such thing." Nicolaus playfully punched Brison's arm and stole the crate from his hands. "Come along, little brother. No doubt Mother wishes to kiss her youngest son's cheeks."

Nicolaus took long strides in order to quicken the pace. Brison was quick on his heels. In a matter of moments they reached the terrace, and Nicolaus turned to his brother. "See how quickly one can move when he has the strength to bear his burdens."

"I was doing fine." Brison clenched his hands at his sides, and then he looked past Nicolaus. His mouth fell open.

Nicolaus turned to see what had caused his talkative brother to lose speech, and all the air left his lungs. Instead of her light-colored hair artfully piled about her head, or braided like his mother was wont to do, it hung loose down Ada's back. Two gold clasps closed the chiton over her shoulders, leaving her slender arms bare. The loose fabric gathered at her waist with a leather belt, flared at her hips and hid her legs from his sight. The difference in their clothing was stark. If she was not standing before him in the flesh and blood he'd have thought one of the marble statues his people were so fond of had come to life to torment him. However, she was more lovely, more beautiful than any woman, statue or not, that he'd ever seen. No wonder his men had been captivated by her.

He'd much prefer his men catching glimpses of her ankles than her entire arm. At least her ankles were not within easy sight unless a man was lying on his belly. He'd much prefer her hair tied in knots than hanging loose, but then everyone would notice her slender neck and the graceful tilt of her chin. He'd planned on taking her back to the vessel on the morrow while he finished up a few chores before he took Galen on an exploration, but no doubt he'd have to cover her from stem to stern before he did such a thing.

"Would you like it if I took that from you, Nicolaus?"

Jasen stepped in front of him, blocking his view. He peered around Jasen for one last look. Ada's cheeks turned pink, and she bowed her head. Jasen shifted in front of him. Nicolaus blinked the haze of Ada from his eyes and tried to focus. "What?"

Jasen laughed. "What did I say, Mother?"

Nicolaus glared at his brother. Jasen winked as he lifted the crate from Nicolaus's hands. "All the way from Egypt? Or so he says."

"I brought you wool, as well, Mother."

"My thanks, Nicky, but let me first greet my boys before you report to your father." She kissed his cheek. "It is glad I am to have you return, Nicky." And then she gathered Brison into her arms. "It is not easy seeing the last of your womb become a man. Look at the hair on your chin." Her eyes watered. Recalling her emotions when Jasen and Nicolaus began to grow beards, he felt sorry for his younger brother. "Come along, your father wishes to see you first."

Jasen gave Nicolaus one last look and then nodded. He had no idea what his brother was approving. He hadn't won this challenge, at least not with speed. "Father will expect you soon."

He watched Jasen's back until he disappeared into the shadows of the courtyard. His gaze flung to where Ada remained. His pulse quickened. He struggled for air.

She'd grown more beautiful as the light faded across the sky. The lavender oil on her heated skin created a new scent, something exotic to his senses.

He blew out an exasperated breath. What was he doing? He could not think of her in such a way and keep his head. Not when he was about to speak with his father and discover if he'd truly won or lost.

"Ada, would you mind crushing these?" Rena asked. She took the bowl of almonds and pestle from Nicolaus's mother, found a spot on the floor and sat. Rena smiled. "What is it you are doing? You can stand here beside me, there is plenty of room."

Ada moved to stand beside Rena and ran her hand over the smooth table. "We do not have tables such as these at home." She bowed her head. "And slaves rarely work so close to the family at my home. My father's wife does not tolerate slaves in her presence unless they are performing a chore for her."

Rena laid her hand over Ada's. "I am sorry, Ada. As I said, you are my guest and will be treated as such until you leave my home. Besides Nicolaus's father, my slaves have become my closest friends. I expect we'll become great friends, too."

Not knowing what to say, Ada ground the pestle against the almonds. She'd never had a friend before, not even her sisters.

"Do you miss them, your family?"

The pestle clattered to the table. She snatched it up and continued grinding the almonds. At first she had missed them, but only because she feared what was ahead of her. Now…she would know if her father chose the actions of her sisters, but… "No, I do not miss them. I have not thought of them much except to compare their character to Nicolaus's, which I now realize is unfair to him."

"I do not understand." Rena halted Ada's actions with her hand. "You are not close to your siblings?"

Ada glanced to the floor, embarrassment burning her cheeks. "No. I am not like them. I am the daughter of a Hebrew slave. Their mother is free. They did not like that I received the same privileges as they did."

"How did my son end up purchasing you?"

"He thought to rescue me." She explained to Rena how Dina and her other sisters had traded her for a gold band. One corner of Ada's mouth curved upward. "I suppose he did considering the alternative. My other bidder was a procurer. I'm afraid I was none too kind to Nicolaus. I even accused him of stealing me from my home. At the time I was consumed with grief over the death of my mother and anger over my sisters' betrayal."

"I am sorry."

"I am not. She is now free to rest with our ancestors." Ada lifted the pestle and grimaced at the fine powder she'd turned them into. "I think I should try again."

Rena smiled. "No, it is fine. We will sprinkle it over the fish along with the garlic. It will make for a delicious aroma." She pointed toward cloves of garlic in a bowl. "You can grind those now, if you would like."

"Of course. After days of being idle I am glad to have my hands busy."

Unfortunately her mind continued to wander to Nicolaus. The way he'd looked—stared—at her when he had arrived still left her stomach fluttering and her knees wobbly. If she could get that consuming fire burning in his eyes out of her thoughts she'd be all right. She'd be able to draw in air with ease, she'd be able to convince herself she wasn't already in love with him, because surely that look hadn't conveyed his love for her. It couldn't. She wouldn't allow it, but if he did…

"Ada, would you take the hydria and fill it with water? The well is in the center of the courtyard."

"Yes, of course." Leaving the pestle in the bowl,

she took up the black painted jar that looked like their earthenware jars at home and carried it to the courtyard. She placed it on the ledge of the well and drew up the bucket.

"Father." Nicolaus's voice bounced off the courtyard walls. She looked around for him but did not see them. "I do not argue that I lost. However, I purchased her with my own coin." There was a moment of silence. She imagined Nicolaus spearing his fingers through his hair or running his hand over his beard. "You must understand, I was broken when Desma was taken from my protection. When I saw Ada on that auction block I knew the only way to ease my guilt was to save her, there is nothing more."

The sound of pottery shattering against the marble made her jump. Pain sliced down the center of her chest. She was nothing more than an object to assuage his guilt. How had she thought he longed for her love? Had the look in his eyes deceived her?

"The challenge was all merchandise on the winning vessel would go to the winner. That includes your slave."

Ada gasped. Was she now to become Jasen's property? What would he do with her? She did not wish to know any more. Even though Jasen and Nicolaus looked alike, she would not have the problem of loving her master if she did become his property, which was just as well with her, especially since she seemed to be a guilt offering for Nicolaus.

And nothing more.

She filled the hydria with water and rushed back into the kitchen. "Where would you have me place this?"

Rena glanced over her shoulder. "Are you well, Ada?"

Ada drew in a ragged breath and nodded. "I am tired from the journey."

"Of course you are." Rena took the hydria from her. "Why don't you cut the onions? We break with custom here and eat with the men."

Ada's eyes grew wide. Was she to further suffer by breaking another meal with Nicolaus?

"Even our house slaves dine with us. Once a week we invite all of our slaves to eat with us. It is nice, living here and being able to make our own customs. As I said, they are my friends as well as my husband's."

If Nicolaus's father was so friendly then why was he giving her to Jasen?

Rena propped the hydria on her hip and grabbed a bowl of cakes. "I would suggest you seek your rest. However, my husband is anxious to meet you."

## Chapter Nineteen

His father paled as did Jasen. Brison's cup shattered on the marble floor. He hadn't meant to say his sister's name, but he was furious. How could his father give Ada to his brother? She belonged to him. He was more slave to her for she had bound his heart. He knew that now. Had known it since they had sat beside each other watching the sea at Yaya's. He just hadn't been ready to admit it to himself. Now he was. However, he needed to find the courage to defy his father and the ways of their ancestors, and yet honor him the way a son should.

First, he needed to speak to his father. Alone. "Will you both allow me a moment with Father?"

One of Jasen's eyes narrowed before he glanced at their father. Nicolaus understood his brother's hesitation since they'd always taken care of the family business together, but he would not question his father in front of his brothers. Even if there was little truth to what Knosis had told him, Nicolaus did not want his brothers having doubt about their father's character.

Nicolaus looked his father in the eye. "I would not ask if it were not important."

"Very well. I will see you boys when we break for our meal." His father glided toward Brison and kissed his cheek. "You did well, son. You did well."

Jasen wrapped his arm around Brison's shoulders. "How about a game of knuckles whilst we wait for Nicolaus to plead his case?"

They walked out of the *andron*, the only room where women were not allowed. Jasen tossed one last look over his shoulder before slipping beyond the door. Nicolaus didn't like leaving his twin out of this conversation, but it was not his tale to tell. *If* there was one to be told.

His father took a sip from his cup, his eyes peering at Nicolaus over the rim.

Nicolaus crossed his arms over his chest and drew in a breath to fortify his nerves. "Knosis boarded my ship."

His father's brows rose slightly. He set the cup down on the table and paced to the window overlooking the port. "He is bold."

"That he is. He surrounded my ship with three heavily armed ones."

His father swung around. "What did he want?"

"Desma."

"She was tak—"

"I know this, Father." Nicolaus scrubbed a hand over his beard. Never before had he dishonored his father with his speech or his actions. Until the moment he had failed to protect his sister. "He believes there was trickery involved."

"That is absurd."

Nicolaus walked to the courtyard window, and he looked around to see if his brothers hovered in the shadows. He raised his palm and laid it flat above the window, resting his head against the crook of his arm. "I must admit if I were him, and knowing what I know, I would believe the same."

"What is it you are saying, Nicolaus?"

He twisted around to face his father. "Knosis told me how you won Mother's hand, and that I believe. He also claimed you cheated." Nicolaus raised his hand to keep his father from speaking. "I do not believe that. What I do not understand is why you would promise Desma, my sweet, delicate sister, to a man who has outlived a passel of wives."

His father hung his head, drew in a shaky breath and then collapsed onto one of the couches. He buried his face into his hands. Nicolaus sat beside him and rested his elbows on his knees. He stared at the seams of the tiles near his feet.

"I was young," his father said. "You are right that I did not cheat. However, that did not stop Knosis from his accusations. He claimed I poisoned their water, causing his men to become ill—many died." His father shook his head. "I never would have done such a thing. Your grandfather favored Knosis and believed him, but there was no proof. He left the decision up to your mother. Without her knowledge he required us to sign contracts giving our firstborn daughter to the son of the other upon their coming of age. If there were no sons then the other could claim her as his own if he wasn't already married."

Nicolaus looked at his father. "Knosis bore no sons."

His father shook his head. "Nine wives and no sons. I wonder if his wives died naturally." His father rose from the couch and paced to the other side of the room. "I was beside myself when Knosis sent a message upon

Desma's last birthday. What little choice had I when I signed the contract?"

Nicolaus crossed the room and laid his hand on his shoulder. "You have always been honorable, Father. You taught us that a man is nothing without the honor of his word. There is nothing you could have done."

A tentative smile formed his father's lips. "Except pray to that God my brother Oceanus is forever speaking about. When Knosis sent word that you never arrived, I had thought—had hoped that you chose to take her elsewhere. Jasen reminded me you were the dutiful son and would never have done such a thing."

The tips of his ears burned at his brother's assessment. "He is right, although I wish I would have."

"I find no fault with you, Nicolaus. It is what it is. Ironically, my prayers to Oceanus's God were answered. She never made it to Knosis."

Had his sister met a much worse fate? "I will be honest with you, Father. If I had won this challenge I had planned to search for Desma until I found her."

His father looked him in the eye with great sadness. "Then it is a good thing you lost, for I fear it is hopeless. Your brother searched for months while searching for you. We were overjoyed when he brought you home."

"About Ada—" Nicolaus's words were cut off by the raising of his hand.

His father straightened his robes. "She seems important to you, almost as important as your mother is to me. What is it you would do with the slave if I allowed you to keep her?"

He'd marry her if he could, but he did not wish to push his father's good graces. "She reminded me of Desma's circumstances. The only man bidding was one who would force her into prostitution. I would not wish that on my sister."

His father grimaced, and Nicolaus immediately regretted his words, but he pressed on. "I only purchased her to save her from prostitution. I would free her if I could, but then she would lose the protection of my name." The word *marriage* clung to his tongue. Why could he not just tell his father how he felt about Ada, that she made him feel alive again? That he cared for her. He shook his head. "I do not know."

"Then I do not know, either. I will consider my actions and inform you of my decision on the morrow before the sun goes down."

It was the best Nicolaus could hope for at the moment. And if he somehow gathered the courage to tell Ada he loved her, then perhaps he could tell his father that truth, as well.

"Come, let us wash our hands. We are dining with the women this eve." His father smiled. "I cannot wait to meet this woman who has your thoughts twisted."

Laughter echoed through the *andron* as his father slipped into the courtyard. Nicolaus did not think the way Ada made him feel was at all humorous. If only he knew the right course of action in order to become himself again. Whether she went back home to her family, remained a slave with him, or whether he married her, something told him he would never return to his old self. He was no longer Nicolaus captain of the Great Sea, or the Sea Dragon, but Nicolaus a man falling in love.

His chest filled with joy and the corners of his mouth lifted. Nicolaus, a man in love, was not as frightening as he first thought it would be. In fact, he liked the sound of it.

* * *

Ada hovered near the doorway, just behind Rena and her servants. She'd been given permission to check on the children and found peace in doing so, but now her nerves were causing her stomach to feel as though she were being tossed around on the waves.

The women at her home never dined with the men. They weren't allowed to eat until the men had finished their repast. It was a custom never broken. Not even for special occasions. What would it be like sitting at the same table, sharing from the same bowls? Would her hand brush against Nicolaus's as it had when they ate at his grandmother's? She sucked in a breath at the fluttering in her stomach. Every time she had grabbed for an olive, so had he. A cake of bread, and his fingers had been there. She would not survive the tug on her heartstrings or the intensity of his gaze if that were to happen during this eve's meal. She'd have to take care to not remove food when he did.

"The table is prepared. All we must do now is wait for the men to take their places." Rena touched her arm and then tucked a strand of Ada's hair behind her ear. That one small touch created an ache in Ada's heart. She missed her mother, and had had little time to mourn her passing before her sisters traded her for a gold band. "I do not know how it was done at your home, but as I told you we do not hold to customs here. I would have you sit beside me to ease your concerns."

Ada dipped her chin. She doubted much would ease her concerns, even sitting beside Nicolaus's kind mother, especially knowing that his father was intent on giving her to Jasen.

Rena tugged on Ada's hand, bringing her to stand

beside her, and then tucked her arm through Ada's. If Ada had not already been nervous, Rena's fortified inhale and elongated back would have made her so. It was as if Rena herself was uncertain of how the meal would go. She was about to ask to leave when Rena stepped through the kitchen and into the dining area, pulling Ada with her.

Ada feared she would stumble and fall when her toes caught in her garment as she moved beside Nicolaus's mother. It was her blessing that Rena did not travel far, taking the couch closest to the kitchen's door. She sat on right side of the bench. It looked much like the padded one on Nicolaus's boat. Ada sat beside Rena and nearly melted into the cushions.

No sooner had she settled onto the bench than the servants moved tables before them. They were laden with cut figs, olives, cakes of honey bread and bits of fish Rena had fried in olive oil and almonds.

The meal had tantalized her senses while she'd helped prepare the food and it did even more so now, causing her stomach to grumble. Male laughter filled the room, startling her. Heat rose in her cheeks. She was tempted to cool them with her palms, but did not wish to draw any more unwanted attention to herself.

"You are the reason for my son's delay."

Ada wanted to allow the tears stinging the backs of her eyes to stream down her cheeks, but Rena's gentle squeeze on her hand gave her the fortification she needed to look Nicolaus's father in the eye. She swallowed past the knot of linen in her throat and emulated Rena's posture. "Is it fault of mine that you raised your son with a compassionate heart?"

No sooner were the words off her tongue than she

wished to call them back as Nicolaus's father stared at her without even blinking an eye. Someone cleared their throat—she was certain it was Nicolaus—and another barely held back their laughter—which she most certainly believed to be Jasen. She had not meant to sound rude, only to give credit where it was deserved. "You should consider it an honor that you have raised your son in such a manner. No doubt a lesser man would have tossed me into the sea."

"No doubt," Jasen said as he burst into laughter. Ada swung her gaze to him. Was this man who so easily laughed at her to be her new master? She'd much prefer her sisters' abuse. She'd much prefer Nicolaus with his never-ending kindness, even if his manner was somewhat rough, but that was not her choice.

"You are bold for a slave. Perhaps my son should beat you into submissiveness."

Ada sucked in a sharp breath. Even Rena seemed taken by surprise. "My apologies. Six days ago I was the daughter of a wealthy merchant."

"I do not understand. If you father is wealthy, how is it you've come to this fate?" He chose a plump fig from a bowl and took a bite.

Ada glanced at the tiles, and then back to Nicolaus's father. "My father journeyed to Judah to bury my mother, his slave, with her ancestors as he had promised." Nicolaus's gaze warmed her, but she dared not look at him lest she break her resolve to distance herself from him. "My sisters invited me to the market in Ashkelon. Hoping it would take my mind from my grief, I went, even though my father had never allowed me to journey to the city before."

"Perhaps your father should beat you."

The corner of Ada's mouth twisted upward as she twisted the fabric of her chiton. The white tunic began to wrinkle with all the knotting she'd been doing with her fingers. "Perhaps. It was in Ashkelon where my sisters sold me to a slave trader."

Nicolaus's father took a sip from his cup. His eyes turned thoughtful, and then glittered above the rim. He set the cup aside, and then smiled. "I admire you. I can see why my son broke with character and purchased a slave. Shall we eat?"

Everyone in the room, except Ada, seemed to breathe a sigh of relief. She should have known Nicolaus's father would test her, but for what purpose?

"Allow me this question, Ada. If you were freed from your bondage what would you do?"

Her eyes immediately went to Nicolaus. Her heart longed for him, longed to stay by his side whether slave or servant, but she would not say such and embarrass herself further by declaring her love for a man who thought of her as nothing more than an offering to assuage his guilt. She also did not wish to go home where she was despised by her sisters. Somehow she had found joy in her bondage. Was that how her mother felt toward her father? Had he brought her joy even though she was a slave? "I—I do not know."

"She is exhausted from her journey, Gavros," Rena said. Ada blinked, having heard this man's name for the first time. "Perhaps she'll have an answer come the morrow."

Given the way she yearned to remain by Nicolaus's side she did not think the morrow would bring her a better answer. The correct one was to return home to her father, to no longer be indebted to these people if they were to grant her freedom. She did not have coin to return the price Nicolaus had paid for her. Nor did she think her father would part with his riches for any daughter, especially the daughter of one of his slaves.

# Chapter Twenty

The sky was beginning to lose the light of the day and the moon was peeking above the sea as they walked toward the storehouse where he and Jasen spent their evenings. Thinking back on Ada's responses to his father's questions made him smile. However, her lack of answer as to what she would do if freed was not what he had hoped for. He wanted to hear her say she'd stay. Did she still long for a home where her family rejected her?

"What has you in deep thought, brother?" Jasen nudged his arm. "Or need I ask? You should tell Father your intentions."

Nicolaus stopped and looked at his brother. "I do not know what you mean, Jasen."

"Do you not? Tell Father you wish to marry her."

Nicolaus laughed and resumed walking. "She is not Ionian."

"Neither is our mother, or have you forgotten?"

"At least she is Greek." Nicolaus shook his head. "Father would never approve of a marriage between one of his sons and a Hebrew woman. Especially his oldest."

"Only by a few moments, brother. I believe you underestimate our father."

"Perhaps I do." He certainly didn't expect him to treat Ada with respect and admiration, but he had. Of course, she'd earned it. Not many dared speak to his father as she had. "No matter. I cannot marry her even if he allowed it."

"I do not understand, Nicolaus. You watch her every move, you threaten your men—yes, I've heard the tales from Brison—you lose speech and thought when in her presence. It is obvious you are taken with her."

*Taken with her* were not exactly the words Nicolaus would use, but he wouldn't argue with his brother at the moment. "There is a chance she no longer belongs to me to free."

Nicolaus opened the door to the storehouse and began climbing the stairs to their room. "If that is Father's decision then I will free her so you can take her as your wife," Jasen countered.

Halting on the stairs, Nicolaus turned and glanced down at his brother. "I will not take her if she does not wish to be taken. Besides, I have a vow I must honor before I can consider a wife." Even if Ada was his only chance at the love his parents seemed to share.

"What vow would that be, Nicolaus?"

Nicolaus ignored his brother. He did not want him to think he'd lost faith in his abilities to search every port from here to Egypt for their sister. If he told Jasen the truth trust between them would be broken.

Jasen stomped up the stairs and spun him around. Concern showed in his eyes. "Nicolaus, what vow is it that would keep you from Ada when it is obvious you love her?"

Nicolaus closed his eyes; an image of his sister as she was being taken off his ship pierced his thoughts. The quiet acceptance as she'd been led away still caused an ache deep in his chest. She'd been as calm still waters. "Desma."

"What?" Jasen's brows knitted together as he shook his head. "What does our sister have to do with Ada?"

"I have spoken with Father. I must search for her. I cannot bear the thought of her in bondage to a cruel master or worse—" he bowed his head and whispered "—prostitution."

"Nicolaus, she is well."

He snapped his gaze to his brother's, uncertain of what he'd heard. "She's what?"

"If you do not marry Ada, I will." Jasen swiveled and ran down the stairs.

Nicolaus was fast on his heels. He grabbed hold of his brother's arm to halt him. "What have you done?"

"Oh, brother, how will you ever forgive me?" Jasen sank onto the carved bench sitting against the storehouse.

"You are my brother," Nicolaus said as he sat beside him.

Jasen leaned the back of his head against the storehouse and looked up at the stars. "I only thought to rescue her from Knosis. I overheard Father and Mother. They were both crying. Father had confessed to her about a contract."

Nicolaus nodded. "Father told me of the contract."

"Mother was angry. I'd never heard her in such a rage. She even threw things at our father. He left the house that day. I followed him to Oceanus's home where I heard him confess his concerns about Knosis's previous wives. All deceased. Our uncle was grieved as well but counseled Father to keep his honor."

"You should have shared this with me."

"I could not. I did not know myself whether I wanted to kill Knosis for his demands or allow Desma to go without so much as a word. I could not share with you because you are much like our father. Honor is your badge, ever since you buried the Sea Dragon. You would have insisted on upholding the contract."

Nicolaus leaned his shoulders against the storehouse. The soft waves lapped the shore around them. Men continued to unload merchandise from their ships while others finished hammering planks into place on the ships being constructed. "I wish I would have had your courage. My former self would have, but as you said, he is long gone from this life. I was young and full of vigor. I craved victories when we warred with those against Greece. I did things I could never be proud of, not now. However, if I had known about Knosis and his many wives I'm not certain I could have given him my sister, even to uphold Father's honor. It wasn't until I heard Knosis wished to speak with me that Xandros told me of his dead wives."

Jasen groaned. "He should not have told you."

Nicolaus glanced at his brother. "Knosis boarded my vessel and demanded Ada in exchange for Desma."

Jasen's mouth fell open. "He did not."

"He did, with three armed ships." Nicolaus smiled. "Fortunately she suffered from a fever. Her mad rantings scared him back to his own boat."

Jasen squeezed his eyes shut. "I did not mean for

you to be taken into captivity. I hired David to take Desma only, nothing more. When he brought her to me he said nothing about you."

Nicolaus thought back to that day. The way Desma carried herself with grace, yet fear tinged her eyes, as he fought against the thieves, made sense to him now. "Did she know?"

"No, I did not even know if David would send his men."

"What of Xandros?"

Jasen shook his head. "He confronted me upon his return. Seems he recalled a jest he'd made about stealing her away and wondered if I had done it. Will you forgive me?"

"Desma is secure?" Nicolaus asked.

"Hidden from men such as Knosis and David."

"Then, there is naught to forgive, Jasen. My time in captivity is more than worth knowing our sister is well." Well worth knowing he could now face his father and request the freedom to offer marriage to Ada.

"Does Father know?"

"No," Jasen said as he looked Nicolaus in the eye. "That is a truth he cannot discover. Not yet. If anyone were to discover Desma's whereabouts, Knosis would demand the contract to be fulfilled. And if Father discovered the truth, his honor would demand he fulfill it."

"Then I will not ask where she is, but the truth is bound to come out. I pray to Ada's Almighty God that Father's wrath does not demolish you."

"You love her enough that you've been won over by her God?"

"Love her, I had not thought much on that. All I know is I want to be near her." His pulse beat a little harder against his chest. Did he love her? He rushed on before his brother read something in his silence. "However, if you look at all we've seen all of our lives, the sun, the moon and the stars, the sea and all the creatures within it, the butterflies that flit from one flower to the next, the birds, even the flowers and all their various shades, do you not see a God much greater than those we've created with our hands?"

Jasen scratched his fingers through his beard. "You sound like our uncle."

Nicolaus laughed. "He makes much more sense now that my eyes have been opened." And he couldn't wait to share his belief with Ada. "Our people create statues with their hands and then give them a story. Consider there is an actual God, not created by our hands but one who created us and everything around us? The heavens, the seas and all within. Those curious creatures that greet us with such excitement nearly every time we come home, the ones we call dolphins."

"Oh, now you've convinced me, for no Greek god would create one of those beings. They are too happy."

They laughed. Nicolaus wrapped his arm around Jasen's neck and rubbed his knuckles against his head. Soon they were lying on their backs, staring up at the starlit sky and gasping for breath. "You always did beat me at wrestling."

"And you always beat me at sailing. I do not know why I even accepted Father's challenge."

"If you had not you would not have found Ada."

A star twinkled and Nicolaus wondered if perhaps God had brought them together. "Ay, that is true."

"What will you do?"

Nicolaus sighed. "I must discern her wishes. If she

wishes to stay then I will offer her freedom and then marriage."

"If she doesn't?"

Nicolaus didn't know what he'd do. Keeping her in captivity seemed cruel, but could he let her go?

Ada lay on the soft sheepskin mat and stared at the flickering shadows from the oil lamps. She'd been surprised when Rena ushered her into a private sleeping room and not into the slaves' room. She'd been even more surprised to find Edith and the babe, under Chloe's care, waiting for her.

Ada's arm cradled Edith's head. The poor child mumbled, and Ada was certain the nightmare she'd lived only days ago when her mother was taken continued to play out in her sleep. Ada ran her fingers over the girl's clean, soft curls. She wished she could right all in Galen's and Edith's world. She had no ability to search for their mother. However, she was beginning to see how important it was to Nicolaus to find his sister.

She was also beginning to understand why Nicolaus had purchased her. She hadn't realized the full of it until she'd spoken the truth to Nicolaus's father. Nicolaus had a heart full of compassion. He could not have left a leper to the mercies of what Ada had faced.

The babe made a little sucking noise, bringing a smile to her lips. They still hadn't given him a name. It only seemed right to leave that honor to Nicolaus and his family. Nicolaus had seemed at ease carrying the infant. The sight was as new and exciting as seeing the dolphins had been. That same excitement filled her when she watched him play with Edith and Galen.

Perhaps even more so considering the way she felt just at the thought of Nicolaus cradling the babe again.

One thing was for certain: no matter what her future held, she could rest in God's peace knowing these little ones were being cared for by a wondrous family. Ada rolled onto her side, curling around Edith. A tear slid from the corner of her eye. What she wouldn't do for a family such as this. However, the one thing her mother had taught her was to be content in her circumstances. Although it wouldn't be easy, she would try. If only she weren't a slave, the daughter of a Hebrew slave. If only her father treasured his daughters as much as he had his sons then perhaps she could have married, but then who would have been willing to marry her? Certainly not a Hebrew man and most certainly not a Philistine. Either way her blood was tainted.

She would not regret her past. She'd had a caring mother and although her father was distant and cold, he had provided for them. It was more than Edith and Galen had at the moment. At least she would not have the memory of her mother being stolen by cruel men who would most likely sell her into slavery.

Slavery…hadn't she watched her mother endure the hardships of slavery? Was Ada not now a slave herself? Ada's eyes widened as she covered her mouth with her hand. Nicolaus had not once treated her as a slave should be treated. Nor had he beaten her when she well deserved it.

She slipped her arm from beneath Edith's and instantly missed the comfort the contact had brought her heart, but she needed space to think. Rising from the mat, she walked onto the open balcony and gasped at the way the moon rippled against the waters.

Although there had been some moments of discomfort, she had a sense of belonging here. True shalom. Well, as true a peace as possible. She had no sisters to torment her or a father to ignore her. There was nothing missing or broken here. The only things broken were the relationships with the family she'd left in Ashkelon.

She leaned against the railing and watched the ships bob in the water in the light of the moon. There were many in the port all nestled together as if they were the best of comrades, much like Nicolaus and his brothers.

Leaning against a column, she looked up at the stars and sighed. For as long as she could remember she wanted to be a part of her family, to be one of the sisters running through their village chasing each other. To be, in truth, one of her father's daughters who played *senet* with him each night, not just one who sat in the shadows watching her father pat her siblings on the head in approval when they stole his pawns. Not that he would have rejected Ada if she would have sought him out, but the torment she received from her sisters wasn't worth her father's attention.

Now, if given the chance to return home, would she? She pulled her lip between her teeth and shook her head. Of course she would. They were her family. Besides, even if her heart longed to be here with Nicolaus, even as nothing more than his slave, it would cause an incurable ache to be so near him. To watch him bond with a wife in marriage, to play with his children as he did with Edith and Galen.

No matter how much she wanted to stay here and be a part of this loving family, she knew if given the choice to go home she'd have to return.

# Chapter Twenty-One

Nicolaus leaned against the doorpost separating the kitchen and the dining room. Ada's hair was pulled back and piled around her head, revealing the small bits of dough caked at the top of her ear.

"Good morning." He smiled when Ada jumped. The pestle fell from her hand and clattered against the pottery. Her shoulders rose and fell with a breath of air. She picked up the pestle and resumed grinding the wheat. She'd lost the natural movements of only moments ago, and he willed her to relax the stiffness in her shoulders and turn around so he could feast his eyes on her beautiful face. To see the expression in her jewel-like eyes.

"Nicolaus!" His mother pulled her hands from the dough in the bowl and wiped them on a cloth. She glided across the room, stood on the tips of her toes and bussed his cheek. A smile lifted the corners of her mouth. Her gaze flitted toward Ada, as did his, and she patted his arm. "What brings you here so early?"

He laughed. "It is not so early, Mother. The sun long ago rose above the horizon."

Ada glanced over her shoulder. A dusting of flour

coated her cheek. Last night all seemed so simple when he'd talked to Jasen, but that was before a ship from Ashkelon made port this very morn. One, he was told, carried men looking for Ada. According to word traversing throughout port, a man was looking for his sister called Ada. Another was looking for his daughter by that same name.

Nicolaus halted the urge to rake his fingers through his hair lest his mother know not all was well with him. His sleep had been all but restful. His gaze constantly roaming toward his parents' home until he'd made his way up the path and rested in the courtyard. However, it wasn't until word of her father and brother's arrival in port that he understood just how infused into his being she was. The thought of her returning home with her father was unbearable.

He had yet to speak with Ada's father as he wanted to speak with her first, but he intended on asking her what she wished; if she longed to stay he would offer marriage. If not —his mouth twitched at the ache forming in his chest—he'd be left with no choice but to let her go.

"Of course it has, Nicolaus. However, the noon meal is some time away. You will have to wait if you are hungry."

"I did not come for food, Mother. I broke my morning fast with Jasen and Father earlier." He swallowed the doubt filling his throat. "I would take Ada for a walk to view our beautiful home." He glanced down at his mother. "If you no longer have need of her."

"Of course. One of the servants can finish up."

Ada laid the pestle inside the bowl. Turning to face

him, she narrowed her eyes. "I wish to carry out my duties. I would not be seen as an idler."

"Nonsense, Ada." His mother smiled. "Clean your face and hands in the bathing chamber. My son will meet you in the courtyard."

Ada bowed her head. She averted her eyes as she neared the door. He moved aside but not before he caught a whiff of the lavender water she'd obviously bathed in. The warmth of the kitchen cooled with her absence.

"She is a rare creature, Nicolaus." His mother moved back toward her bowl and began kneading the dough. Joy beamed from her, making him feel a little guilty.

"I know, Mama."

She halted her task and looked him in the eye. "You love her?"

He shook his head. "This, I do not know."

She moved close to him and placed her palm against his cheek. "Nicolaus, my son, she brings you joy. Happiness. This is good. It is enough."

Was it? He clasped his mother's hand in his and kissed the back of her hand before dropping it. He welcomed her confidence. However, the confusion warring within his mind and the heaviness pressing against his chest as if he was crushed beneath a mast kept the door locked against any hope he might have that happiness was enough.

He knew his mother only wanted her children to be happy, and for some reason, perhaps because of the way his gaze continually sought out Ada, she believed Ada was his source of happiness. Although Ada brought him joy and made the air around him easier to breathe, his joy could not be dependent upon her. That was a burden he would not place on her, not after the way her sisters had treated her as if she were the source of their sadness. Besides, ever since realizing there was a one true God who had created everything, including the skies and the seas, and even him, he'd held more joy than he could ever remember. Ay, Ada had something to do with that.

"Nicky, if she brings you joy you must keep her close. Take her as your wife."

He shook his head. "Father may not agree. Besides, I would give her a choice, Mama."

"Of course, Nicky. I would not expect you to force her into marriage just because she is your slave. I have no doubt she will accept your quest. Just ask her."

"If only it were that simple."

She patted his arm. "Love is never simple, Nicky. If it was we would not understand the extent of our love for the other. We would take it for granted. Even now, the love between your father and me is not simple. Pure, yes, but never simple. However, our trials bring us closer together."

Pain flickered in her eyes, and he imagined she spoke of his sister. He longed to tell her Desma was alive and well, that Jasen knew where she was, but it was not his secret to tell, no matter how much that revelation would ease his mother's pain.

"We make mistakes, your father and I, but we love each other. I thank the one true God each morning that He provided me with a man such as your father to help carry my burdens. And to bring me joy."

Nicolaus was surprised at his mother's revelation at believing in God. That knowledge brought him greater joy than he thought possible. He grabbed hold of his mother's hands and squeezed them as he pressed his lips to the top of her head. "My thanks, Mama."

"You will ask her?"

He pulled back to look down upon her. "Her father and brother have arrived. I only assume to retrieve her."

"I am sorry, Nicolaus." She wrapped her arms around him as she'd always done when he was a boy. He'd thought he had outgrown her tenderness, but he had missed her greatly during his captivity, had longed for her motherly touch.

"I am not." The ache in his chest expanded. "Not if it will bring Ada some peace about her family. She needs to know her father's heart. Whether or not it is good remains to be seen, but she deserves the truth from him and I would give Ada that choice." His lips twisted. "If she wishes to return home, I would let her go."

"What if she does not wish to go?"

Then he would do all in his power to keep her with him.


Ada splashed the cold water against her heated cheeks. After tossing and turning much of the night, she had finally drifted off to sleep only to dream of Nicolaus. The palm of her hand still burned from his touch, and her pulse continued to race from the images she dreamed last eve. A dream where he'd stolen a kiss out on the balcony beneath the stars.

Fortunately, she'd been asleep and that kiss had not happened.

For the kiss in her dream had been much more than the one they had shared near his grandmother's home.

It was the sort of kiss shared between spouses, which they could never be. Not when she was his slave. She wouldn't be her mother, couldn't, even if she already loved Nicolaus. If only there was a way for her to gain her freedom and to love Nicolaus.

Ada swiped her fingers beneath her eyes. Even if she gained her freedom they could never be together. She would accept nothing outside of marriage, and she'd heard enough times no man would marry her because of her mixed blood. Her mother often taught her to see the blessings over the curses, but Ada could not see the blessing in this. Not when she longed for a family to call her own. A husband and children such as Edith, Galen and the babe.

She waved her hands in front of her face to dry her cheeks, drew in a breath of air and then walked out into the courtyard. He stood with his arms crossed, staring out toward the sea. A breeze blew across the courtyard, ruffling his curls, stealing her breath. The urge to dance curled her toes, yet the tears stinging the back of her eyes held her still. Would she always be standing in the shadows longing to belong? What sort of fate did God intend for a being such as her? Would there never be one to love her as she so longed to love others?

"Shall I call for Galen?"

He glanced out her. Creases formed between his eyebrows.

"You promised him you would show him the ships."

Nicolaus uncrossed his arms. "Ay, that I did. However, I have something of great import I must speak with you about, and I'd prefer not to do it here among listening ears."

Ada's gaze shifted around the courtyard, and she re-called with embarrassment how she'd overheard the ar-gument between Nicolaus and his father. "Of course."

He motioned with his hand for her to come along-side him. They walked along the paved path for sev-eral long minutes in silence. As soon as she heard the gurgling of a creek he halted, parted some foliage and motioned for her to step beneath the canopy of green-ery. "We oft times came here as children. I thought you would like to see it."

Ada took a few steps and then gasped at the beauti-ful scenery. Sunlight danced as the wind breezed over the canopy of leaves. Various flowers with different colored leaves dotted the banks of the small spring. "It is beautiful."

"I thought you would like it."

She turned toward him. "We have a spring flow-ing near our village but very few trees and even fewer flowers. Everything back home is…desolate." Guilt pricked her nape at betraying her home. "Do not mis-take me, even though my home is rugged it is still beautiful. This is—" She held her hands out wide. "Is beyond anything I have ever seen, even more beauti-ful than the islands I saw as we made port."

"It was one of my sister's favorite spots." He paused and then cleared his throat. "I thought it would give us a bit of privacy to speak."

"What is it you would speak, Nicolaus?"

"Come, let us sit." He started to reach for her hand, but she pulled away and rushed to the other side of the creek. She didn't need any more reminders of how much she loved him, especially in the midst of his sister's favorite spot. He needed to search for Desma, and she did not need to feel the jealousy raging in her heart at his feelings for his sibling. And as much as she wished to bring healing to Nicolaus's heart she did not wish her heart to be a sacrifice for his guilt.

She sat on a patch of green ground and ran her fingers along the top of its softness. Nicolaus sat on a rock and plucked a flower from its stem, causing her to blink. How could he destroy such a delicate plant without thought? Much the way he sought to destroy her heart. That was not fair to Nicolaus. He had no knowledge of her feelings for him. He rested his elbows on his knees and tilted his chin to look at her. The soft curls falling across his brow gave him a boyish charm, and she quickly forgave him for tearing the petals from their mooring.

"Ada…" He hesitated, seeming to consider his words. "If you could do anything at this moment, if you had the freedom to choose, what would it be?"

*To love you.*

She felt her eyes grow wide at the words clinging to her tongue. It was a confession she could never speak. She bowed her head and stared at the grass, the earthy scent as foreign to her as the sea had been, yet she had grown to love the sea, long for it, even. If her heart did not ache at the sight of him she would stay with his mother where she was treated better than a daughter in her father's household. And if Jasen did not look just like Nicolaus she would choose to be his slave, but the daily reminder of a love she could never have would be torment.

"To go home." She didn't lie exactly. If she couldn't spend her days with him as his wife, she would not be able to serve in his mother's household. She could only wish for home.

His gaze warmed her and she brought her head up to look him in the eye. For a moment, she thought she witnessed the pain in her heart in his eyes, but it could not be for her. Could it? No, perhaps it was only this place that reminded him of the sister he'd lost that caused such an emotion.

He flicked the flower into the water; the petals swirled around and then glided away. Standing, he crossed his arms over his chest, his gaze focused somewhere in the distance. If they had not been sheltered by the trees she would have thought he gazed upon the waters he loved. Nicolaus twisted his lips and then cleared his throat. "It is not my nature to purchase humans, Ada."

Hardness etched his tone. She stood and crossed over the water. Her hand hovered over his forearm before she dropped it to her side. "Nicolaus, I do not blame you for my plight."

He dropped his gaze to hers. The blackness of his eyes swirled like the storm they encountered when at sea.

"I thank you for rescuing me from a fate much worse than this."

One corner of his mouth curved upward as he ran his fingers over the top of her ear, tucking a piece of hair back. He wrapped his arms around her and pulled her close. Her ear nestled against his heartbeat. Every bit of her being oozed like warm honey, yet her muscles screamed to run far from him. How could she finally feel as if she belonged? Belonged with him, only to know in her mind that she did not?

The warmth of his mouth pressed against the top of her head as his hand smoothed down her back. "I would keep you with me always if I could."

She stiffened. There were too many things keeping them apart. As long as she was his slave, she could never freely love him. The scars on her mother's heart had encompassed Ada's, as well. Even if she was not his slave, he could never marry a woman who was not Greek, just as her father could never marry a woman who was not a Philistine. Just as no man would ever be free to marry her because she was neither Hebrew nor Philistine. As if those barriers were not enough, she would not keep him from searching for his sister. Desma was too important to him and to his family.

She stepped from the comfort of his arms and turned from him. Her gaze caught site of the ships bobbing in the port through a break in the trees. "I would not have you keep me to appease your guilt, Nicolaus."

"That is not—"

She held up her hand. "I overheard you speaking with your father, and I know why you purchased me. And it does not matter. What does matter is that you now have a dilemma. Your conscience will not allow you to remain my master." She turned toward him and smiled. "Truth be told, although my captivity has not been oppressive, I do not wish to be any man's slave."

Especially to one she loved.

He clenched his teeth and a muscle at the corner of his jaw ticked. "If you were to return home you risk your sisters selling you once again."

"You speak a great truth." She sighed. "Nicolaus,

you would know your sister is alive and well just as I would know if my father wished such a fate upon me."

"If he does?"

She squeezed her eyes shut, and then opened them. "Then I would have been better off here as your slave."

He growled. "Not once have I treated you as such."

"No, you have not, but the fact remains that is what I am." She shrugged her shoulders. "I understand that as a woman I have little to nothing to say. As a daughter I am ruled by my father. If I were to marry I would be ruled by my husband, as a slave I am ruled by you. My worth is not dependent on how I care for your household. It is dependent on the price you paid for me."

"Then I would set you free."

Ada blinked up at him. He couldn't discern what she was feeling. At first he thought she'd been pleased, and then he saw a hint of sadness before she veiled her eyes from him. She bowed her head. "My thanks, Nicolaus." Turning from him, she wrapped her arms around her midsection. The tension in her muscles returned and her shoulders stiffened. She seemed to place a barrier between them. It was as if she'd donned a man's armor. "How will I repay you for the coin you have lost?"

Her words were no more than a whisper above the rustling leaves and the water flowing down the mountain. She should be celebrating her freedom. He raked his hand through his hair. He should feel the peace he'd hoped to obtain by granting her freedom. However, a sense of loss bore down upon his shoulders. "It is a gift, Ada."

Her spine straightened a little more, but she did not say another word. He never should have mentioned her freedom until after he'd spoken with her father. What if the man wanted nothing to do with her, leaving Ada without the protection she needed to keep her from another master? What if her father only desired more money?

He would have gladly given it, but now, because of his rash speech, she was free to do as she wished. Free to stay, free to go. If only the guilt plaguing him over his part in her captivity had not been so great, especially in the face of her confession…she needed to know she was worth more than the price he'd paid for her, more than all the riches contained on this island. Worthy of a thousand men's hearts. Worthy of his. If only he was worthy of hers. "I would escort you back to my mother."

"Nicolaus." His name whispered from her lips. The longing in her voice tied his stomach into a large knot. He waited for her to say more, to tell him she did not wish for freedom but to remain with him.

He neared her and placed his palms upon her shoulders. The scent of lavender water combined with the heady fragrance of the flowers surrounding them left him feeling light-headed A feeling he hadn't known since before his own captivity. He leaned closer and inhaled. The tip of her ear called to his lips. "Ada, I would keep you with me. I would grant you the protection of my name. Tell me that is what you wish and I'll make it happen."

How, he did not know. At least, not until he spoke with her father. But one thing was for certain, he'd move mountains to marry her, if only she would grant him permission. She tilted her head as if she would look at him. Her hair, piled around her head, danced at her shoulders. He could not see her eyes or even the soft curve of her cheek. He gave in to the desire to press his lips to the flesh peeking through her hair. "Ada."

Pulling from him, she shook her head. "I cannot, Nicolaus." She turned toward him. Tears shimmered in her eyes. It was like a blade to the gut. Their time together neared its end. He saw it in the way her eyes pleaded with him. "I cannot."

She hugged her arms tighter around her waist and bowed her head.

"Come, I will take you back to the house."

"No," she said, shaking her head. "I would stay here a moment."

"Although this is my home, it is not safe for you to be alone." His tone was sharper than he intended, but he would not see her harmed in any way. Or stolen from him before he had to let her go.

"I understand your concern." Her gaze rose to his. "I am now free to do as I please, am I not? Or have you decided to go back on your word?"

He clenched his teeth, nodded and then swiveled on his heel. He shoved the branches aside and stepped out onto the path. He should count his blessings that Ada had the wits about her to know she could not stay with him. She drove his emotions to confusion. He shook his head. If she stayed with him he'd no doubt lose all his teeth from gnashing them together.

He was tempted to return to the storehouse and leave her truly alone. However, the port was active and he would not wish Ada to wander toward the ships where an unsavory fellow could happen upon Ada, or any man for that matter. One look upon her beauty and even the most good-hearted and compassionate of men could lose their heads.

Plopping down onto the pathway, Nicolaus plucked a blade of grass from between the stones and twirled it between his fingers. An image of Ada's tears forced its way into his thoughts. He'd seen the longing in her eyes. Had that longing been only for her freedom? Then why did she look pained at the mention of their parting, of her returning home?

He dropped the blade of grass and rested his elbows against his knees. Why did he not tell her of his love for her and his wish to marry her? Because she needed the freedom to choose her own will, and he needed to know that choice was made without the binding of his words.

Voices mumbled from the twist of the path, and Nicolaus rose. Crossing his arms over his chest, he waited for the men to round the bend. When they did, he wasn't surprised. However, it seemed as if they were.

The men halted their steps. Both were large and imposing. The younger, who seemed to be a few summers shy of Nicolaus's age, clasped his finger around the hilt of his dagger and allowed his gaze to travel over Nicolaus.

Nicolaus twisted his lips at the young man's daring. "What business do you have here?"

He didn't need to ask. He knew who they were as they had the same color eyes as Ada, and their language was that of hers.

The older man nodded his graying beard. "I am

Manus of Ashkelon and this is my son Asher." He held his hand out in front of the younger man. "We are in search for Nicolaus, son of Gavros."

Nicolaus narrowed his eyes. "You have found him."

# Chapter Twenty-Two

Ada tilted her head and listened to the familiar voices from the path. The prayer she'd lifted to God only moments ago had been a request for an answer. She loved Nicolaus, there was no doubt in her mind as to that fact, but she would not see him choose between her and searching for his sister. She would do all that she could, even speak with Nicolaus's father, so he could search for her.

Her heart had rent in two when he'd pleaded with her to stay. Although she knew she couldn't, she also knew she had no other place to go. Not until now. She tiptoed toward the edge and peeked through the shelter of the branches. She blinked, uncertain if her eyes deceived her. Her father, who was almost as tall as Nicolaus, stood next to her brother Asher, who was just as tall. Their cheeks bore the brunt of days in the sun. Asher's cheeks and chin, which he normally kept smooth, were now sprinkled with the beginnings of a beard. The change surprised her. He no longer looked like a youth but a grown man.

Her father looked as if he'd aged since she'd last

seen him. No longer did he look the giant she always believed him to be. Perhaps it was the wrinkles lining his face or the way his shoulders slumped or even the walking stick he leaned heavily upon. How had her father come to be here so far from home? She parted the foliage and stepped out onto the path. Her gaze darted to Nicolaus. A muscle ticked beneath his beard. She turned toward her father. "Father, Asher."

The corner of her father's left eye twitched as he straightened his spine A certain sign he was irritated and on the verge of rage. Asher's cheeks turned crimson. Wishing she would have stayed hidden, she began to take a step back, but Nicolaus grabbed her arm and thrust her behind him. She fought the urge to kick him in the leg at his arrogance. Why did he always feel the need to move her around as if she were a crate of merchandise? She pressed her fingers against Nicolaus's side for balance and peered around him to garner her father's reaction.

The sharp contours of her father's nose became more prominent when he narrowed his eyes farther. His staying hand on Asher's arm was the only proof he remained reasonable. "I see the rumors about you and my daughter hold some truth."

The muscles beneath her fingers quivered in controlled anger. She moved to stand beside him but stopped when a rumble vibrated through him.

"Of what rumors do you speak?"

"Your treatment of my sister." Asher's gaze flicked to hers. "And she allows it."

"I—"

"Ada." His low command halted any further words from her but it did not halt her movement. "As far as I am concerned she is my slave. My treatment of her is of no consequence, especially since your own daughters sold her into slavery."

Her father flinched, and her brother paled. She gave in to her urge and stomped on the top of his foot. "You granted me my freedom."

His nostrils flared. "Not yet, my love. If you recall, I offered but I have yet to grant your freedom."

Ada gasped at his words.

Asher nudged their father. "You see."

"Yes, it is a mystery to be solved." Her father smiled, and then took in Nicolaus.

"I believe there are matters we must discuss between us." Nicolaus shifted his weight. He did not want to take these men to his father's house, yet he did not feel comfortable with Ada walking home, even if the distance was short. What choice did he have? Although he'd sought out his daughter, Nicolaus did not trust her father, nor her brother. "Ada, you can find your way to the house?"

She blinked, her gaze moving from Nicolaus to her father. She was more confused than she had been moments before. "Yes, of course."

"Then I will take these men to the storehouse where we can have our discussion."

Her father shook his head. "That will not be necessary, my son. I will not leave my daughter alone to your care, and I have need to speak with your father."

Nicolaus's body seemed to expand. "Very well," he said as he grabbed hold of her hand and stepped aside to allow her father and Asher to go before them.

"His home, where Ada has been staying, is at the end of this path," Asher informed her father.

"This I know." Her father took a step forward. Ada laid her fingers against the fabric of his tunic on his forearm. He glanced at her and she immediately bowed her head. "What is it, daughter?"

She swallowed the knot in her throat and risked a glance at him. "Why is it you have come?"

"To see that my daughter is well. After I heard what your sisters had done…I could not believe my own ears. You may be assured they are receiving a just punishment. One fitting their crimes." Ada shivered as her father sighed and then smiled. "I am overjoyed to see you are better than I could have hoped for."

She drew her brows together and wondered what it was that he meant. Certainly he did not wish any of his children to endure slavery. Although she had to admit she could have obtained a worse master than Nicolaus. One much more like her father had been. And why he seemed pleased with himself she could not fathom. Had she ever seen him truly smile, like he did now?

"I do not understand." She wrapped her fingers around her father's arm, so thin beneath his tunic, and then looked to Asher for answers, but his angry gaze was focused on Nicolaus. They would be fortunate if these two did not draw their weapons. She did not wish for Asher, the only champion she had among her siblings, to be harmed by the hands of the man she'd given her heart to.

"Do not worry yourself, Ada. All these troubles will, no doubt, be resolved shortly." The warmth of his palm covered the back of her hand. "You'll soon be a bride."

Ada jerked away from her father. "What? No, I cannot marry."

* * *

Ada paced the bedchamber. She did not appreciate the fact that she'd been barred from the conversation, especially considering it concerned her. She sat on the cushioned mat and pulled her knees into her chest. Such was the lot of women. At least she held confidence that Nicolaus would defend her in any manner he could. She just wished she could be sure he and Asher would not destroy each other. How would she ever face Nicolaus if he brought harm to her brother or Asher if he harmed Nicolaus?

She sighed. If only she understood what Nicolaus meant by his endearment. Did he, in truth, love her, or were his words nothing more than…words? Would she be able to leave him if his heart belonged to her? Would her father allow her a choice? What of Nicolaus's sister?

"Ada," Chloe said as she walked into the room, the babe nestled against her chest. "Have you seen Galen?"

Ada shook her head. "I've only just returned. When is the last time you saw him?"

Color rose high in Chloe's cheeks. "I cannot be certain. He and the babe were asleep when I took Edith down to bathe and break her fast. When I returned Galen was gone." Tears formed in the nursemaid's eyes. "I've looked everywhere as have a few of the servants. He is not to be found. I would inform Nicolaus, but he is in the *andron* with his father and brothers."

As well as with her father and brother. She rose from the mat and ran her hands over the fabric of her chiton. "No bother, Chloe. I believe I know where Galen has taken off to. I will find him and bring him back posthaste."

Searching for the boy would keep her mind from wandering to the men below and the fate they would ultimately decide for her.

"My thanks, Ada. I have been beside myself with worry."

"As would I if I did not know this young man's curiosity." Ada offered the nursemaid a hug. "Now, if I do not return before the men are done with their discussions please inform Nicolaus I went to search the port for Galen."

Chloe gasped and grabbed hold of her hand. "You cannot go down there, Ada. It is too dangerous."

Ada nodded. "So it is and even more so for a curious little boy."

Nicolaus ran his hand over his beard. He opted to lean against the wall and stare out the window overlooking the bay. Asher, Ada's arrogant brother, took up a spot near the door leading to the courtyard as if to keep Nicolaus locked in his father's home. He'd been glad when Jasen and Brison had arrived, perhaps, smug even. He could not help the way the corner of his mouth lifted at the tipping of the scales. If this young man chose to challenge him, his brothers would no doubt stand beside him.

Ada's father lounged on one of the padded couches and plopped a grape into his mouth. He was like a dog with a meaty bone. Problem was Nicolaus could not figure out why. Did he think forcing Nicolaus to marry his daughter such an onerous task for him? "Pfft."

He crossed his arms over his chest and expanded his muscles. If that was his thinking, he was wrong. Nicolaus would like nothing more than to spend the rest of his life in Ada's company. He just wasn't going to let Manus know that.

Jasen finished his game of knuckles with Brison and strode toward him. "What is the matter with you, Nicolaus? Father will not be too happy with the way you treat his guests."

The corner of his eye twitched. "Hah, guests. More like thieves."

Jasen shook his head. "I do not understand."

"The elder," Nicolaus said, motioning his head toward the man, "is Manus of Ashkelon. Ada's father."

Jasen laughed. "The glowering giant guarding the doorway must be her brother."

"I find nothing humorous." Nicolaus shoved his fingers through his hair and pushed from the wall. "What is taking Father so long?"

"Hmm." Jasen tapped his chin. "Believe it or not, Mother said he was praying."

A breath of air whooshed from Nicolaus's chest. "As should I be."

His brother clamped him on the shoulder. "Then do so. I'll keep the giant from bothering you."

Before his brother made it across the room, their father entered. "Manus, my old friend!"

Nicolaus froze and then glanced at Jasen, who seemed as surprised as he was. How did his father and Ada's know each other?

Ada's father rose from the reclining couch and clasped his father in a quick embrace. "Gavros, it is good to see you. However, I do wish it were under different circumstances."

His father's gaze shifted to Nicolaus, and then back

to Manus. "Yes, yes, of course. However, I can assure you my son's intentions were of good nature."

Manus returned to the reclining couch and took a sip of water from his goblet. "I have no doubt they were." His gaze shifted to Nicolaus. "I wish to thank you for rescuing my daughter from Ashkelon's darkness."

"I would do it all over again."

"Of course. I did not realize the discord between my daughters. They have been punished for their part in Ada's captivity. Harsh as it may seem, we received a fair price for them at Delos, all but my oldest, Dina, who will remain a slave in my household."

The contents of Nicolaus's stomach revolted in disgust. "A harsh punishment I would not wish on my worst enemies."

"You may be assured they will consider their actions. Besides, I do not intend to leave them there. Once I am finished here I will return to Delos and retrieve my daughters. Now, I was prepared to offer thrice the price you paid for my daughter as I have a neighbor willing to pay that much for her hand in marriage."

Nicolaus clenched his hands at his sides. Heat rose into his cheeks.

Manus fused his gaze to Nicolaus's. "It is much more than I could have expected given she is the daughter of a Hebrew slave."

His heart lurched into his chest at the implications. He now understood why Ada fought against the affection between them. Had her mother loved Ada's father during her captivity?

"However, I fear rumors of my daughter being slung

over a man's shoulder and carried onto a boat have ruined her reputation, one I did all in my power to guard throughout the years." He plucked a grape from the bowl. "If that were not enough, I hear rumors of how you carried her off your boat and into port, and then proceeded to reprimand your men for daring to look at my daughter."

He recalled well the moment when he swept her into his arms and carried her from his vessel. Nothing could have prepared him for the way his heart had lurched at the comfort of holding her close, not even that small kiss they'd shared.

"I do not know about you, Gavros." Manus looked to his father. "But I have never treated my slaves with such grace. If they refused my orders they were beaten, especially if they were as disobedient as my daughter."

Nicolaus stiffened. Ada would never survive the beatings he'd received while in captivity.

"You must forgive my son. He was kidnapped and forced into slavery. It is fortunate his brother found him and paid a ransom for him. He bears the scars of brutality and would not treat another as such."

"Gavros, we are old friends, are we not? We sailed together, traded together and went our separate ways. You made your riches and I mine. We helped make the world as it is."

Thorns pricked Nicolaus's neck. He did not like the tension in the air, and the way his brothers stood at attention showed they did not, either. "What is it you ask, Manus of Ashkelon?"

"Direct, much like your father, Nicolaus, son of Gavros."

"I have no tolerance for games just as I have no stomach for beating obstinate slaves."

Manus laughed. "You know my daughter well." He took a sip from his goblet. "And I find you hidden away with her in the trees."

His nails bit into his palms. "Forgive me, sir, but as my slave, I can do as I wish, and I did. However, as beautiful as your daughter is and as much as I desire to take your daughter as my wife, I respected her virtue." He would not tell him about the stolen kiss. Not when he knew Ada wished to go home.

Manus rose and glided toward him until there was little space between them. The air in the *andron* thickened. "I know the look in your eyes. It is the look of a man in love. My daughters' beauty has been known to weaken even the strongest of men, especially Ada. I've seen men go mad over a glimpse of her. It is why I pushed her away. I have done all I could to keep the dogs from stealing her from my house. Even telling her no man would want her because of her mixed blood. Of course, her mixed blood did little to keep my neighbors from offering. However, it kept her from encouraging them."

Manus tucked his hands into the sleeves of his tunic and paced the room.

"What is it you wish from me?"

"I would see you marry my daughter. However, given her protest, I would seek her wishes."

"I have already done so." Nicolaus swallowed. As much as he disliked her marrying a neighbor, he would not keep her bound to him when she had no desire to. "She confided that she wished to return home."

Manus tilted his head and started to speak but Jasen interrupted. "Did you tell her you love her?"

Before he could answer, he spied Chloe hovering outside the door in the courtyard. Her face was pale and she worried her fingers together. "Excuse me," he said as he slipped past Asher. The man's looming presence followed him. "What is it, Chloe? Has the babe taken ill?"

She bowed, and then shook her head as tears streamed down her cheeks. "No, it is Ada. She went to search for Galen at the port and has yet to return."

Asher rushed back into the *andron*. Nicolaus squeezed her shoulders. "How long ago did she leave?" Chloe hiccupped on a quiet sob. "Chloe?"

"Shortly after you returned from your walk."

"What has happened?" Manus and his father said at the same time.

"It seems Ada went in search of Galen, a young orphan boy," he added for Manus and Asher. He tilted his head toward the sky. "She's been gone near an hour. Too long for my liking."

Manus nodded his head. "Shall we search for your bride?"

Nicolaus liked the sound of the words, but his heart refused to accept them just yet. When he found her, he would declare his love for her and once again give her the choice of staying with him or returning home with her father.

He took off running down the path.

Perhaps, she'd become lost, or even angry over being sent away while they discussed her future and had decided to find a quiet place to think. Ada may be obstinate, but she was not one to hide during trials. She'd proven that when she cared for the injured on his boat in the midst of her seasickness. Something told him she was in trouble.

He only prayed she'd not been taken out to sea by a band of thieves.

# Chapter Twenty-Three

Ada kicked at her abductor's shin, but he yanked her back by her hair and tossed her to the planks. She clamped her hand to her head to halt the throbbing as she scooted against the side of the boat. Galen glared at the man who'd caused her harm. She pulled the boy down beside her and wrapped her arms around him. "We should not anger him further."

The sailors busied about the deck, heeding the commands of their captain. Ada arched her neck and tried to look over the edge. Sighing, she sank down. Her insides quaked in fear, a fear she'd never known in the presence of Nicolaus, not even when he'd carried her on board his vessel. The captain's shadow loomed over them and she glanced at him. A soiled cloth covered half his face, leaving one eye unsheltered. Fresh wounds, barely scabbed over, marred his forearms.

"You'll fetch a nice coin."

She scowled. "I already have a master." Perhaps that bit of knowledge would cause the captain to release her and Galen.

He threw his head back and laughed. "I would challenge him for the rights to you, unless of course he does not care. What sort of master would allow a prize such as you to roam the port unattended?"

Heat rose in her cheeks. Nicolaus had warned her of the dangers, and yet because she did not heed them she was captured by an unsavory sailor. "Nicolaus, son of Gavros."

His laughter died. Ada glanced up. The man's eyes narrowed. "Brother of Jasen?"

She furrowed her brows and then nodded. The captain rested his chin against his fist and smiled as if he'd found a bag of silver. "He'll pay a heavy ransom for you, especially after what he did to me"

Ada shook her head. Nicolaus had already spent a king's ransom to rescue her from Ashkelon's slave trader. She would not ask it of him, not when he needed coin to search for his sister. Her only hope was her father. She shivered. Rarely had her father parted with his riches and she doubted he'd do so now.

The captain snapped his fingers and motioned for the man who'd taken her to approach. "Do you know who this woman belongs to?"

The sailor tilted his head while he looked her over. "No, Captain."

The captain burst into laughter. "You've done well, Joseph." He glanced at Ada, his eyes narrowing to slits. "I'd come to speak with your master about some unfinished business between us. However, I had little hopes of success. With you in my hands, I do believe I may have a chance." He crossed his arms over his chest and turned toward Joseph. "Inform the crew we leave now."

"Captain, what of the men who remain on shore?"

The captain swung his arm out and grabbed hold of his man's tunic. "Do you wish to face the wrath of Nicolaus in his own port, surrounded by his men? If you recall, the last we saw him he was none too happy with us. Just look at my face. He even threatened to hang us by our toes for all the vultures to feast upon, and now we have something which belongs to him."

The man paled several shades and his eyes bulged as he glanced at Ada. The knot below his chin bobbed. "He'll kill us."

"Ay, if we do not leave now. If I lose my head because of your lack of haste, I will order yours to be lost, as well."

Ada's eyes grew wide. The blood drained further from the sailor's face, and he looked to be ill. The captain spoke of Nicolaus as if he feared him. The captain knelt in front of her. She leaned away from his foul odor. "Did my man cause you harm?"

She shook her head as Galen spoke, his childlike voice carried over the planks. "The captain will kill that man for pulling Ada's hair."

Ada clamped her hand over the child's mouth. "Do not provoke him, Galen."

The captain ruffled Galen's hair and then laughed as he rose. "I have no doubt that he will, boy. No doubt he's killed greater men for lesser offenses."

She sucked in a sharp breath. The Nicolaus she knew and loved could not be the fearsome man this sailor spoke of, could he? The man she knew was gentle and kind. Compassionate. Although she'd seen hints of his temper, he had never raised a hand to her. It was hard to fathom he'd cause harm to this man, unless he done something like take Nicolaus's sister.

If the captain feared Nicolaus then why were they leaving port? Why not return her and Galen? Perhaps this captain intended to lure Nicolaus and cause him harm for the threats he'd made to the captain. Tears pricked the backs of her eyes.

Ada reached deep into her soul for courage. "It would serve you well to release us before you leave."

Reaching down, he gripped her chin, forcing her to look into his soulless eyes. His calloused fingers squeezed, bruising her flesh. "Your master has something that belongs to me, and I would retrieve it. Besides, I would not miss another chance to capture the deadliest captain of the Great Sea, not after what he's done to me."

Ada sucked in a sharp breath, the salty air stinging her lungs. Had this man caused the scars slashing Nicolaus's back? The man straightened once again. "He cost me a lot of coin and my pride when he freed my slaves, tormented me and stole my map."

Ada recalled the small piece of leather with pictures drawn on it, but knew if Nicolaus had taken the map it was for a good reason. "You stole him, did you not?"

"Ay," he said as he grinned. "My men did. Right from his ship. Stole his sister, too. I could not pass the chance to humble the great Sea Dragon. After years of service with Nicolaus I never thought a woman would be his ruin, not even his sister."

Ada pressed her palms against the planks and stood. She laid her palm on his arm. "You know where Desma is?"

His upper lip curled. The corner of his eye twitched as he glanced at her palm against his arm. He jerked back a step. "No."

"You stole her, and you do not know where she is?"

His gaze roamed over her, from head to toe and back again until he stared into her eyes. "Ay, I stole her. That does not mean I kept her."

Ada shivered. Her hope at finding Desma plummeted to the bottom of the sea. Queasiness rocked her back on her heels. What sort of fate had this man sentenced Nicolaus's sister to? The same Nicolaus had rescued her from? "What kind of a monster steals a man's sister and sells her into slavery?"

"I am no different than Nicolaus, son of Gavros."

"No greater falsehood has been told." Her heart told her that truth about Nicolaus, even if the fear in their eyes when speaking of him lent to an unsavory past. He was no longer that man. She caught sight of Nicolaus approaching the wharf. Even from this distance she could tell it was him. Knew by the hardness of his jaw. He squeezed past men carrying crates and then stopped to speak with several young boys.

"I've no time to convince you otherwise." The captain gave her a slight shove, forcing her to stumble before she landed on her backside. "Watch her," he said to Joseph, and then he walked away.

She stood back up and shifted her gaze around in search of Nicolaus.

"What are you doing?" Joseph grabbed hold of her upper arm. "Where did the child go?"

Ada swiveled around. The child no longer sat at her feet. Had he fallen into the water?

"Galen?" She pulled from her captor and rushed toward the side of the boat. Wrapping her fingers over the rail, she climbed onto a wooden crate and looked down, and then to the right leading out to the sea before looking toward the shore. The men hastening along the wharf were many. How was she to find a child? "Galen!"

A man walking toward the shore snapped his head around. *Nicolaus.* She inhaled a sharp breath. A mixture of emotions flitted over his face as he squeezed between several men carrying merchandise away from the boats. Her pulse stuttered to a halt, and she shook her head. He couldn't board this vessel, not alone. "Nicolaus, no! No!"

Joseph yanked her away from the side. "You are going to get us killed."

At the moment she didn't care, she would do anything for Nicolaus to not suffer the abuse he had at the hands of the man who now held her captive. The captain called out a command and the boat lurched, causing Ada to stumble. She fell to the planks. The boat lurched again and again as a shipman released the rope keeping it moored. She climbed to her feet. Her gaze flew to the wharf, seeking Nicolaus. She breathed a sigh of relief even as her heart sank. His arms were held by Jasen and her brother Asher. But where was Galen?

Dropping to the planks, she buried her face into her hands and shuddered. Nicolaus had asked her what choice she'd have, and if she could go back she'd tell him the truth. She'd tell him that if she could have anything her blood would be pure; Greek even. She'd tell him if there were no bounds keeping them apart she would wish to become his bride and to love him for all of her days.

Now it was too late. She choked back a sob and lifted her face to the sky. Perhaps, she should thank

God for taking the decision from her, for she would not have to endure all that her mother had, loving her master. Nor would she have to endure her sisters' abuse.

The captain's voice boomed over the rolling of the sea. The vessel rose and dipped as it fought against each wave. Once again Ada's stomach churned. Once again she was left wondering about her future. However, although she should be, she wasn't angry. At least Nicolaus was safe from this man. Yet she was disheartened that she'd never again face the man she had come to love.

Nicolaus struggled against his brother's hold as the boat rowed away. He didn't need to see the name on the vessel or the distinct red eye at the front of the bow. The wicked grin on the captain's face was enough. If David didn't have Ada in his possession, Nicolaus might have even taken pleasure at the sight of the bandage covering part of his face. Every scar marring his body burned. It was as if he was once again being flayed. He should have killed David when he had the chance. The Sea Dragon would have done so and more. Nicolaus pulled his arm from Asher's grip and then glared at his brother. "You should have let me go."

Jasen's hand came to settle on his shoulder, but Nicolaus pushed him away. Shaking his head, his brother drew in a breath and crossed his arms over his chest. "I will not allow you to sacrifice yourself."

*Sacrifice!*

"You would not understand. Having her by my side makes me a better man. It's as if the sun shines all hours of the day. Even when she is contrary." Fifty oars cut through the waves pushing ashore. Once David reached the open sea, there would be nothing to stop his former tormentor from escaping. "You have no idea what he will do to her, especially if he knows she belongs to me." Belonged to his heart.

He raked his fingers through his hair and darted his gaze toward Asher, pleading with him for understanding, but his eyes remained blank. Did Ada's brother have no care for her?

"I know what he did to you, and I'd not have him do it again."

"I have seen David's treatment of his female slaves. Trust me when I tell you, what he did to me is nothing compared to what he will do to her." Especially after what Nicolaus had done to David.

A hand came down on his shoulder. The touch shocking considering it did not belong to his brother but to Ada's. "I would like nothing more than to swim after them. However, wisdom tells me that even if I were to come close to their vessel I would not live long. Nor would you, my friend. His archers would not allow it."

"Asher is correct, Nicolaus. We know where David ports. I know of his home. We must devise a plan."

Every muscle in his body tensed. A plan would take time, time he did not have if he was to rescue her before David discovered Ada belonged to him. If he had not already.

"Ay, we will retrieve your bride, Nicolaus." Asher removed his hand from Nicolaus's shoulder. The way his voice quavered did not leave Nicolaus confident.

The air filling his lungs halted at the knot in his throat. Many times he'd felt alone, had done things alone. Survived alone, fought alone. Failed alone. Although he still did not trust his brother at the moment because of his association with David, he loved Jasen and had no doubts of his loyalty. But could he trust Jasen to help rescue Ada? Especially since his brother had hired David to take Desma. The fact that Nicolaus had been taken, too, had only been a consequence of his brother's action. One Nicolaus would not change given Desma was far from Knosis.

"I do not think David will deny my request for Ada. Although, it may cost some silver, he never has before." Jasen said.

Nicolaus stared at the boat as it shrank in the distance. "I fear it will cost much more than a few silver coins."

"What are you not saying, Nicolaus?" Jasen asked.

"I was not the only one who escaped his captivity." The longer he stood here staring at the vessel carrying his heart away the longer it would take for him to prepare his men and make chase. He turned to walk away. They'd need their fastest rowers. He thanked the Lord both his and Jasen's men were ashore.

"What madness is it you speak, Nicolaus? I was there. My memory recalls you being tied and beaten to near death. I did not ransom another soul that day."

"No, you did not." Waves lapped against the wharf, bathing his feet with their salty spray. He drew in a breath as the scars marring his body ached, reminding him of their existence. "Why do you think I was beaten with such harshness? Because I had tried to free others from David's cruelty."

He would not hang his head in shame, not even with his brother's eyes watching his departing back in disbelief. Nicolaus had broken a code, a code among merchants. A man did not interfere with another man's slaves. However, in his defense, he had not been acting a merchant, but a slave. And slaves did what they could to survive, especially under the treatment of cruel masters such as David. What would his brother think once he knew helping several of David's slaves escape was the least of his transgressions? "Besides, dear brother, I returned right after Father issued his challenge. And as you will soon see, David did not fare well."

Nicolaus's shoulders slumped at the memory. He had vowed to never torment another man as long as he had breath in his body, but the sight of David reclining on his couch as a female slave fed him figs and another fanned him with palms had filled him with irritation. The sight of women chained in his *andron* had filled him with rage. At the time, he'd no doubt in his mind that Desma was in David's possession. He had not wanted to consider how David might use her. It was not until later, after the sun had long slipped beyond the horizon, that Nicolaus had returned and demanded Desma's whereabouts. How was he to have known that David did not know? And for some reason David did not speak of Jasen's deed. "What did you do?" Jasen asked.

Nicolaus ignored the accusation in his brother's tone and walked toward one of his father's fastest vessels, one that would be well armed in minutes. If his brother had told him the truth after he'd paid the ransom, Nicolaus would not have entered David's house in the dead of night and tormented him.

"Nicolaus, what did you do?"

"Captain! Captain!"

Nicolaus spun around to find Galen pushing through the sailors. "They've taken her."

Nicolaus swept the dripping wet child into his arms. The boy gasped for breaths. "They took Ada. I didn't mean to be stolen. I only wanted to find you so we could go to the beacon like you said. But they took her, took her like they took my mother."

The child's eyes brimmed with tears, and Nicolaus could not help but feel the anguish this child felt. He wrapped his arms around the boy and hugged him tight. "It is no fault of yours, Galen."

"We have to save her. We have to, Captain."

Nicolaus set the boy on his feet and crouched in front of him. This child was too young to feel the weight of his burdens, burdens not of his own making. "I must ask that you stay here and keep watch over your sister and your brother. I will rescue Ada and return her to you even if it is the last thing I do."

## Chapter Twenty-Four

Ada loosened her grip from the edge of the wooden bench and lifted her face to the sun. The illness that plagued her with the motion of the sea had lessened now that the mountains of Nicolaus's home had become nothing more than a speck of dust on the horizon. The seas seemed to smooth the farther they moved from shore, bringing with them a calmer stomach. However, each jolt of the boat as the rowers cut their oars through the waters deepened the ache within her breast. How would she survive the pain?

Was this how her mother felt each time her father seemingly rejected her? Was this why she gave up her life to death so easily, because the pain of loving another was too great? No, loving Nicolaus was no hardship. It was the losing of Nicolaus that threatened to destroy her. Even if he never truly belonged to her, but her to him. A slave.

"Why the tears?"

Ada swiped the wetness from her cheek and glanced at the figure standing in front of her. She twisted her lips before lifting one corner. "I am uncertain."

In that, she spoke the truth.

He glanced toward the direction of Nicolaus's home. Lines creased around his eyes as he squinted. "If you worry as to whether or not you will see your love again, do not. He is a man who retrieves what belongs to him, and when he does I'll be waiting for him."

"Have you not caused Nicolaus enough pain?"

He threw his head back. His shout of laughter rumbled like the waves carrying the vessel. He crouched before her and looked her hard in the eye as his fingers bit into her arms. Ada held her breath, refusing to allow her fear to rake across her skin. "What is it you know of pain? Your body has not known the abuse of a whip, nor the sting of a blade. I have known the pierce of a dagger. His dagger. He not only caused these cuts on my arms, and the damage to my eye, but he is responsible for these, as well."

He pulled his hand away from her and removed the clasp holding the pieces of his tunic together. The fabric fell to his waist revealing several thick scars on his chest. The injuries were not as bad as the ones she'd seen on Nicolaus, but it was obvious the marks were intended to cause the captain much suffering when inflicted. "Your master, the man you care for, is no different than I. Perhaps, he is even worse, as I have never stolen into a man's home and attacked him while he slept."

Ada gasped at the captain's insinuation.

"Come," he said as he reached for her hand. "I have something I wish to show you."

Pulling her hand from his, she stood on her own. The corner of his mouth lifted. "I see why Nicolaus likes you. Your temperament is wild." Before she could deny the captain's observations, he held up his hand. "Tales of your master's behavior have surfaced all over the Great Sea. It has left many to wonder at his change. Not I, though. I'd no doubt it was a woman, especially when I had heard he allowed Knosis to board his vessel without raising arms."

He motioned her toward the back of his boat where the helmsman sat.

"From what I was told, the man had three heavily armed ships." Ada stepped past him.

The captain laughed. "You do not know your master well. I doubt twenty ships would have kept Nicolaus from fighting to keep any man from boarding his ship after I caught him unaware and captured his vessel. Desma was entrusted into his care for a reason. Nicolaus is honorable and would see the deed done, but no man would dare board one of the Sea Dragon's ships, not without fear of losing his life."

"You dared."

He halted before the ladder leading up to the helmsman's platform and looked down upon her. "Ay, I will tell you, Ada, I knew exactly how many men were aboard his vessel, and how many armed men he had. I knew he'd cut straight across the sea to avoid thieves. Most important, I was paid well and hired many mercenaries. Most of whom sailed and fought for the adventure of saying they felled the Dragon. Ten ships I had that day. All heavily armed with archers. He did not have a chance."

She furrowed her brows. "Who paid you?"

"That is a question not mine to answer." He placed his hand on a rung and climbed to the platform. He stood above her, his hand resting on the rail. "Come, you'll wish to see this."

Ada climbed the ladder and pressed against the railing to keep from touching the captain. Although the helmsman's perch was much larger than Nicolaus's commander's post it was still small and the close proximity made her uneasy. She would have defied him and remained where she sat but she dare not test his patience as she had Nicolaus's. "What is it you wish me to see?"

An endless sea of blue spread out before her in all directions, broken by islands jutting toward the sky.

"There." The captain pointed.

Everything quieted around her, even the whisper of waves pressing against the wooden boat. The birds perching on the rail stilled their chatter. Her pulse halted as her breath held. "What is it?"

She knew. Even though she could not discern what the dark spot was, her heart knew.

"I've no doubt it is your master come to retrieve what belongs to him."

A white bird hovered in air above the railing, squealing as it struggled against the breeze. Her eyes watered. Nicolaus was coming for her, even after he'd promised to set her free. Or was it her father and Asher? After all, they had followed her from Ashkelon to see that she was well. "It is nothing more than a speck of dust. How do you know it is Nicolaus?"

"Because there is an entire army following in his wake."

Ada leaned against the rail and squinted. "I see nothing."

The captain rested his elbows against the rail. "I do

not sail much, but I've sailed enough to know there are many ships chasing us."

Ada felt his confidence waver, heard it in his tone. "If you are scared of Nicolaus then why tempt him?"

"I told you, Ada. We have unfinished business. He took something that belongs to me, and I would have it back. You are my means of having it returned to me."

She shook her head. "I do not understand. If he has an army at his command, then he'll destroy your ship."

His lips twisted in a wry grin. "He will do anything to rescue you, even become my slave once again, if I so choose."

Ada recalled the puckered scars covering Nicolaus's back and the pain in his voice when he'd told her of losing his sister. She could not ask him to suffer at the hands of this man again, not after all he'd lost to keep her safe. He needed the chance to find Desma, to save her from the cruelty of slavery.

One thing this captain did not know—she would do anything to keep Nicolaus from coming anywhere near this man. All she needed to do was figure out exactly what that something was.

"What are you going to do?"

Nicolaus kept his eyes on the boat carrying Ada. For near an hour he'd been left in silence and now his mother, who had insisted on coming, wanted to know what he was going to do. He would have preferred that she, along with his father and Ada's father, had sailed with his brother, or with Asher, or with one of the many ships that had followed him out of port. None of which he had invited on this adventure. He dared not glance around him lest he discover the whole island of Andros had joined them. At least Galen, Edith and the babe were safely ensconced at his parents' home. "I will offer him a trade. Myself for her."

His mother laid her hand over his folded ones. "Nicky, you are not thinking rationally."

He glanced down and looked her in the eye. "Mother, I have done nothing but think. There is no other choice. I am all he seeks." As well as the partial map hidden beneath his tunic.

"There are other options." Her fingers tightened around his hand. The sadness in her eyes tore at him. He did not wish for her to witness the loss of another child, but she'd insisted on coming and Father had allowed it. If only he could reassure them that Desma was well, but it was not his secret to keep. He would have to trust Jasen would set all right in due time.

"Leaving her to the mercies of David is not one."

"I have not asked you to do such, Nicky." She pulled her hand from his and brushed a lock from his brow. "I only ask that you talk to the others before you act."

"What would they say? Wait until David ports before we do anything as Jasen suggested? His island may be small, but his home is vast. Many unsavory men owe David fealty. The risk of her being lost to me forever is too great. I love her, Mama. I know this now and would not see her suffer slavery as I have already done." He would not tell his mother about the abuse he'd witnessed David inflict upon his slaves. He would not have her worry further over Desma's well-being. "I must do what I must."

"As must I, Nicky." With Haemon's assistance, she climbed down the ladder. He watched as she glided toward his father and Ada's. Their gazes shifted to his.

A grim line formed on his father's lips. Manus's jaw fell open a little.

"Xandros!" His father's voice boomed across the ship.

Nicolaus followed his friend's movement as he leaned his head toward his father. Xandros's chest rose, but he dared not look at Nicolaus. He strode across the planks, climbed the ladder and stood in front of him. The hair on Nicolaus's arms rose in warning.

"I am sorry, my friend." He motioned to Haemon and Argos standing guard on either side of the commander's post.

"What? What are you doing?" Nicolaus tried to pull his arms free from the men holding him. *His men.*

"Your father has ordered you to be bound until the matter with David can be resolved."

"Xandros," Nicolaus growled as he fought against the hands holding him. "If you value our friendship—"

"I value our friendship above all other things, Nicolaus. I am in agreement with your father. I will not allow you to be enslaved by that man again."

"Then you must understand why I cannot leave her in David's hands. She does not have the strength to bear what I did."

Xandros clamped his hand on Nicolaus's shoulder. "Have faith in us to rescue your bride."

"You have nothing to bargain with. If he believes I did not come for her, he'll likely kill her."

"Bind him beneath the helmsman's perch," Xandros said to Haemon before turning away from him. "Nicolaus, I warn you, if you make trouble I'll have them lock you in a storeroom below where no one can hear your bellows."

"Xandros, do not do this."

The corner of one of Xandros's eyes twitched. "Bind him in to the mast in the hold."

"Xandros!"

His friend turned away and climbed the ladder to the commander's post. His second-in-command, ordered by his father, no doubt, had expelled him as captain. What was worse, they were holding him captive.

"Come, Captain." Haemon tugged on Nicolaus's arm. "We do not like this any more than you do, but it is for your own good."

"Ay, I doubt that, Haemon," Nicolaus said as his guard led him down the stairs and into the dark hold void of merchandise.

"Our apologies, Captain." Argos bound his hands behind his back and then tied them to the mast.

A muscle ticked in Nicolaus's jaw. "I have never questioned where Xandros's loyalties lay. He's been my friend since I can remember but he owes much to my father. However, you two I do not understand. We fought together in battles. We have saved each other's lives."

Haemon flinched and Argos paled.

"How is it you would betray me?"

Argos glanced at Haemon, but kept his mouth from uttering a word.

Haemon grinned. "Your mother promised us a wedding feast upon our return to Andros if we protected you well."

Nicolaus drew in a breath. "Leave me be."

They both glanced around the ship and then at him as if he'd somehow grown fins.

"Now! I've no means of escape. I wish to be left to my thoughts without you two hovering."

"If you have need of anything we will be standing guard at the top of the stairs," Haemon said as knelt beside him and tugged on the ropes binding him to the mast.

"The only need I have is my freedom so I can re-trieve Ada."

Rising, Haemon dropped his gaze toward their feet. "If it will ease your mind, I will keep you informed of what is going on."

Nicolaus waited until his guards disappeared above the deck before leaning his head back and closing his eyes. "Lord, how have I come to this? Does not Ada believe that whoever has Your help finds joy? Help us, Lord. Help her. I beg of Thee, make my men swift in their rescue of her. I only wish my hands were not tied so that I may be of some help. However, I'm guessing You have other plans. Whatever they are, Almighty God, keep Ada safe and please return her to me quickly."

He stretched his legs out before him. His feet bumped against an object, which quickly scooted away. Nicolaus lifted his head and peered into the shadows. "Who goes there?"

# Chapter Twenty-Five

David had called for the anchors to be dropped shortly after he'd shown her the ships. Ada had waited, her gaze focused on the shapes propelling toward them for what seemed like hours. Her fingers ached from squeezing the railing for so long. Her lips were numb from the constant prayer uttered in silence over Nicolaus.

She had hoped for peace to overcome her. Instead, the more distinct the multitude of ships became, the more her heart unsettled. Did one of those ships belong to Nicolaus? Had he come to sacrifice himself in order to gain her freedom?

A tear slipped from her eye and was quickly dried by the warm breeze. Freedom would mean nothing without Nicolaus in her life. She almost understood how it was her mother could have loved her father, except her father had not been kind, not like Nicolaus had been. But Ada knew now that she could have given her heart completely to Nicolaus if he offered her marriage. However, if her father tried to force Nicolaus into an agreement, she would never know if he returned her love, and that was unacceptable. She couldn't suffer the way her mother had, to love a man who did not love her. She wasn't strong enough.

"I do not see Nicolaus."

Ada blinked to clear her thoughts, and then glanced at David, who had come to stand beside her. "What is it you said?"

"Nicolaus, he has yet to show himself."

Ada's heart dropped to her stomach. Had Nicolaus decided to abandon her? Her gaze roamed over each of the boats in hopes of seeing him, and yet of not seeing him. They were close enough that she could make out the helmsman and the captains standing at their posts as well as the rowers, but she could not discern who was who. They were still too far. "Perhaps you were wrong about how my master felt about me."

Her heart sank a little further at the possible truth.

David scratched his beard. "Perhaps. I guess we will see."

"What will you do if he has not come?" she asked even though she feared his answer.

"I will have no choice but to keep you until he has a change of heart. Of course, by then he may no longer want you."

Ada's spine stiffened at his threat. However, it was not out of fear, not from this man; he was nothing more than a coward hiding behind cruelty. She straightened her arms. Arching her back, she lifted her face toward the heavens and smiled as the sun warmed her skin. The peace she had sought earlier finally settled over her. Something deep within her heart told her Nicolaus had not abandoned her. He had not left her to such a fate when she was nothing more than a stranger to him, and he would not do so now.

"Are you mad? Why are you smiling?"

Laughter filled her but she dared not allow it to take root. "I have faith that Almighty God will rescue me."

She just had to find a way to keep Nicolaus from sacrificing his life for hers.

"Galen, is that you?"

A whisper of movement scooted farther away.

"Ay, Captain." Galen's voice trembled. "It is me. I am sorry I disobeyed you, but Chloe is taking care of my siblings, and I wanted to help Ada."

Nicolaus almost laughed aloud. He must consider retiring as captain. No one had ever dared to defy his commands until he'd brought Ada aboard his ship, and now it seemed as if everyone chose to do so, even this little mite of a child. However, he could not be more grateful than he was at the moment. And he owed it to the Almighty God for His divine providence.

"You would not happen to have a blade with you, do you?"

"Of course, Captain. How else would I fight?"

His own daggers pressed against his hips. If only he had thought to use them against his men when they took over his ship. Of course, that was something he would never do unless they truly meant him harm. Besides, his father had ordered their actions. "You are wise for one so young." And a little daring for a child of his age. Nicolaus would have to take care and teach him well before he grew into a young man. "Now, will you cut me loose?"

The rhythm of his rowers slowed, and Nicolaus

knew they must be close to David's ship. Galen had yet to move. "Galen? Will you cut me loose?"

The child's face appeared from out of the shadows. The boy worried his lip. "Are you going to punish me for disobeying you?"

The corners of his mouth slid upward. "I should. My commands are meant to keep you safe from harm. The next time you disobey me, you will be banished to your chambers for a time. Is that understood?"

"Yes, Captain." Galen crawled forward, and then moved behind Nicolaus. His blade sawed through the ropes binding Nicolaus's hands.

A muffled shout from Xandros came from above, followed by one from his helmsman. The sound of the oars halted. The boat bobbed with the waves. Nicolaus pulled his hands apart, severing the last threads of the rope. Rising, he patted Galen on the head. "My thanks. Now, stay here until I call for you. I would not wish to be distracted by you while I'm trying to rescue Ada."

The boy's eyes turned sad. His shoulders slumped. Nicolaus understood the need to help. Sitting here with his hands bound, he'd felt helpless, but it had also given him time to think about his original plan. He would trade positions with her if he must. However, he'd prefer to save her without giving up his life so he could spend the rest of his life loving her.

Nicolaus crouched in front of the boy. "I have an important document." Nicolaus reached his hand between the folds of his tunic and pulled out a piece of the map he'd stolen back from David. "Are you willing to keep it safe? Do not tell anyone you have it."

Galen's eyes lifted to the scrap of leather. His face shone with excitement as he nodded.

"Very well." Nicolaus handed him the map and rose. "You stay here. Hide if you must. I will fetch you when Ada has been returned to us."

Several vessels surrounded them. Archers crowded onto the roofs with bows in their hands. Her brother stood at the commander's post of one. Jasen stood on another, his arms crossed over his chest. She could not say how she knew the perfect image was not Nicolaus, other than his gaze did not warm her or melt her knees. And perhaps it was because Jasen did not command the boat she'd become accustomed to over the days of sailing the Great Sea. Instead, that particular boat was captained by Xandros, Nicolaus's second-in-command. Her father and Nicolaus's stood beside Xandros.

Her father moved in front of Xandros. His white hair ruffled in the wind. "David of Delos, I completed my business with you several days ago. Have you found me guilty of theft to steal my daughter from me?"

Ada swung her gaze to David, who seemed to pale beneath her father's frightening stare. "Forgive me, Manus. However, this woman was found roaming freely along the wharf. Fair for anyone to take captive." David pulled her close. His hand roamed over her hair. "A treasure such as this should be locked away, should it not?"

Her father's lip twitched. "That it should. However, I fear my daughter disobeyed orders to stay in her chambers and went in search for a wayward waif. Her affection for those less fortunate often causes her to be misguided."

Ada flinched. She knew her father held no compas-

sion for those beneath him, she'd seen the evidence of
it when her mother died, but hearing the truth struck
her heart.

"I would ask that you release her as she is not for
sale."

"Rumor has it she's already been sold. My apologies, Manus, but I cannot release her until my terms
are met." David shifted, pulling Ada with him. "Jasen,
I've no doubt your brother is hiding among all these
ships. It surprises me he has chosen to hide his face
like a coward. But then, only cowards would sneak
into a man's house while he slept, torture him and
steal from him."

Jasen narrowed his eyes, and Ada thought for a moment he might in truth be Nicolaus. "My brother is of
no concern to you."

"Ah, but he is as I will not release this woman until
I have him in my possession."

"She no longer belongs to Nicolaus. Therefore you
have no means to bargain with."

Ada pulled her brows together in confusion. She
wanted to stomp her foot and shout that she belonged
to no man, but that was not the truth. She just did not
know whom she belonged to; her father, Jasen, Nicolaus...the man holding her captive by her hair.

"I'm afraid I do. My sources have informed me this
woman does belong to Nicolaus. Perhaps, not as his
slave, but from all I hear she owns his heart. A man
in love will do anything to protect his woman, am I
not right, Nicolaus?"

David twisted toward the boat holding her father
and Xandros. Nicolaus stood near the edge, his fingers white from the grip on the rail. She closed her

eyes against the tears forming. Although more beautiful than all she'd seen thus far, she had not hoped to see him. Had hoped he would stay far from this man who had caused Nicolaus much torment.

"What is it you would have me do, David? You are surrounded with over a hundred arrows aimed at you."

The laugh tumbling from David caused shivers to race down her back. He jerked her tight against his chest. "Your orders would see her killed."

Nicolaus's chest rose, and then he nodded. "In that, you are correct."

"I would have the map you stole from me."

Nicolaus grimaced. "A map rightfully belonging to me."

David wrapped his arm around Ada's neck. "Swim over and I will release her."

Nicolaus began to undo the clasp holding his tunic together at his shoulder.

"No!" She elbowed David in the stomach and then stomped on his foot. He released his hold. David's helmsman jumped from his seat and swung his fist out to grab her just as an arrow hissed through the air. He stumbled backward.

"I will kill you." David snatched the back of her tunic, but quickly released her with a bellow.

She glanced over her shoulder to see an arrow piercing his shoulder. She climbed onto the top rail and jumped. Water covered her head. She swept her arms downward and kicked her feet. She broke the surface, gasping for air.

"Grab her."

She turned around. Two of David's men had jumped into the water after her. She kicked her feet, catching one in the chest. The other man grabbed her foot and yanked her toward him. An arrow pierced his chest and she kicked free from his hold. Thick arms grabbed hold of her. She swung around, her hand connecting with a solid jaw.

"Ada, it is me," Nicolaus shouted over the waves lapping against her ears. "You are safe."

Her body lost all of its tension. She wrapped her arms around his neck and hugged him. "I was scared he would capture you. I could not stand the thought of him tormenting you again."

The warmth of Nicolaus's lips pressed against her brow. "Nor I you, my love."

She pulled back and gazed into his eyes. "You love me?"

"Ay." He pressed his head against hers. His breaths warmed her lips. Their hearts pounded together. "I would have you be my wife if you are willing."

"What of Desma?"

"Jasen assures me that she is well."

"Oh, Nicolaus of Andros, that is good to hear." She knotted her fingers in his hair. "I love you, Nicolaus, and I am willing," she whispered as she pulled his mouth down to hers. Their lips melded for several long seconds, until the roar of her brother's laughter rained down upon them.

# Epilogue

Nicolaus leaned his shoulder against the tree and watched his bride as she danced in circles with Galen and Edith. Haemon and Argos stood near the roasting pit, waiting for the meat to finish cooking. Their smiles said they were not disappointed with the wedding feast his mother had promised them.

"She looks happy," Asher said.

"She does," Nicolaus said. "I only wished she would have allowed your father to stay and witness the wedding."

Asher rolled his shoulders. "What my father did to our sisters was unthinkable, but I stood by and allowed it to happen. Of course, we were angry over what they did to Ada and thought the punishment fair."

"I do not blame you." Jasen approached them with cups in his hands. "However, their actions brought my brother a bride. Perhaps, now Mother will quit trying to marry me off."

Nicolaus laughed. "Unlikely. The quicker she sees all of her sons married the sooner she can fill her house with grandchildren."

"She has Edith, Galen and the babe." Jasen sipped from his cup. "What of the babe? You have yet to name him."

"Agapios."

Jasen's eyebrows knitted together. "Love. The boy will suffer teasing from his playmates."

"I'm certain she'll relent and allow us to call him by another name, but for now it stands." Nicolaus glanced at Asher. "What of your sisters? Surely your father does not intend to leave them in slavery. Although they treated Ada with contempt, I know my bride would not wish them to suffer and will never be content until she knows they are safe."

"I intend to leave for Delos on the morrow. Perhaps, David's injuries will keep him in his home and away from the traders. However, I do not know the island and I was never able to conquer the language as Ada has. I fear I'll fail before I begin."

"If you wait a day, I will go with you."

"No."

"No."

Nicolaus glanced at both men. "It is important to Ada."

"You have a bride to tend to." Jasen gazed off toward the sea. "I would not have you face David again so soon. I will go. It is the least I owe you after what my actions have caused you."

"You owe me nothing, brother. I am content with the outcome." Knowing his sister was safe was enough. Ada giggled, drawing his attention. His arms ached with the need to hold her. "I only wish you would ease our parents' minds."

"This is a conversation I should not hear." Asher

clapped his hand onto Nicolaus's shoulder. "I am glad to call you brother. I hope to one day return." The man's eyes darted toward Chloe, the wet nurse, with longing and Nicolaus wondered if there was an attraction between them.

"Hold a moment, Asher. I would discuss our plans for the morrow." Jasen nodded toward Ada. "Go to your bride, brother. Keep her close lest another man seeks to steal her from you, and love her well."

Loving her was easy. He only prayed he was worthy of her love.

"That I will do, brother." Nicolaus handed his cup to his brother. "Asher, may all go well with your travels. I hope to hear good news from you soon."

Nicolaus pushed away from the tree and strode toward Ada and the children. She threw her head back and laughed at something Galen had said. He was content with his new family, especially with Ada at his side. Her face radiated with such joy and by the smiles of all the people around the terrace he'd say her laughter was infectious.

"Ada." He grabbed hold of her hand. He itched to sweep her into his arms and carry her away from the festivities. "Will you walk with me a moment?"

She stretched onto her toes and kissed his cheek. The softness of her lips pressed against his flesh weakened his knees. "Of course, Nicolaus. Where is it you'd like to walk?"

Away from here, from prying eyes so he could kiss his bride with all the passion thrumming through his blood. "Come and you will see."

He guided her to a path behind his parents' home. For several long moments they walked in silence. The pulse of her palm beat against his, sending waves of delight to his heart. How had he become so fortunate as to have a bride such as her? They reached the stone stairs, and he gave in and swept her into his arms. Hers snaked around his neck as her head leaned against his shoulder. He carried her up the steps leading to the top of the mountain and reluctantly set her on her feet.

He kissed her forehead, her eyes and the tip of her nose before he sought out her lips. She melded against him, her body fitting perfectly against him as if God had made her just for him. Pulling away, he gazed into her eyes. "I love you, Ada, my heart."

"And I you, Nicolaus."

One corner of his mouth slid upward and he spun her around so she could see the magnificent beauty of his home. Their home. Her sharp inhale told him she agreed. He snaked his arms around her middle and pulled her against his chest. Her hands settled over his. "Are you truly happy, Ada?"

She tilted her head to look at him. "Of course, why do you ask?"

"I never officially freed you and…" Words clung to his tongue. The deed was done. They were married and he didn't think he could ever let her go, but he knew how much she did not want to become her mother.

She turned in his arms. One palm rested on his cheek, the other over his heart. "Nicolaus, I have no fear of suffering as my mother did. She loved my father without his love in return. I love you, and I have no doubt that you love me. That you will love me for the rest of our lives."

He covered her hand on his cheek with his and then

threaded their fingers together. He kissed the back of her hand. "That I will, Ada. That I will."

Dropping her hand, he wrapped his arm around her waist and pulled her tight. His lips captured hers. The squeal of the birds, the wind through the trees, the waves pushing against the shore below all disappeared. The only sound he was aware of was the beating of their hearts.

\* \* \* \* \*

Dear Reader,

I hope you enjoyed reading Nicolaus and Ada's story as much as I did writing it. It was inspired by the Bible story of Joseph and his brothers as well as my love for ancient history and my intrigue with pirates from all eras.

Writing a story set on the ancient Mediterranean had its challenges where research was concerned. Given that details from this time period varied, much of the story, as well as many of the details, were created from my overactive imagination. I will say that Nicolaus's ship was fashioned after several different Greek ships, including the trireme as well as the Greek merchant ship. However, I did take some creative license with his ship in order to accommodate Ada and the children.

If you do not know the Lord, or if there is something hindering your relationship with God, remember Psalms 145:18, "The Lord is nigh unto all them that call upon him, to all that call upon him in truth."

I look forward to hearing from you. You can send mail to me in care of Love Inspired Books, 233 Broadway, Suite 1001, New York, New York 10279. You can also find me at authorchristinarich.com and threefoldstrand.com.

Many blessings,
*Christina*

SPECIAL EXCERPT FROM

*Love Inspired* HISTORICAL

*James Wallin's family is depending on him to find
a schoolteacher for their frontier town.
Alexandrina Fosgrave seems to be exactly what he
needs to help fulfill his father's dream of building a new
community. If only James could convince her to accept
the position.*

*Enjoy this sneak peek at*
FRONTIER ENGAGEMENT *by* Regina Scott,
*available in August 2015 from Love Inspired Historical!*

"Alexandrina," James said, guiding his magnificent horses
up a muddy, rutted trail that hardly did them justice.
"That's an unusual name. Does it run in your family?"

She couldn't tell him the fiction she'd grown up hearing,
that it had been her great-grandmother's name. "I don't
believe so. I'm not overly fond of it."

He nodded as if he accepted that. "Then why not
shorten it? You could go by Alex."

She sniffed, ducking away from an encroaching branch
on one of the towering firs that grew everywhere around
Seattle. "Certainly not. Alex is far too masculine."

The branch swept his shoulder, sending a fresh shower
of drops to darken the brown wool. "Ann, then."

She shook her head. "Too simple."

"Rina?" He glanced her way and smiled.

Yes, he definitely knew the power of that smile. She
could learn to love it. No, no, not love it. She was not here

to fall in love but to teach impressionable minds. And a smile did not make the man. She must look to character, convictions.

"Rina," she said, testing the name on her tongue. She felt a smile forming. It had a nice sound to it, short, uncompromising. It fit the way she wanted to feel—certain of herself and her future. "I like it."

He shook his head. "And you blame me for failing to warn you. You should have warned me, ma'am."

Rina—yes, she was going to think of herself that way—felt her smile slipping. "Forgive me, Mr. Wallin. What have I done that would require a warning?"

"Your smile," he said with another shake of his head. "It could make a man go all weak at the knees."

His teasing nearly had the same effect, and she was afraid that was his intention. He seemed determined to make her like him, as if afraid she'd run back to Seattle otherwise. She refused to tell him she'd accepted his offer more from desperation than a desire to know him better. And she certainly had no intention of succumbing to his charm.

*Don't miss*
*FRONTIER ENGAGEMENT by Regina Scott,*
*available August 2015 wherever*
*Love Inspired® Historical books and ebooks are sold.*

SPECIAL EXCERPT FROM

*Love Inspired*

*Reuniting with her high school sweetheart is hard
enough for Tessa Applewhite, but how much worse will
it get when she realizes the newly returned cowboy has
brought with him a baby son?*

*Read on for a sneak preview of* **Deb Kastner**'s
*THE COWBOY'S SURPRISE BABY,*
*the next heartwarming chapter in the series*
**COWBOY COUNTRY**.

"So you'll be wrangling here," Tessa blurted out.

"Yep." His gaze narrowed even more.

Well, that was helpful. Tessa tried again.

"You've been discharged from the navy?"

He frowned and jammed his fists into the front pockets
of his worn blue jeans. "Yep."

She was beyond frustrated at his cold reception, but
she supposed she had it coming. She could hardly expect
better when the last time they'd seen each other was—

Well, there was no use dwelling on the past. If Cole
was going to work here with her, he would have to get
over it.

So, for that matter, would she.

"Well, I won't keep you," she said, reaching back to
open the office door. "I just wanted to make sure we had
an understanding about how our professional relationship
here at the ranch was going to go."

He scowled at the word *relationship*. "Just came as a
surprise, is all," he muttered.

"I'll say," Tessa agreed.

"Didn't expect to be back in Serendipity for a few years yet. Maybe ever."

He sounded so bitter that Tessa cringed. What had happened to the boy she'd once known? Who or what had darkened the sunshine that had once shone so brilliantly in his eyes?

"Cole? Why did you come back now?"

He tipped his hat and started to walk past her without speaking, and Tessa thought she'd pushed him too far. Whatever his issues were, clearly she was the last person on earth he'd talk to about them.

He was almost out the door when he suddenly swiveled around to face her.

"Grayson." His gaze narrowed on her as if weighing the effect of his words on her.

She scrambled to put his answer in some kind of context but came up with nothing.

"Who—"

He cut off her question and ground out the rest of his answer.

"My son."

*Don't miss*
*THE COWBOY'S SURPRISE BABY by Deb Kastner,*
*available August 2015 wherever*
*Love Inspired® books and ebooks are sold.*